Photo Bombed

Bianca Wallace Mysteries, Volume 1

Daria White

Published by Daria White, 2020.

Photo Bombed

A Bianca Wallace Mystery, 1
(A Cozy Mystery Novel)

---

1.   http://www.crimsonfoxpublishing.com

DARIA WHITE

Turner, Oregon

Photo Bombed
(A Bianca Wallace Mystery, 1)

3

Chapter 1

"Excuse me, young lady?" Bianca Wallace eyeballed her daughter, who had her phone in her hand. Who knew how many texts her sixteen-year-old had sent because Alyssa's thumbs moved at every ping that sounded from her phone?

Alyssa met her mother's dark brown eyes. She placed her phone back on the table, face down. "Sorry."

"No phones during dinner." Bianca picked up her fork just as her own cell phone rang.

Alyssa smirked as she folded her arms over her chest. "Well, well, well."

Bianca pointed her fork at her. "Not one word." Loud laughter filled the air of the Italian restaurant, Bello Italian, along with servers taking orders. Heat emerged from a pulled apart breadstick on Bianca's plate.

Alyssa giggled. "Sorry, Mom, but that was Chloe. We're meeting some friends after dinner."

"You're just *now* telling me this?" Bianca would never get used to her daughter becoming an adult. Two more years and her only child would graduate high school. Though Alyssa didn't know her major yet, she'd mentioned plans of either studying medicine or architecture. Bianca hoped her daughter decided soon.

"It's only a party." Alyssa bounced in her seat.

Bianca watched her. "With whom? Do I know the parents?"

Alyssa groaned. "*Mom.*"

"Don't *Mom* me. Who's chaperoning this party?" she asked. Bianca had been young once too, wanting to hang out with friends. High school was where she'd met Alyssa's father, Malcolm Cook.

"Mom," Alyssa continued unabated. "We have a new kid at our school, and they invited us. Chloe and I will look out for each other. Don't worry."

"Be home by eleven."

"*Mom!*" Alyssa's eyes bugged, as if realizing her outburst. She leaned across the table. "I'll be seventeen soon. I at least thought you'd bump the curfew to midnight."

"I would have if you'd put up the dishes last night. Guess who had to empty the dishwasher?" Bianca twirled the fettuccine on her plate.

Alyssa sat back in her seat. "Fine."

"I'm only thinking of you," Bianca said. It was the truth. She'd been thinking about her since she'd become a mom, even more now that she was single.

"Can we negotiate on the curfew?" Alyssa asked.

"I don't do that. I'm the mother."

Alyssa rolled her eyes. Then she took a gulp of her iced tea.

Bianca didn't take pleasure in being the bad cop, but if she didn't raise her daughter with boundaries, she'd only run wild and make careless mistakes. Though some things were inevitable since her daughter had to learn, Bianca did her best to guide her daughter to be a well-rounded person. Then she cocked her head to the side. "Does this have anything to do with that boy?"

Alyssa's head jerked back. "What boy?"

"The boy who met you this morning at the door when I dropped you off at school."

Alyssa looked down at her plate. "He's just a friend."

"I know that look."

"Mom, please don't say anything."

"Why would I do that? I was young once. I remember having crushes and wanting to fit in. I didn't forget," Bianca said.

"His name is Kendrick." Alyssa's eyes glowed. "He plays basketball and football. Before you say anything else, he's the nicest boy ever. He's not cocky at all. He's so smart."

Bianca smiled. "I see. Is he hosting this party tonight?"

Alyssa bit her bottom lip. "Yes."

"Now we're getting somewhere." She gazed at her mini me. Alyssa had her dark brown eyes and naturally curly hair. Smooth brown skin, but Alyssa had faint freckles on her nose. Like her father. "You can tell me anything. I'm always willing to listen."

"I know." Alyssa laced her fingers together. "Please, can I stay out a little later? I'll be home by midnight, Mom. I'll even text you when I get there."

"This boy must be something."

"He is. He's amazing. And mature. Do you know how many jerks are in high school?"

Bianca laughed. "I can only imagine." She swallowed the last of her pasta. "I'll give you until eleven-thirty, and you have to make sure you unload the dishwasher."

Alyssa practically squealed. "Thanks, Mom!"

Bianca flipped her medium-length brown hair. "I know. I'm the best."

They both laughed

Bianca continued. "Just promise me that whomever you end up liking or dating, it won't hinder our mother-daughter nights. They're important to me. I know you're growing up, but don't forget."

Alyssa's eyes beamed. "I promise, Mom. You're the best." Taking her phone out, Bianca figured Alyssa confirmed her plans with her best friend. "She's picking me up here. Is that okay?"

"That's fine," Bianca said.

Once the ladies finished eating and Bianca had paid the bill, they exited the double doors. Chloe pulled up to the restaurant and let down her passenger-side window to her Toyota Corolla. How her parents had gotten her a new car at sixteen, Bianca didn't understand. Thank goodness Alyssa hadn't asked for a car. She needed to pass the driving test first.

"Hey, Ms. Wallace!" Chloe waved. The girl's long layered black hair framed her olive skinned face. Her loose curls rested on her shoulders. Alyssa joined her friend inside the vehicle.

"Hi, Chloe." Bianca leaned to look at her daughter. "Remember your curfew. Don't make me change my mind."

Alyssa clicked her seatbelt. "I will. I promise." The girls waved and Chloe drove out of the parking lot.

Bianca threw her keys in the air and caught them. With the night sky free of clouds, the stars sprinkling above lifted her spirits even more. The gentle night breeze kissed her face. She turned her head for a moment as the murmurs of waiting customers heightened in her ears.

Sitting on benches and standing near the entrance, they either waited for a table or chatted with their party. Others walked to their cars with plastic takeout bags. Bianca walked the semi full parking lot to her royal blue 2018 Kia Soul.

Where had the time flown? It was as if it were only yesterday that she'd had her daughter. Now Alyssa was almost out of the house.

Bianca would be an empty nester. Her breathing slowed as the memories took over. Alyssa's gurgles and toothless smiles. She was such a happy baby, squealing and bouncing with excitement when she played with her toys. A shallow sigh escaped Bianca's full lips as the engine hummed in her ears while she drove home.

A night to herself, and since she was caught up with work for the week, she'd watch reruns of her favorite sitcom, *Living Single*. Home. One of her favorite places. Pulling into the driveway, she hit the button for the garage door to her modern farmhouse home. With a hanging swing bench on her front porch, it was the perfect place where she could sit with a steamy tea cup in her hand.

A mix of vinyl shingles and cement board siding covered the house and the garage. To her surprise, the garage came attached to the house, at the request of the previous owners. Bianca parked. Grabbing her phone again after cutting the engine, she saw a text from her mother. How did she not hear her phone? Lost in thought with memories about baby Alyssa.

Mom: Check your porch. Left a surprise!

Just now? Perhaps her mother had been in a hurry and couldn't stay. Typically Bianca entered her one story house through the garage, but she marched to her front door. She stopped in her tracks as she stepped on her porch. An open cardboard box. What?

She heard whimpers. What did her mother leave on her doorstep? She looked inside to see a puppy. A white and chocolate puppy with a red bow around its neck. Bianca's mouth fell open. She didn't do pets. Even when Alyssa had asked for one in middle school, Bianca hadn't cared to take care of one, when trying to support herself and a child.

She focused her eyes on the dog. A Beagle? It sat on its hind legs, with his paws hanging on the end of the box.

"Uh…" Bianca pulled out her phone. When she saw another text from her mother, she inwardly winced.

Mom: You'll love Casper. Enjoy!

Bianca called her mother. "What's this?"

"Mrs. Pruitt's dog had puppies. I thought you would love Casper, so I dropped him off a few minutes ago."

"Mom—"

"If you don't want him, I'll take him, but I know Alyssa's had her heart set on a dog for years."

"Why now? You wait until she's sixteen? Who will take care of him once she leaves home?"

Her mother huffed, never ceasing to surprise her. Just when she had her mother figured out, she threw a curveball. "Bianca, I thought it would be a fun gesture. He's young, so you can train him. But like I said, if you don't want him, I'll take him."

"You already have two dogs."

"The more the merrier. You'd be surprised what great company they are."

Bianca didn't mind dogs, but since she'd grown up with them, she didn't care to have any of her own. They were a lot of responsibility.

"Fine. He can stay for one night, but I'm bringing him over to your place in the morning after I drop Alyssa off for school."

"Enjoy him, dear. He's such a sweetie." Her mother hung up.

Bianca released a deep breath and picked up the box. Casper licked her chin. "Not the face, please." She carried him inside. Not the evening she'd expected.

Chapter 2

Alyssa *had* to ask to keep Casper. She arrived on time for her curfew, but when spotted the puppy asleep in the living room's corner, she pleaded with her mother to keep him. Bianca said she would consider it and they had to weigh in the opinion of her younger sister. Melanie. Her one and only sibling.

The sisters hadn't shared a home since Bianca moved out to marry Malcom, but it was nice to be together again. Even when she texted her, *Mom left us a dog*, her sister sided with their mother and Alyssa. Three against one. Casper was staying.

When she dropped Alyssa off at school that morning, Casper rode in the back seat. A puppy in the family? Would it be so bad? Alyssa loved him already, and as Bianca glanced at him in her rearview mirror, her mouth twisted into a grin. He was adorable. When she dropped him off at her mother's home, her mother practically busted with excitement at the news of Bianca keeping him.

Pulling into the parking lot of R&J's Restaurant and Bakery, she entered through the glass door, hearing the bell chime above her.

"Good morning, Judy." Bianca paced to the front counter, grateful that the morning rush was gone.

"Bianca." The redhead's eyes beamed. For a woman in her late fifties, Judy didn't look a day over forty. Five eight, emerald green eyes, and a pleasant smile. "Good morning. What can I get for you today?"

Bianca pulled out her card. "It's my turn to bring donuts for the teachers. PTA."

Judy bobbed her head. "How many?"

"At least two dozen." Bianca's eyes wondered about the combo restaurant and bakery. Aside from the tall glass cases filled with donuts, she noticed the collection of cookies on red plastic trays. Customers chatted as they ate, and Bianca couldn't help but inhale the smell of toasty bread.

"Are you excited about Nicole's bridal shower?" Judy asked.

"Yes. Besides, I get to eat your cooking, but..." Bianca rubbed at her toned stomach. She wanted to keep it that way. "I may stay clear of the pastries. Most of them."

Judy giggled. "You look great, so don't even try that with me."

"Thank you."

"Makes me think of going to the gym."

"It can be fun once you find an exercise routine you like," Bianca said.

Judy tapped her forehead. "I said *think*. Thinking and going are two different things."

Bianca laughed.

"Looks like a new face in town." Judy stared out the front door as the bell chimed. Someone had just walked inside.

Bianca pivoted out of curiosity, only to have her eyes widen slightly. She stared for a moment at his almond skin against his gray suit. Fresh haircut, tall but no more than six feet she assumed. His muscular frame filled his suit.

How old was he? He couldn't be no older than thirty if she had to guess. Though his groomed beard made him look older. She didn't recognize him, either, so he had to be new in town or a tourist. Or he could have been lost. His eyes intrigued Bianca even further. Were they gray too? She couldn't tell, but staring wouldn't help. She faced the counter. She felt a presence behind her.

"Is that all for you, Bianca?" Judy asked.

"That'll be all." Bianca took back her card and returned it to her purse. Judy handed her two boxes, and Bianca secured them in her hands. The man behind her backed away. "Excuse me."

Next thing she knew, he walked ahead of her and opened the door. Bianca swallowed. A gentleman. She could appreciate that. "Thank you."

"You're welcome." His voice was smooth, and she could not ignore his woodsy cologne. Her chest heaved as the scent filled her lungs. Was there a smolder to his eyes? Bianca didn't stick around to see. She had to get back to work and drop off the donuts to her daughter's school.

She didn't waste time getting into her car and pulled out of the parking lot. Whoever this new guy was, she'd met enough attractive men in Edenville. One more didn't matter. None of them sparked her interest until... she blinked. Hearing her mother's ringtone, Boyz II Men's "Mama," through her car, she answered. "Yes, Mom?"

"I forgot to ask you before you left. With my matchmaking event, I got behind cooking for our family meal. If you can come over after church this Sunday, I'd appreciate some help in the kitchen."

Deborah Wallace never missed cooking a family meal.

Bianca agreed. "I don't mind coming over."

"I'll tell you something else too. I'm so excited for Nicole's wedding."

Bianca's eyes widened. She'd forgotten to call Nicole back last night. Her best friend since college. How long had it been? At least sixteen years since the day they were roommates. Practically another sister to her and she was getting married. As matron of honor, Bianca stayed on call if the bride-to-be needed anything, and thank goodness her friend wasn't a bridezilla. Even with the wedding coming up next weekend and Nicole scrambling with her wedding planner to finish all the details, she didn't unravel.

"Me too. I'll call her as soon as I get home."

"Think you'll meet some eligible bachelors at the wedding?" her mother asked.

Bianca stopped at a traffic light. Her mother meant well, but she wasn't ready to get back into the dating scene. At first, Bianca had told herself she'd try once Alyssa was older. Now that she was, Bianca's stomach only roiled at the thought of dating again. She wasn't supposed to be divorced. Malcolm was supposed to be here forever.

Thinking they'd been in love, she'd married him right out of high school. Though they'd made it to twelve years of marriage, he'd come home one day asking for a divorce. His reason? He'd fallen in love with his secretary.

Now Malcolm lived with his new wife in California. No kids that Bianca knew of yet. Though he called on Alyssa's birthday, their relationship had never been the same. Alyssa didn't talk about him much to her, as if she didn't want to bring up memories. Bianca didn't press her either. At least Malcom made the effort. She couldn't say that about most men.

"You never know, Mom, but I'm not looking."

"Bianca?"

"Mom?"

"I think it's time. You've done well for yourself since Malcolm left. You've raised a wonderful daughter. Your graphic design business is doing great. I think it's time to think about you for a change."

"A relationship helps me do that?" Bianca asked.

"No, it doesn't have to. If this is a choice, then fine, I'll respect it. I just don't want you to give up."

Bianca pulled into the parking lot of Edenville High School. "Mom, I'll call you later. I need to drop off these donuts and I have to get back to work. I have to finish some work for clients."

"I'll let it go for now, but remember what I said. I'll see you when you pick up Casper."

"Okay." Bianca rolled her eyes.

"Are you rolling your eyes at me, young lady?"

Young lady? Didn't Bianca say that to Alyssa? Oh, no. She was turning into her mother. Though the notion wasn't *too* bad since everyone in town loved Deborah Wallace.

"I'll stop by later for Casper." She hung up, only to see Nicole's name on her screen. "Hey, I was going to call you later."

Nicole sighed. "I can't wait for this wedding to be over."

Bianca secured her Bluetooth in her ear, carrying the donuts to the front doors of the high school. "Are you and Chad all right?"

"We're great. It's his mother. She can't go two minutes without giving her input."

Bianca smiled at the high school secretary and placed the boxes on the counter. She waved goodbye and exited the building. Her heels clicked on the concrete. "She *does* know it's *your* wedding, right? And Chad's."

Nicole groaned. "Something told me we should have eloped." Was that a gasp? "Hey, I've got to go. I'll talk to you at the bridal shower. Okay?"

Why the rush? Bianca could tell her friend sounded overwhelmed. "No problem."

Nicole hung up.

Bianca thought of calling her back but gave the bride-to-be some space. She continued the walk to her car. She had more designing projects to complete. Bianca hadn't thought she would be in another wedding, but when Nicole had asked, she couldn't resist her friend.

She was certain she could stand and watch another couple exchange vows. Besides, this was Nicole's first marriage. In college she didn't think she would find true love, so now in her thirties, it seemed like a distant dream. That was until Bianca introduced her to Chad Lee two years ago. He hadn't met the right one either, and when Bianca paired them together, there was no doubt they were meant for each other.

A wedding. If only her stomach didn't burn, but she would put on a happy face.

BIANCA PULLED INTO the long circular driveway of the Davis mansion. Robust ivy trailed along the brick walls. Manicured hedges framed the entrance. A large, healthy lawn with pruned trees, and the red rose garden added the perfect pop of color. Though Bianca had visited before for the engagement party, she couldn't get over how huge the house was.

Nicole's bridal shower. Cutting the engine, she grabbed her gift for her friend and stepped onto the driveway. Despite her friend marrying into money, she breathed easy knowing Nicole would appreciate her practical gift. A custom photo album with her and Chad's names on the cover, designed by Bianca. They could fill it with their honeymoon pictures in Rome, Italy, along with the many memories they would make as husband and wife. Bianca spotted the balloons tied to the columns on the front porch. Grinning, she walked past the parked cars lining the driveway.

The maid greeted her at the door, no older than her. What was her name again? Mandie if she recalled. Smooth tanned skin, curvy body with her jet black hair brushing against her shoulders. Her pearly white smile grew as she welcome her inside.

Mandie pointed to her gift. "Want me to take that for you?"

"I got it. Thank you." Bianca brushed past her and entered the large entryway, with high ceilings.

Bianca's ears filled with the music, particularly 90s hits that she remembered listening to when she was in college. Even though she was in college in the mid-2000s, the 90s hit never went out of style for her. Laughter, and the murmured voices of the women in town whom Nicole had invited to share in her joy caught Bianca's attention. She smiled at a few faces and hugged the necks of her friends.

"Bianca!" Nicole shrieked.

Bianca embraced her friend. "You look amazing!"

Nicole planted her hands on her slim hips. Her sundress flowed to her knees and flattered her waist. Long blonde hair, five seven, and flawless ivory skin. Her blue eyes shined. The woman could have been a model if she wanted to, but found her passion as a beauty blogger. "Thank you. Come on in."

Looping her arm with hers, Bianca walked with Nicole to the kitchen after setting her gift on the designated table. When they entered the kitchen, Bianca spotted Judy.

"Bianca! Welcome." Her red hair shined as always.

"Let me help you, Judy. I can't just stand around and let you do all of this for me." Nicole stood in front of a plate of ham and grabbed the butcher knife from Priscilla's, Chad's mother, kitchen set.

"Nicole." Judy sighed. "You're the bride. You should be mingling with your guests."

"There will be plenty of time for that." Nicole nudged her shoulder and sliced the meat onto a serving tray.

Bianca made herself comfortable on a bar stool. "Having fun so far? You seem more relaxed now." That was a good sign.

Nicole beamed. "I am. I can't believe the wedding is next weekend." She exhaled. "I'm so nervous."

"Not about marrying Chad, I hope," Judy said as she tossed the salad.

"Can I help?" Bianca stood.

Judy pointed for her to sit down. "No, I won't have the both of you helping. Nicole's the bride so she can get away with it."

Bianca returned to her seat and folded her hands in her lap. She figured Judy was in her zone so she wouldn't offer again to help her in the kitchen. "Everything looks amazing."

Judy touched a hand to Nicole's shoulder. "I can't tell you what it means to me that you asked us to cater your wedding. Thank you."

Nicole smiled. "Are you kidding? I wouldn't have anyone else cooking for me."

Bianca's heart warmed at the friendly exchange. With Nicole marrying into the high society Davis family, she could have chosen top-notch caterers to serve her reception meal. Yet, she'd chosen Edenville's best. There was no one better than Judy, who could cook and bake along with her husband, Richard.

"I do have a question for you my friend." Nicole directed her attention to Bianca.

"What?" Bianca asked.

"I think you could get along with at least one of Chad's—"

Bianca held up a hand to stop her. "Before you start setting me up with all of the groomsmen, I'll pass."

"Oh, Bianca. Really?" Nicole huffed.

"I'll let you know if I change my mind." Bianca winked at her.

Nicole paused in her slicing of the ham when her phone rang in her dress pocket. She stared at the screen but didn't answer.

"Give me a minute, ladies." Judy picked up the salad bowls and left to place them on the dining table.

Nicole's face fell. Whoever had called had changed her mood.

"What's wrong?" Bianca asked, standing to move beside Nicole and offering a gentle hand on her shoulder.

"Jordan." She stuffed the phone in her pocket.

Bianca sighed. "How is he?"

"He's fine." Nicole bit her bottom lip.

"Nicole?" Bianca raised an eyebrow.

"I just... didn't think it would be this hard. Don't get me wrong, I don't have any second thoughts about marrying Chad, but Jordan's taking it harder than I thought."

"He's loved you for as long as I can remember." Bianca met Jordan through Nicole, who had been her best friend since they were children. They were considered a trio in college, but Bianca couldn't help but notice how Jordan paid more attention to Nicole. The longing in his eyes couldn't be denied, but by the time they graduated, he left. According to Nicole, it was his way of giving her space since she didn't feel the same about him. Now he was an accomplished writer. Thrillers were his specialty. He appeared to accept Nicole's new relationship, but there was no negating the heartbreak he'd suffered.

Nicole shook her head. "He's an amazing friend, but... that's all I feel for him."

Bianca gave her a side hug. "You told him the truth. That's all you can do. It may be hard, but Jordan will understand. I'm sure of it."

"I know. He respects my wishes. Sometimes... I still see his face when I told him about my engagement." Nicole admired her solitaire diamond ring. "I'm happy, Bianca. I want him to be happy too."

Bianca assured her. "He will be. Just give him time to heal from this. A broken heart needs time."

"I'm not interrupting anything, am I?"

Both women turned to see Priscilla's husband, Martin Davis. Fit for a man in his mid-fifties. He towered others being over six feet, and his salt and pepper hair stayed in a buzzed cut. His mustache stayed trimmed and his long face was either serious or expressionless. Though Bianca had seen him chuckle occasionally.

"Martin, nice to see you again." Bianca forced a smile despite her prickly skin. She took a few steps away from Nicole.

"And you." He winked at Bianca. "Priscilla can't wait to see the photos."

As an extension of her graphic design business, Bianca offered her own photo copyrights, so her customers had unique designs and she didn't have to rely on stock photos. Even recently she'd expanded her skills with video editing. She didn't do it often, but only when requested for her unique photo service or a special video. Priscilla had requested Bianca's services for her twentieth wedding anniversary to Martin. Bianca didn't tell her she had a special surprise for the couple. A video based off the pictures she'd taken of Priscilla and Martin.

Bianca responded. "I'm glad. I'll keep you posted."

Martin then directed his attention to Nicole. "The beautiful bride to be."

Nicole's body stiffened.

Bianca's eyes shifted between them, and to avoid the awkward silence, she continued. "I didn't think I would see you here. The house is full of women for a bridal shower."

Martin chuckled and the laugh lines in his face increased. "I'm just checking in with you all. I'm leaving for a golf game in a few minutes." He focused his eyes on Nicole. "Everything to your liking?"

She cleared her throat. "It is. Thank you for sharing your home."

"You're practically family, my dear." Did his voice drop?

Bianca's eyes widened slightly. "Nicole, do you need me to take anything into the living area?"

Nicole picked up the plate with the sliced ham. "If you can help me with this, I think we'll be fine."

"Anything I can do?" Martin asked. His eyes never left Nicole.

"I thought I might find you here." Priscilla entered the room with her short blonde bob haircut, white dress slacks, and sleeveless turtleneck. Her heart-shaped face was wrinkle free. Botox maybe?

Bianca never asked since it wasn't her business, but she admired the woman for keeping her slim figure despite being past fifty. Priscilla's chic style never failed. Even on a casual day, the woman always dressed to impress. Then again, a former actress, Priscilla's style was part of her trademark on Broadway. Her five-five presence commanded the room when she entered.

Priscilla's eyes focused on her husband. "What are you doing?"

He walked over to her. "Looking for you." Martin circled an arm around his wife's waist and kissed her cheek.

"We were just taking these to the guests." Nicole slipped out of the kitchen with the serving plate.

Bianca followed her friend, but the faint voices of Martin and Priscilla stopped her. She stepped to stand behind the wall, separating the kitchen from the hallway.

"I thought you were leaving," Priscilla said.

"I'm on my way out. Don't worry,"

"I don't have to worry about you, do I?" Priscilla asked.

Bianca's eyebrows furrowed. Worry? Why would Priscilla worry about Martin?

"I see no reason why you should," Martin said.

Priscilla added. "Let's keep it that way."

Bianca wouldn't listen anymore. Her heels clicked as she proceeded into the main living room.

Chapter 3

The weekend passed quickly. The final countdown to the wedding started with only four more days until the nuptials. At least the bridal shower was a success and Nicole loved Bianca's gift.

Tapping her fingers on the tabletop, Bianca listened to the classical music playing through the speakers. If only she hadn't agreed to come to her mother's latest matchmaking event. This time? Speed dating. She didn't expect this many people to show on a Tuesday evening, but men and women crowded the ballroom.

Blowing through her cheeks, she raised her tapping fingers to cup her face. Her other hand toyed at the hem of her silky plum-colored dress. One hour. That was the agreement she'd made with her mother. Thank goodness Alyssa was old enough to stay at home by herself.

Then again, Bianca missed the excuse of having a small child and not having time to date. Her mother wouldn't hear of it now. She had a perfect record of matchmaking ever since Bianca's father had passed away. Bianca thought it was a hobby, but her mother couldn't resist a possible love story.

Next thing Bianca knew, her mother had opened her matchmaking business. Good for her. Bianca was proud, but did she have to be a guinea pig? She stared at the custom moldings along with the painted abstract artwork on the walls. Perfume and cologne filled the air and Bianca touched a hand to her chest.

"Thank you, ladies and gentlemen, for coming," her mother said into the microphone. At five-seven, her mother's brown skin glowed. Her pixie haircut fit her round face, while her little black dress complimented her curvy body. Bianca eyed her mother's peep-toed wedged heels. Sixty years of age didn't matter. Her mother wore them whenever she wanted to.

The audience applauded.

"We're ready to get started. You all have your assigned numbers." Her mother rang her trusty bell. "Everyone will be seated but is welcomed to move around and mingle. Then afterward, each attendee will write down the numbers of the person they'd like to pursue. That way everyone gets a fair chance to meet everyone!"

Bianca forced a smile at her mother's energy. Swallowing despite her dry mouth, she counted down the minutes. Next time, she would find something better to do than attend one of her mother's events.

"I guess I can make the most of it," she said to herself. It wasn't a marriage proposal. It wasn't a committed relationship. If she met a nice guy, at least she made a new friend. What was the harm in making new friends?

Straightening in her chair, Bianca recalled her main reason for showing her face at a speed dating event. It wasn't so much to support her mother's business, but to prove to herself that she had something to offer. Her life wasn't over because her marriage had ended. She wasn't damaged goods.

Would she remarry? Bianca toyed with her earring. Alyssa was getting older day by day. Would Bianca want someone in her life once her daughter had moved out? What kept her from pursuing something now?

"Good evening," a tenor voice said.

Bianca raised her head and acknowledged the man taking a seat across from her. "Good evening." She folded her fingers on the clothed table.

The man extended his tanned hand. His bright smile made him charming. "I'm Simon."

"Bianca." She shook his hand, ignoring his sweaty palm.

His face softened as his tone contained wonder. "Tell me something you love about yourself."

His question surprised her. "Well... I think I love my creativity. I'm a graphic designer."

His smile grew bigger. "How long have you been doing that?"

"I've been drawing since I was a kid, but I opened my business a few years back."

"Same here." Simon ran his fingers through his short, brown hair. He grabbed at the small bowl of nuts on her table, popping a few in his mouth without even taking his baby blue eyes off of her. "I got into photography in high school, but now I travel for the magazine I work for."

Bianca didn't mind this conversation so far. "That's amazing. I know for me, graphic design wasn't my first choice. I thought about the law, but when I had my daughter..." Her eyes bulged as Simon's mouth fell open. "Are you all right?"

His spoke as if in disbelief. "You have a child?"

"Yes. She's a teenager."

"So you're...?" He blinked rapidly as if trying to process what she was saying.

"Divorced. Almost three years now." She tilted her head to the side, trying to read his expression. "Are you alright?"

He ran a hand down the back of his head. "Yes, I just wasn't planning on dating a woman with children. I never wanted kids of my own."

Bianca froze momentarily. Not everyone wanted children. She could understand that, but this was the first time she'd heard it out loud and to her face. It never crossed her mind until now that if she got into another relationship, would the man accept her daughter? If he didn't, it was his loss. Her daughter came in the package deal.

"Thank you for sharing," she said.

He gave a faint smile and stood to his feet. "I hope you find what you're looking for." He extended her hand. "Have a good evening."

She returned the gesture. "You too." Bianca returned to her chair as he walked away. She hadn't expected that. As she adjusted in her cushioned seat, another man approached her table. Chin high and shoulders back. Bianca didn't know whether to describe him as confident or cocky based off the smolder he gave her. With an earring in one ear and a gold chain hanging around his neck, he took the seat across from her.

"Having a good time?" he asked. His voice was slightly deeper than Simon's.

"I'm still thinking about it." She focused her eyes on him.

He licked his full lips. "I'm Duane." His amber eyes shined and the way he leaned in made Bianca sit back in her chair.

"Bianca."

"Tell me: What is a beautiful woman like you doing here?" he asked.

"I could ask why you're here too."

Duane chuckled. "Let's say I'm always willing to meet new people. I hear this town is full of nice people."

"You live here?"

He shook his head. "No, but my parents do. I'm visiting and saw this event was going on so I figured why not give it a shot."

"Well I'll confirm that Edenville is filled with nice people."

"Have you lived here long?" he asked.

"Since my divorce. So almost three years."

He did a double take. "What man in his right mind would leave you?"

Bianca chuckled, despite the stung that lingered in her chest. "That's a long story."

"He didn't know what he had?" Duane asked, as he leaned his elbows on the table.

"I guess. You never know what you have until it's gone," she said.

Duane ran a hand down his bearded face. His face slackened as if he took her last words in deeper thought. His mouth twisted and he bit his bottom lip. "I'm sorry. I can't do this." He stood to his feet.

"O... kay," Bianca said.

"Now I see what my fiancée was talking about. She told me the exact same thing."

Bianca jerked. "What? Fiancée? You're engaged?"

"I was, but we called it off. She did. I didn't realized what I had so I took her for granted. It's like you said, 'we don't know what we have.'" He extended his hand to Bianca. "Thank you. Have a good night. I hope you find what you're looking for. I've got to find her and apologize." Once he shook Bianca's hand, Duane marched off and out the door.

Bianca held her hand up in midair but brought it back to the table. So far, this speed date event wasn't working in her favor. The first man didn't care for kids, and the second had to make amends with his ex-fiancée.

"I hope you all are enjoying yourselves," her mother said into the microphone. "Don't forget to keep your tickets close by. We'll have our first raffle giveaway in the next ten minutes."

Bianca played with the neckline of her dress. Her heels tapped underneath the table on the hardwood floors. She sighed and popped a few peanuts in her mouth.

"Is this seat taken?" Another man asked.

Bianca tilted her head to the side to stare at him. Olive skin, cropped cut hair, and a goatee. His cold eyes made him appear closed off. She couldn't hold back her questions after the first two men. "Are you against single mothers?"

He shook his head. "No."

"Do you have a fiancée? Ex-wife?"

The man backed away as his eyes widened. "No, but um… good luck to you." He moved on to the next woman.

Bianca waved at him. "You too." Adjusting in her chair, she checked her watch on her wrist. A dull headache kicked in, so she ran a hand down her neck. Not wanting to remain in the torture chamber any longer, she picked up her assigned number and returned it to the main table. She caught her mother's eye, who didn't hesitate to march her way.

"And where do think you're you going?" her mother asked. "The evening is just beginning."

"I have a date with a chocolate shake and a large order of fries," Bianca said, wrapping her shawl around her shoulders.

"Bianca? You promised to give it a chance." Her mother touched a hand to her arm.

"I'm not ready. At least not now. Not when most of the men here are looking for a hookup."

"That's not fair. I have some of the greatest men as my clients looking for meaningful relationships."

Bianca scanned the crowd behind her. The murmurs of the people at the tables filled her ears along with the music. "Well, I didn't meet one of them tonight."

Her mother's brow wrinkled. "Is it wrong that I worry about you?"

"There's nothing to worry about. I'm fine." Bianca dropped her shoulders and took her mother's hands. "We have Nicole's wedding soon, right? Maybe I'll meet some nice guy there, but for now, I want to go home."

Her mother released her grip and clapped her hands. "I'm so glad. I asked Nicole about Chad's groomsmen. So far, I think—"

"Mom, I'll meet him on my own."

Her mother pressed a hand to her chest. "I'm a professional. I have a ninety-five percent success rate. All the couples I match are either in committed relationships or married."

"And the remaining five percent?" Bianca folded her arms, waiting for her mother's answer.

Her mother narrowed her eyes at her. "No one is perfect, Bianca. I can't control what my clients do once they meet and start dating."

"Exactly, and I'm asking for that same freedom. You did your job tonight. I came like I agreed and I'm leaving early." She kissed her mother's cheek.

"Fine. I need to get back to my guests anway." Her mother's mouth twisted into a grin.

Bianca knew her mother wouldn't stay disappointed for long. Now if there was a way to get off her mother's matchmaking radar. Bianca sighed as she paced to her car. Not likely.

Chapter 4

The following evening, a stargazing party. Bianca had never understood Judy's need to host parties for the town, but she was creative. Perhaps it was her and Richard's way of promoting their bakery and restaurant in Edenville. Bianca didn't mind either way. Though trying to be mindful of the foods she ate, she couldn't resist Judy's cinnamon rolls.

With it being a family gathering, Judy encouraged a pajama party theme. Bianca wouldn't dare show her real pajamas in public, so she'd chosen a simple black-and-white pinstriped pajama set. Judy would owe her big time, but since Bianca had done the graphics for the party invitations, at least she'd gotten some publicity for her business.

"Are you there yet?" her mother asked through the speaker of her car.

Bianca disconnected her Bluetooth and held her phone to her ear. "I'm here. Don't know why you couldn't come."

"You know my self-care routine. It's my pamper me day," her mother said.

Bianca had to give her mother credit for taking care of herself. Was that why she didn't look a day over fifty? "If you say so.

Sometimes I think you let me come to these events alone so I can meet a man without my mother."

No answer.

"Mother?"

"Enjoy the party, sweetie." Her mother hung up the phone.

Bianca walked around to Judy's backyard. Three-dimensional star and meteor ornaments met her at the open gate. Cylinder vases with candles decorated the round tables. Bianca grinned as the ring of wind chimes filled her ears.

"Nice pajamas." A deep voice made her turn around.

Bianca faced Chad, Nicole's fiancé, and hugged his neck. His strong arms embraced her back. His sleep attire consisted of a hoodie and sweatpants. Slick back haircut, fit frame, clean shaven, and six foot one. "I can say the same thing about you."

Chad chuckled. "I keep it simple. Nicole wanted us to match, but I'm not into that."

"What about compromise? You two will be married soon."

Chad's face tightened.

"What's wrong?" Bianca touched a hand to his shoulder. "Is everything okay? You're not having second thoughts, are you?"

He shook his head. "No, it's just all this wedding stuff."

Bianca looped an arm around his and walked beside him. Who would have thought working with Chad as a client would have her introduce him to Nicole? Working on his real estate business logos and advertising graphics, Bianca got to know his charming and chivalrous ways.

The one time she imitated her mother's matchmaking skills paid off when she realized Chad's love for Renaissance art and traveling fit Nicole's interests. Once Bianca completed her job with him, she asked if he wanted to meet her best friend. Chad agreed, and he thanked Bianca more times than she could count when he fell in love with Nicole.

"Not really your thing, huh?" she asked him.

"Not at all," he said.

"One question."

"What?" he asked.

"Is Nicole happy?"

He grinned. "I hope so. She's been under some stress, but my mom's been helping as much as she can."

"I'm glad they're getting along." Bianca's mind flashed of her once-relationship with her former mother-in-law. While Malcom had never believed her, his mother had never missed an opportunity to criticize and nitpick how she'd treated Malcom. Bianca had never understood why when she'd done everything she could to make their marriage work.

"Me too. The last thing I need is my future wife and mother at each other's throats," Chad said.

She patted his arm as they approached a long table with casserole dishes. Was that lasagna? Bianca's mouth watered. Chad walked to the other side of the table and served his plate while Bianca did the same with hers.

"Bianca." Another man's voice came from behind her. Richard Long, Judy's husband and an exceptional chef. If he'd cooked the lasagna, then Bianca's taste buds were in for a treat.

"Please, tell me you cooked this." She pointed to her plate.

He winked at her.

"Thank God." Bianca couldn't wait to dig in.

Richard chuckled. "Enjoy, and great job with the invitations. We've gotten so many compliments."

"Anytime."

He leaned in. "And thanks for working with us on the payments. We should be able to get the rest to you soon."

"You're welcome. I know you will," Bianca said.

"Welcome, everyone." Judy stood farther ahead in front of the crowd. "Thank you all for coming. As you can see..." She looked upward. "The stars are perfect tonight, so enjoy the party. We've got plenty of food." When her eyes widened slightly, Bianca turned around to see whom Judy was staring at. Priscilla and Martin walked into the backyard, hand in hand.

"Excuse me," Richard said to Bianca and Chad, turning to leave.

Bianca's stomach quivered, but she only found an empty seat at a nearby table. Chad got caught talking to a few more friends who were over the moon about the upcoming wedding. Richard walked over to his step-brother and greeted Priscilla with a kiss to her cheek. Martin extended a hand to him, but Richard didn't take it.

Odd. This was the first time Bianca noticed tension between the men. Would Richard cause a scene at his own party? Though he kept his hands down, both of them clenched on either side of his body. Taking a forkful of lasagna into her mouth, Bianca reveled in the marinara sauce with just the right amount of seasoning and ricotta cheese. Glancing back at the exchange between the brothers, she wondered why Richard reacted the way he did to Martin's presence.

"I didn't think he would show up." Nicole slipped into the seat next to her.

"No?" Bianca didn't want to pry, but even Martin's presence made her own stomach jumpy. She didn't mind being cordial, but nothing further. She preferred to stay away. Martin appeared to have a wondering eye.

For an older man, he showed no shame in flirting with other women. His eyes bored into Nicole at the bridal shower. Even in front of his wife he didn't hesitate to comment or let his eyes linger longer than necessary. How did Priscilla put up with that?

Nicole shook her head.

"I won't ask if you don't want me to," Bianca said.

Her friend gave a faint smile. "But you're going to."

Bianca winked at her.

Nicole ran her fingers through her hair. "It's just... Martin is... Well, I don't think he approves of me and Chad."

"I don't think Martin's opinion matters to Chad. I would think his mother would have more say so."

Nicole added. "Chad and Martin can be a bit... icy to each other."

Priscilla married Martin when Chad was a fifteen years old. His biological father, a pilot, died in a plane crash. Despite his mother moving on with Martin, Chad never appeared to accept his step-father.

"Have they gotten better any?" Bianca asked.

"I think they're civil for Priscilla's sake. I just don't want any problems on my wedding day. Believe me, we have our good and bad days, but—"

"Your wedding day will be great." Bianca patted her hand.

"How can you be so sure?"

"I remember mine."

"Please, Bianca, I don't think that's a good..." Nicole covered her mouth for a moment. "I'm sorry. I shouldn't have said that."

Bianca felt a twinge in her chest. "I didn't think you would go there."

"I'm sorry. You have to understand I'm under a lot of stress. I don't know what I'm saying half the time. I didn't mean to hurt you. We both know Malcom was a jerk."

"He's still Alyssa's father." She swallowed the last of her lasagna.

"You still defend him."

She shook her head. "No, but I don't see the point of holding on to anger when he's clearly moved on."

"What about you?"

"I have a dog," Bianca said.

Nicole grinned. "Not just that. You know what I mean."

She did. "Not yet."

"Why not?" her friend asked.

Bianca's gaze wondered back to Martin, who walked away from Richard. Priscilla trotted behind him. Were they leaving? "I guess they're not staying."

Nicole looked in the same direction. "I guess not."

"Are you glad?" Bianca asked.

Her friend shrugged.

Chad joined them and bent over his fiancée in her seat. "Is this yours?" He held a charm bracelet in the air between his index finger and thumb.

Nicole grabbed it. "I didn't even notice it was gone." She fastened it back on her wrist. "This clasp won't stay put for some reason."

"Glad I found it?" Chad asked. Then he leaned in closer, and Nicole giggled as he whispered something else in her ear. He kissed her cheek.

"You two are so cute," Bianca said.

Chad looked back at her. "Thanks to you."

"Stop thanking me." Bianca joked, but when she winked back, they all laughed.

Nicole reached out and touched her hand. "I can't tell you how I much I appreciate the photos you're doing for us. You blew us away with the invitations and I wanted a personal touch for the thank you cards. I know we already hired a professional photographer for the wedding, but I love your unique graphic designs. You add the personal touch and I knew you could pull it off."

Bianca's chest swelled with pride. Her camera would be by her side during the reception as she was to snap photos and pick the best one to include for Nicole and Chad to send as "thank you's" to their guests. "Of course. I wouldn't miss the opportunity to do this for you both."

"You're the best," Chad said to Bianca. Then he held out his hand to Nicole. "Have a dance saved for me?"

"Always for you." She stood from her seat and clasped his hand.

Bianca leaned back in her seat as she watched the couple. Chad snaked his arms around Nicole's waist. The bride-to-be beamed at her future husband, teasing the nape of his neck with her fingers. Bianca's ribs squeezed tight, but she would be happy for her friend. Though she wasn't ready for something serious again, she remained hopeful that if she wanted to, she could have love again.

"YOU KNOW THEY SET ME up, right?" The next day, Bianca took Casper to the park. The newest addition to the family, and while she acted like the puppy wasn't winning her over, he was. She'd decided a walk would do her some good.

Other dogs barked around her as the wind sighed through the trees. Bianca inhaled the fresh-cut grass. She didn't rush Casper, who apparently took pleasure in digging his paws into the dirt.

The cool breeze caressed her skin, and Bianca checked her phone. Another email from a potential client. Logo request for a family business, compliments of a referral. Her chest swelled, excited at the possibility of a new project.

Why hadn't she started her business right out of college? A *hmm* escaped her throat. Marriage. A child to raise. While she could have pursued it then, being a mother had been her priority. So she'd settled for the drawings in her notebook.

A notebook that had been collecting her pictures since she'd been three years old. Bianca had surprised her parents at a young age, being able to see an image or a photo and replicate it almost exactly within a few hours. An artist in the family? She would have been the first, but coming from a family of educators on her mother's side and law enforcement on her dad's, she'd wanted the practical.

Then she'd gotten married right out of high school. Both parents had thought she and Malcom had been too young, but that hadn't deterred their decision to get married before college. She had been so sure Malcom had been the one.

Rolling her shoulders back, Bianca scrolled to another email. She did her best to check them twice a day. She would need another assistant soon. Her last temporary one married and moved to another country, and finding one with her specifications proved challenging at the moment. Bubbly, five feet, and red wine color hair, Marianne was the perfect assistant, almost predicting Bianca's needs. Thankfully, Bianca's schedule wasn't on overload, and if she couldn't take on any more projects, she declined them. This wouldn't last though as Wallace Designs grew in clientele.

Casting her eyes to her dog, she asked. "Are you done?"

Casper paid no attention to her. At least before work she could walk him through the park with no problems. Besides she had flexibility since she worked from home.

Then Casper barked. Bianca looked in his direction. What had caught his attention? A squirrel.

"Okay, let's go." She tugged at his leash, but she was careful not to hurt him. She didn't need anyone recording her for animal cruelty. Not that Bianca would do that. Her mother would be the first to press charges against her.

A giggle escaped her mouth. "Casper, let's go. You've done your business." She pulled a little harder as she shuffled backward. Bianca only bumped into something hard.

She heard a yelp. The man must have tripped over his feet since he tumbled to the ground. Bianca lost her own footing and fell with him. *Thud.* She only hoped she wouldn't bruise. Casper barked even more.

"Oh, man." A man's voice grunted, but his deep and husky tone sent shivers up her spine.

Bianca did her best to stand, but Casper's leash had tangled around their legs. "I'm so sorry. Are you all right?"

"Nothing's broken. At least I don't think it is." He groaned.

"Give me a second." She did her best to untangle the leash around their legs. What did Casper do? Jump through hoops? "I'll have it in a minute." When she felt a twinge in her low back, she paused. "Oh my."

"Are you okay?" the man asked.

"I will be." She eyed Casper, who wagged his tail. "I'll remember this one."

Bark, bark.

Bianca turned see the man from the bakery. Her breath caught, but she swallowed. His muscled shirt showed his defined abs, but she looked away as quickly as she spotted them. Her scalp tingled. Judging by the smirk on his full lips, he wasn't annoyed with her dog's antics. Bianca finally untangled their legs. "Got it. Are you all right?"

"No permanent damage." He dusted the dirt off his hands.

"I don't know what happened."

He faced her with his gray eyes. His back still on the ground. "I remember your face. The bakery, right?"

He did? "Right." Her eyes bugged as Casper trotted closer to the gentleman. He licked his face.

The man gave a smile. "He's friendly."

"That's Casper. The newest addition in my life. Let's hope he's learned his lesson here not to tie up strangers." Bianca stood to her feet as Casper jumped on his hind legs. He must have been amused too by his little trick. Thank goodness the leash was still in her grip and he didn't get away. She didn't want to report a missing dog.

The man chuckled as he followed to stand, taking care not to step on her dog. "And you are?"

She extended her hand. "Bianca. Bianca Wallace."

He shook her hand. "Lamar Sims. Pleasure. Finally, we meet." Finally? Did she cross his mind since their first encounter? Had he been wanting to meet her officially?

Bianca ignored it. If she didn't know any better, her mother may have paid him to run into her. Not her mother's usual style, although there was a dentist last year who'd "happened" to meet

Bianca at the movie theater during her "me time" on her day off. Not to mention the personal trainer who'd caught her during her occasional morning run in the park. The matchmaking would never end, unless Bianca met a man on her own. Judging by her current dating life, that wasn't happening anytime soon. "Are you new to Edenville?"

"I am." He dusted off the front of his black workout shorts. "It'll be two weeks this week."

Bianca's eyes lowered as Casper pawed at her feet. "Welcome. Sorry again about bumping into you. Casper is still learning."

He bobbed his head and met her gaze. "No problem. I'm good, so don't worry about me suing."

She laughed. "We don't do that here unless it's necessary."

"No personal injury lawyers around?" He scanned the park as if he were looking for one.

Bianca shook her head. "You're out of luck."

"Well, hopefully, next time we'll meet with both feet on the ground. Unless this little guy has a different idea." He bent down and scratched Casper behind his ears. Her puppy licked his hand. "Looks like I made a new friend already."

"It's a friendly town. We pretty much embrace newcomers."

"Good to know." Lamar straightened to his feet. He had a handsome face, and his gray eyes were captivating. Then he cleared his throat. "I'll see you around then."

He smiled, backed away, and resumed his pace for his run. Bianca turned since she didn't want to stare. Casper wagged his tail.

"What was that?" she asked her dog. They made no more stops on the way home. After a quick shower and change of clothes, Bianca opened her emails. Two more clients had sent in requests.

She spent the rest of her day sketching designs, answering emails, and mapping out her calendar for the next quarter. Wallace Designs had taken off for her in the last four years, and she'd been able to support herself and Alyssa. Bianca hadn't thought she could after depending on Malcom as the breadwinner. What had she known about owning her own business after their divorce?

The fear of failure had almost held her back from starting her own company. But what pained her more than failure was not trying at all. She had held back enough in life, putting her dreams on hold for her husband and child. It had been time for her to realize that her dreams weren't selfish.

Bianca huffed at the thought of her failed marriage. Perhaps she wasn't the same woman anymore. That had been one of Malcom's reasons for filing for divorce. Had he expected her to be the same eighteen-year-old girl who'd gushed at the sight of him forever? She'd grown up. She'd changed for the better, and if that was what had driven him away, then Bianca was better off.

Casper lapped at his bowl of water just as Bianca checked the clock on her wall. Her bridesmaid's dress hung in her closet. The rehearsal dinner was tomorrow evening. Then the wedding arrived Saturday afternoon. Hair and makeup were first, while the pictures would follow the ceremony at the venue.

Bianca would stand next to her friend and watch her exchange vows with the man she loved. She prayed for nothing but the best for the couple. Even if her own marriage hadn't lasted.

Chapter 5

Just like that. The night before the wedding arrived. Bianca didn't expect Mexican food for the rehearsal dinner, but according to Nicole, Chad had insisted since it was his favorite food. He'd already compromised on the reception meal, so Nicole and his mother had caved. Bianca enjoyed her chicken enchiladas Verde.

Her tongue tingled because of the spice, but it was nothing she couldn't handle. Her practice speech was coming soon. Her mind raced with what to say, but she only gulped her iced water to calm her nerves.

Martin caught her eye as he stood by the wall. When did he step away from his table with his wife? Bianca followed his gaze to Nicole. He took a gulp from his glass, as his eyes lingered. Bianca's skin prickled as something didn't sit well. Looking over at Priscilla, she saw her talking with the guests. When a waiter offered Priscilla a champagne glass, she declined it.

Bianca finished her plate, and took out her portable camera from her purse. Walking around the room, she snapped photos. She would take more at the wedding reception, but there were some great shots from the rehearsal dinner.

The wedding planner, standing in her pencil suit, tapped her fork to a glass. Her medium length brunette hair flowed in loose curls. Perfect arched eyebrows, long acrylic nails, and a slender frame. Bianca had met her at the engagement party, and had talked to her briefly when accompanying Nicole to the bridal shop for her dress. "I think we're ready for the toasts, everyone."

Bianca returned her camera to her purse. Dean, Chad's best friend, had already said to her, "Ladies first."

Bianca held up her glass. "Good evening everyone."

"Good evening." The crowd gave her their attention.

Bianca touched her throat but continued. "Nicole and I became friends in college. She was definitely a social butterfly, and we managed to keep in touch all these years. I was so glad to find out that she too lived here in Edenville." Looking over at the couple, Chad draped an arm around Nicole's shoulders. "When she told me she and Chad were engaged, I couldn't help but be happy for her. Chad, you're getting a great woman. Treat each other well." Bianca held her glass higher in the air. "To the bride and groom."

Chad kissed Nicole and Bianca walked over to hug them both.

"Thank you," Chad said. He kissed Bianca's cheek.

"I just hope I remember all of that tomorrow." The group laughed. *Crash!* Bianca's body jerked as she watched Martin storm from the hallway in front of the kitchen. Glass in hand, Richard trailed behind him. Was Richard holding a knife?

"Oh, no." Chad hurried over as the men argued.

Bianca took Nicole's hand. She'd never seen them argue so loudly. Not even at the stargazing party.

"Why don't you get out?" Richard shoved Martin's shoulder.

Chad stood between them, mostly to keep Richard from attacking Martin.

"I don't think so." Martin looked at the crowd. "Don't you see there's a wedding going on this weekend?" He took another swallow from the dark liquid in his medium-sized glass. No doubt it was alcohol.

"They don't want you here anymore than I do!" Richard shouted.

Bianca then spotted Priscilla cover her forehead with her hand. This wasn't good for her. She rushed over and touched her shoulder. "Are you all right?"

Priscilla nodded. "I am. Sometimes my heart..." She touched a hand to her chest.

Heart trouble. Bianca knew that too well from her late father. That was how they'd lost him a few years back. Bianca pressed her lips together, choking up at the memory. This wasn't the time.

Martin walked over, just as Chad got Richard to return to the kitchen. Martin wobbled a bit, but leaned over his wife. How much had he had to drink? "Are you all right?"

Priscilla nodded, not making eye contact with her husband. Bianca didn't blame her.

"No thanks to you." Chad stalked over, taking Bianca's place next to his mother. "Are you sure you're all right?"

"I'm fine, dear." She touched her son's cheek.

Martin chugged the last of his glass. Then he stared at Nicole and licked his thin lips. "Do me the honor of a dance?"

Nicole swallowed. Bianca raised an eyebrow. She wouldn't want to dance with the man, either. Not after his stunt with his step-brother. Bianca's eyes roamed around the room. Apparently, the guests of Chad and Nicole resumed their meals.

"No, thanks. I need a moment." Nicole walked to the ladies' room. Bianca followed her, finding her friend in front of the sink. She sniffled and wiped underneath her eyes.

"Nicole?"

"I'm sorry." She grabbed a napkin from the dispenser and touched up her makeup.

Bianca moved closer and gave her a side hug.

Nicole said, "I'm sure he's only had too much to drink."

Bianca sighed. "Well... I'd focus on what's important."

"What's that?"

"You're getting married tomorrow!" Bianca squealed.

Nicole laughed. "Thank you. I'm glad you're here."

The women stared in the mirror. Bianca heard music through the speakers. Earth, Wind, & Fire's "Shining Star" played. She shimmied her hips. Nicole giggled but tossed her blonde hair from her shoulders as she rocked to the music. They laughed as they had their own dance party.

"Oh, my goodness." Nicole touched a hand to her chest. "I feel better. Tomorrow Chad and I'll be Mr. and Mrs. Lee."

"Keep that in mind despite all this craziness."

A knock sounded at the door. "Nicole?"

Bianca recognized Chad's voice.

"Coming." Nicole's eyes beamed but widened as she felt around her wrist. "Oh, no. Not again. My bracelet's gone."

Bianca stared at the tiled floor. "I'll look for it. Go talk to Chad."

Nicole nodded and headed to the door.

Bianca's eyes scanned the floors, but she didn't detect Nicole's bracelet. Bianca only hoped it wasn't lost for good.

Perhaps it was in the hallway. Leaving the ladies' room, Bianca saw no trace of the bracelet. She bit her bottom lip. It would disappoint Nicole.

"You're just bitter." Martin? Again?

Bianca saw him at the end of the hall with Chad. Bianca lowered her eyes as she walked past them, but she couldn't help but overhear in passing.

"You stay away from Nicole. I'm warning you," Chad said.

Bianca paused just as her phone buzzed inside the pocket of her skirt. It was a text from Alyssa.

Mom, can you pick up some dogs treats for Casper on the way home?

Sure

"Bad news?" Martin's rough voice made Bianca inwardly wince.

She pivoted to face the older man. His fair skin wrinkled around his eyes when he did smile. He must have been amused today, but Bianca's muscles tensed. "No, everything's fine."

Martin extended his hand. "Think you can keep up?"

"I'd much rather I be the one to dance with you," Priscilla said, standing right behind her husband.

Martin unbuttoned the top button on his collared black shirt. "Jealous, my dear?" he asked his wife.

Bianca stepped to the side for Priscilla to dance with her husband. Priscilla shook her head slightly, but Bianca gave a slight smile back. Martin *had* had too much to drink. Perhaps his wife could calm him down. Hopefully, he'd be better for the wedding.

A WEDDING SHE WOULD never forget. Chad and Nicole were now Mr. and Mrs. Lee. Bianca had pressed her lips together when she'd heard the couple exchange vows, but a tear had escaped her eye nonetheless.

Even when her own wedding flashed through her mind, Bianca recalled the smiles and congrats she'd received from friends and family. Her heart had swelled with joy. She couldn't wait to start her life with Malcom. Bianca played with her gold necklace.

That was then. This was now. A new beginning.

Now at Chad and Nicole's wedding reception, Bianca stared at the long, dusty roses and plum flowers standing tall in clear vases on all the tabletops covered in black cloth. The black-tie theme wedding hadn't appealed to Bianca at first, but the decorations had turned out to be amazing. The way the newlyweds danced, embracing one another. Dancing to Dave Barnes' "God Gave Me You," they were happy.

Bianca was grateful the wedding had gone smoothly. Martin was supposed to be seated beside his wife, but she hadn't seen him since the ceremony. Bianca sipped from her glass as she swayed to the music. The day brought back memories for her, but she wouldn't dwell on her failed marriage. She had Alyssa. The best gift she could have received.

"Having fun, sweetie?" her mother asked as she adjusted her shawl on her black floral gown.

Bianca adjusted in her seat. Her strapless black gown accentuated her honey skin, and her updo hairstyle complemented her round face. Bianca tucked a loose tendril of hair behind her ear. "I think so. I got some great photos so far. This wedding tuned out great, despite last night."

"I heard. You know the people in this town cannot keep a secret."

Bianca giggled. "I'm just glad Nicole's doing better. She's been on edge lately."

"I haven't seen Martin since we got here. One moment he was at the bar, and the next he was gone."

"Maybe he left. I don't miss him. Do you?"

Her mother covered her giggle with her free hand. Bianca stared into the crowd as more couples danced along with Chad and Nicole. Priscilla chatted with guests as they stood off from the dancefloor, but she walked over to where Bianca and her mother were sitting.

Priscilla placed her white gloved hand on Bianca's shoulder. "You should be dancing, Bianca. There're so many prospects out here."

Bianca scanned the room again.

There were a few handsome faces in the crowd, but none caught Bianca's attention. Not like Lamar Sims. Bianca swallowed. "Maybe later."

A waiter approached their table with a tray of filled champagne glasses. Stubble on his chin, tall, with olive skin against his black and white uniform. "Ladies?"

"No thank you," Priscilla said. "I don't drink." She tapped a gloved hand to her chest.

Bianca and her mother accepted a glass, thanking him in return.

Priscilla continued. "I still say there are more than plenty of men for you to dance with, Bianca."

"I was thinking the same thing." Her mother then sipped her glass.

"You're both on my case now?" She looked between them both with a grin on her face.

"Maybe I can help with that," a bass voice said.

Bianca squealed at the sight of the man's face. Crew haircut, full dark brown beard, and muscular build. His gentle speckled eyes beamed as his white smile grew. Nicole's other best friend. He came, though she wondered how he was accepting Nicole's marriage after years of his unrequited love for her. The fact that he came showed his support for her in Bianca's eyes.

Bianca exclaimed. "Jordan!"

He chuckled as she hurried to her feet and hugged his neck. "I didn't think I would see you here."

Jordan gestured to the dance floor. "Let's dance." He acknowledged Bianca's mother and Priscilla. "Ladies."

Bianca's mother nodded with beaming eyes, while Priscilla's face grimaced. Adjusting her shawl, she marched to the next table. Bianca didn't ask about her annoyed reaction.

"Not sure what that was about." Her mother gestured to her and Jordan. "Go have some fun."

Jordan walked with Bianca hand-in-hand to the dance floor. He avoided eye contact with the bride and groom. Bianca rested one hand on his shoulder, while the other clasped his hand. Her eyes glanced over his shoulder. She spotted a man dressed in black. Tall, clean shaven, and tanned.

Bianca recognized him as the limo driver who'd dropped them off at the venue after they'd finished their hair appointments at the hair salon. Nicole *had* told him he was more than welcome to attend the reception and serve himself a plate. That was Nicole. She never missed an opportunity to help a stranger, even if it was in a small way.

"Want to tell me why Priscilla looked at you that way?" she asked him.

He shrugged. "Who knows? I can't please everyone." He eyed her dress. "You look amazing. I can't believe you have a teenage daughter."

Bianca smiled. Jordan obviously didn't care about Priscilla's opinion, so she dropped the subject. "Don't tell me about it. I feel old."

"You're not old. You look great for a woman of—"

She squeezed his shoulder. "Don't you dare say *my age*!"

Jordan laughed, but then his eyes diverted to Nicole and Chad.

"Are you all right?" Bianca asked.

"Why wouldn't I be?" He shrugged.

"I remember someone having a huge crush on Nicole back in college before she..."

Jordan sighed. "Yeah, but she turned me down. She didn't feel the same way." He paused as his gazed focused on Nicole and Chad. "You think she's happy?"

Bianca moved with Jordan as the music changed. Brad Paisley's "She's Everything" boomed through the speakers. "I think so."

"I hope so."

Bianca opened her mouth, only to have the DJ make an announcement.

"All right, single ladies, come to the dance floor. The bride's going to toss the bouquet!"

Jordan gestured at Bianca. "You going?"

"I'd rather not."

He wiggled his thick eyebrows. "Don't think you'll catch it?"

Bianca pinched his shoulder.

"Violent, but you're cute when you're angry." He winked at her.

Bianca's eyes narrowed at him. "Only to make you happy, my friend."

Jordan laughed as Bianca joined the other single women on the dance floor. She stood in the back of the group just as Nicole walked in front of them with her bouquet.

"Here we go! One. Two. Three!" Nicole tossed the bouquet behind her back.

Bianca watched as if it moved in slow motion. While others reached up, almost elbowing each other out of the way, Bianca only faced her palms upward. To her surprise, the bouquet landed in her hands. Her eyes bugged. All eyes faced her.

Nicole clapped and hurried to her side. "Awesome!"

Bianca gave a humorless laugh. "You did this on purpose."

Nicole giggled. "No, but if anyone deserves a happy ending next, it's you."

Bianca pointed at her, but her grin gave her away. Heading back to her seat, Bianca saw that her mother was gone. She placed the bouquet on the table as her eyes searched the crowd. Then she spotted her mother coming from the hallway.

"Are you all right?" she asked.

"Priscilla wasn't feeling well. I walked with her to the ladies' room. She has her pills with her so she said she'd be fine." Her mother resumed sitting in her seat. "This wedding may be too much for her."

"Is it really her heart?"

"I think it's the excitement and Chad is her only child. Now he's married and starting a new life."

"Did you feel that way when I got married? That I was leaving you behind in a way?"

"I was happy for you," her mother said. "I think most parents are, but time goes by so fast. One moment your kids are babies and the next, they're graduating and off to college."

Bianca winced. "Don't remind me, please."

"See what I mean?" her mother continued. "Alyssa is not too far behind."

"And now there's a boy."

Her mother grinned. "I see. How's that going?"

Bianca's eyes widened slightly. "No 'she's too young to be dating'? Isn't that what you said to me at her age?"

Her mother waved off her question. "I'm the grandmother, so I can spoil her. I was only strict with you and Melanie."

"Traitor."

Her mother winked at her.

"Well, I want to meet the boy before she goes out with him."

Her mother bobbed her head. "Now you remind me of your father. That's exactly what he said when you told us about your crush on Malcom. He wanted to hire a private investigator."

Bianca's mouth fell open. "He didn't."

"I stopped him," her mother said. "After I told him I would keep an eye on you two."

"I still can't believe you followed us on our first date." Bianca ran a finger over her eyebrow.

"It was either him or me." Her mother paused as her fingers drifted to her now bare ring finger. "Sometimes I can still hear him laughing. Even in my dreams, I can see his face. Hear his voice. To think we almost made forty years."

Bianca touched her mother's hand. "I miss him." There'd been terrible beyond health circumstances. If only his heart had been stronger, but it took him away from the family too soon.

Her mother patted her hand. "Me too."

"Ladies and gentlemen, the bride and groom are heading out!" the DJ announced through his microphone.

Bianca grabbed her small purse and the small drawstring bag that was filled with birdseed. She smiled, knowing her friend didn't want the birds to choke on rice. She followed along with her mother as they tossed the birdseed at the couple. The limo waited for them, but Chad kissed Nicole one more time before opening the door. The crowd cheered only louder.

Bianca managed one last glance at Jordan, but he slipped away from the crowd. She didn't blame him for not staying, but since he was Nicole's best friend, Bianca knew he would show his support. He'd do anything for Nicole.

Tossing more birdseed, family and friends cheered and whistled at the newlywed couple. Bianca's chest swelled. Her friend's bouquet was tucked underneath her arm. Would she get married again? Bianca would think about that later. Right now, she wanted to get out of her five-inch pumps. They'd served their purpose, but she was grateful that she had flats in her car.

Chad opened the door for his new wife, only to hear Nicole's high-pitched scream. Bianca's instincts kicked in and she scurried to her friend's side. Nicole's face paled. Looking inside the limousine, Bianca spotted someone sitting across from where they stood.

She didn't hesitate to walk to the other side. Bianca gasped at the sight. Her eyes bugged. It was Martin, and judging by the blood soaking his collared shirt, he was dead.

Chapter 6

Bianca sat next to her mother on a nearby bench. Police sirens had replaced the cheers and whistles for the newlywed couple. The paramedics now added to the crowd. Bianca had exchanged her heels for her flats, but the police had closed off the area and no one could leave until they received statements. Clouds blocked portions of the evening sky, but at least it didn't rain. It had been one of Nicole's biggest concerns, but the day had been sunny.

"They can't keep us here all night." Her mother huffed. "Who would do such a thing? We just saw Martin earlier."

"You said you saw him at the bar?" Bianca asked.

Her mother nodded. "He got another drink and stepped outside. I thought perhaps he was getting some air."

"That's more than what he bargained for." Who would kill Martin? Bianca bit at her bottom lip. Aside from his argument with Richard the other night, there'd been no apparent threat. Not that she could think of.

Then she recalled hearing his heated conversation with Chad, but the groom had been inside with Nicole on the dance floor. Between greeting and thanking family members, had he slipped away without Bianca seeing? Hearing sobs, she spotted Priscilla crying on her son's shoulder. Bianca's heart broke for the woman.

Speaking of heart, she hoped this didn't make things worse for Priscilla's condition. Losing Martin. How would the woman survive? She loved him, despite his questionable behavior.

Bianca caught a glimpse of Nicole. She rubbed at her covered arms since Chad had given her his jacket. Bianca patted her mother's arm. "I'll be back."

She slipped through the crowd toward her friend. "How are you holding up?"

Nicole shook her head slightly. "I just can't believe it." She folded her arms over her chest.

"Me, neither." Bianca's eyes wondered over the crowd just as a familiar face grabbed her attention. Lamar? Dressed in a dark suit, he spoke to one officer.

"He's new?" Nicole wondered.

"Yeah, he is."

"You've met him? Is he a detective?"

Bianca shrugged. "I'll guess we'll find out."

Lamar finished his conversation and faced where the officer pointed. At Bianca. Her. Lamar's eyes widened for a moment, but then he walked over to her and Nicole.

"Bianca Wallace," he said.

"Yes."

He showed her his badge attached to his pants. "Detective Lamar Sims. We meet again. I'm told that you discovered the body."

"When Nicole, the bride, screamed, I walked over and saw the body." Bianca shivered recalling the blank stare in Martin's hazel eyes. Focusing on Detective Sims, his eye contact stuck with hers for a moment as if taking her in. Bianca glanced at the concrete as her skin tingled. Did he plan to stare?

Then he gestured for her to follow him. Bianca stepped over with him away from the crowd. "Can you tell me exactly what happened?"

Bianca wrung her hands together. "Well... we were saying goodbye to the bride and groom. The groom, Chad, opened the door to the limousine."

Detective Sims wrote on his notepad. They still used those? "And then?"

"Again when I heard Nicole scream, I walked over to see what had happened. Martin was dead."

"Did you check his pulse?" he asked.

"No, I didn't touch him. I just saw... the blood soaking his shirt." Bianca's stomach quivered. She cocked her head to the side. "I didn't see the murder weapon." Recalling the tear in his shirt, her lips parted. "Is it possible they stabbed him? We would have heard a gun."

Detective Sims didn't answer. "Anything else you can remember? Did Martin have any enemies?"

Bianca stared at the concrete. "Well... there was an argument last night at the rehearsal dinner. I don't think Martin had enemies. He would get riled up after drinking too much, but that's all I know."

"Tell me more about the argument." Detective Sims appeared intrigued.

"The caterer, Richard Long, is his step-brother. I don't know what they were arguing about, but we heard something break. Richard wanted him to leave. He was pretty upset." Enough to kill his own family? The notion itself was low.

"Was that the only argument you witnessed between them?"

"There was... a stargazing party at Richard's house earlier this week. Martin and his wife showed up, but they didn't stay."

"Why not?" He cocked his head to the side.

"I don't believe Richard cared to see them there. I didn't hear much, so that's all I know about that." The last thing she wanted to do was point fingers at Richard or anyone in her hometown.

Detective Sims bobbed his head as he wrote. "Does anything else come to mind?"

Bianca shrugged. "Nothing serious. Whom do you think would kill him?"

"I intend to find out. Thank you."

He differed from when they'd met in the park. This Lamar didn't make small talk. He was Detective Sims now. He walked over to talk to more of the wedding guests. Bianca ran a hand down her neck. Who would want Martin dead? Inching over to the limo, she saw that his body no longer was sitting inside, but they had him covered with a white sheet on the ground.

The next thing she knew, the paramedics had placed him in a body bag and on a stretcher. Bianca saw Chad hold his mother as she wept in grief. Bianca then felt her own chest twinge. She walked over to her own mother, who watched the scene with her mouth covered. Bianca draped an arm around her mother's shoulders. This couldn't be good for her.

"Are you okay?" she asked.

Her mother bobbed her head. "Just brings back... memories when I received word about your father."

Bianca rested her chin on her mother's shoulder. "I need to get you home."

Her mother shook her head. "We can't go now. The police haven't questioned everyone." She exhaled. "Poor Priscilla."

Bianca leaned into her mother's embrace as they watched Priscilla cry over Martin's body. Chad stayed by her side, while Nicole bowed her head. Bianca walked her mother back to the bench. They held hands as they waited, but then Bianca stood to her feet to pace.

She continued. "I wish there were something we could do."

"I think it's best we be there for the family as often as we can," her mother said.

Bianca shook her head in agreement. "I'll be back."

"Where are you going?"

"I need to walk around some, Mom. This is a lot."

Her mother nodded and Bianca stepped away for a moment to herself. Her eyes glanced back to see Detective Sims talking to Priscilla and Chad. Getting closer to the street, Bianca hoped she could take her mother home soon. Tapping her foot, her eyes drifted to the ground. She blinked. It couldn't have been. Were her eyes playing tricks on her? She stepped off the curb.

Was that blood on the concrete? Bianca stooped down to inspect. It was. Had Martin been killed and the killer had dragged him to the limo? Had he been trying to get inside for help but hadn't made it in time?

Bianca straightened to her feet. Where was the driver? Her head swiveled as she searched, but she only spotted him with another police officer. Had he seen anything? How long had he stayed inside the venue before returning to his post?

Perhaps Detective Sims could talk to him. Bianca stooped to the ground once more. Was there any more blood? Then her eyes stared under the limo. Was something by the tire? She looked both ways, not wanting to disturb the crime scene. She peeked closer, only to grab her phone and use it for better lighting. Her mouth fell open. It couldn't have been.

"Ma'am, this is an official crime scene. You need to join the others on the sidewalk," a police officer said.

Bianca didn't move.

"Ms. Wallace?" Detective Sim's voice again. "We need you to step away."

She stood to her feet, shutting off her flashlight.

"Ms. Wallace?" Detective Sims only knelt to see what had made her so intrigued. "Do you recognize this?" He stood to his feet. He held a bracelet in his gloved hands. A charm bracelet that she knew well.

Bianca bobbed her head. "Yes."

"Whose is it, Ms. Wallace?" Detective Sims asked.

She closed her eyes. Shaking her head. It couldn't be true.

"Ms. Wallace?"

"Nicole's."

"The bride?"

Bianca nodded.

"Ask the bride over, please." The officer next to him nodded and pushed through the crowd. Detective Sims faced Bianca. "Do you think she had something to do with this?"

"No. She lost this last night. To be honest, I'm not even sure they killed Martin inside the limo." Bianca motioned for him to follow her. She pointed to the small drops of blood on the ground. "How is there blood here? Besides, Nicole was inside the entire time."

He cocked his head to the side. "I'm aware of the blood, Ms. Wallace. What I want to know is are you sure your friend didn't have anything to do with this? Is it possible she stepped outside for anything?"

"I know her. She's not a killer."

"That doesn't mean I can't bring her in for questioning." He stared at the blood on the ground. "If she's innocent, we'll soon find out."

Bianca's chest heaved as he walked back over to Nicole. As soon as he held up the bracelet, Nicole's mouth fell open.

Chad stepped forward. "She didn't do it."

Priscilla covered her mouth in apparent disbelief.

Detective Sims handed the bracelet to another officer, who placed it inside a plastic bag. "I'll need you to come the police station, Mrs. Lee, for questioning."

Bianca stood still as a statue as Nicole and Chad faced each other. He hugged his wife. Bianca's nails dug into her palm. Her friend was innocent.

Chapter 7

"Thank goodness. It's good to be home." Bianca's mother undid her seatbelt, but she didn't get out the car right away. "I can't believe this is happening."

Bianca didn't take her hands off the steering wheel. What a night. A wedding. A reception. A dead body. "I can't believe Nicole is a suspect."

"Are you sure that was her bracelet?" her mother asked.

Bianca's hands dropped from the wheel to her lap. "Yes. She lost it again at the rehearsal dinner. Even at the stargazing party, Chad gave it back to her when it came off her wrist then. I tried to help her look for it last night, but I didn't see it. I wonder if..."

"If what?"

"Did someone... plant it there? They wanted someone to find it."

"Bianca, don't let your imagination run away with you."

It did. She'd pointed the police to her friend for murder. Bianca's stomach hardened at the thought. Replaying the evening in her mind, did she miss anything? Did Nicole step out from the reception? No. This was all a mistake. Her friend wasn't guilty and time would prove that. She hoped.

Bianca turned to face her mother, who had been telling her about her imagination since she'd been six years old. At least when she'd been a child, her mother had encouraged it because that was how Bianca's artistic skills had improved. In the case of murder, she could see why her mother wanted her to back off.

"I'm serious," her mother continued. "Once your wheels start turning, you can't let go of a thing."

"Can you blame me?"

"I love Nicole too. I don't want anything to happen to her, but I believe it's all going to work out. I'm sure the police can take care of this and find out whoever... killed poor Martin." Her mother clutched her purse in her lap.

Bianca reached over and patted her hand. "Are you okay, Mom? Really?"

"I will be. It's just a lot to process. This type of stuff doesn't happen in Edenville."

"What *does* happen, then?"

"The most we've had, Bianca, is an altercation at one of our summer kickoffs. Something about the cook-off being rigged and who knows why oranges were thrown from the fruit table."

Bianca giggled. "Oranges?"

Her mother chuckled with her. "And coolers and lawn chairs. Don't ask how it escalated because I still don't know." Turning to her daughter with a smile, she leaned over and hugged her. "I'm just glad we're okay. I wish I could say the same for Priscilla." Her mother patted her cheek. "Go home and get some sleep. Love you."

"Love you too." Bianca sat in her car until her mother walked inside. Once the porch light turned on, she pulled out of the driveway and headed to her house. She rode in silence. The night didn't seem real. A murder right outside of the wedding venue. She had been close to a killer. She shuddered at the thought.

Once she arrived home, she quickly undressed for a shower. It couldn't wash the day away, but it calmed her frayed nerves. She wiped the steam off the mirror and washed her face free from makeup. False eyelashes? Never again.

She'd check on Alyssa after cleaning up. Hopefully she finished her research paper, which was why she couldn't attend the wedding like she wanted. Bianca peeled off the false eyelashes and tossed them in the trash. Freedom. Nothing against Nicole wanting her bridesmaids to have them, but Bianca preferred her own. Still, the makeup artist had done an amazing job with her look, along with the others'.

Leaving the bathroom in her cotton robe, Bianca paced to her daughter's room. Sound asleep in her bed. Casper next to her. Her backpack hung of one of the bed posts of her full sized bed. Her phone faced up on her nightstand, and her lamp was still lit. The corners of Bianca's mouth turned up and she kissed her daughter's forehead. Then she turned off her lamp and walked out, but left Alyssa's door cracked. Thank goodness her daughter didn't attend the wedding after all. Bianca would have hated for her to see a dead body like that.

Some wedding this turned out to be. Bianca figured a cup of tea would further relax her. Pausing for a moment, she stared into space in her country style kitchen. The clock ticked on the wall. Ten thirty at night.

After the evening she had she was going straight to bed. At least a cup of tea would relax her frayed nerves. After boiling hot water in her tea kettle, she poured it into her favorite cup and added honey to the herbal mix. Chamomile. Her favorite.

She rubbed at her chin as she searched her thoughts for answers. Something didn't add up. Nicole couldn't have committed a murder.

Though Detective Sims hadn't confirmed her suspicions, Martin had to have been stabbed, but why sit him in the limo? Why hadn't Martin called for help? Had the killer worked too fast? Bianca rubbed the back of her head.

Though the situation was different, her dad's face flashed in her mind. Her father had died one year before Malcolm had filed for divorce. He'd been a police officer, but he'd been arrested for murder. Mistaken identity. Despite being a police officer, he'd been mistaken for a shooter.

Bianca closed her eyes. Because of how it had looked on tape, her father had been jailed for murder in the second degree. He'd been awaiting his trial, only to die in prison. Heart disease ran in his family, so it'd been a miracle for him to work on the police force for twenty years.

Buzz, buzz. Bianca's phone rattled on the table. Nicole? She didn't let her friend wait another minute. "Are you all right?"

Nicole sniffled. "They didn't arrest me, but I hated being there."

Bianca touched a hand to her chest. "How did your bracelet get there, Nicole? I thought you lost it."

"I did. That stupid clasp could never stay shut." Her friend groaned. "I don't know what to do."

"We all saw you. There's no way they can prove that you left your own wedding to kill Martin. You were inside the entire time."

Nicole didn't answer.

"How well did you even know Martin? You and Chad only dated for two years, right?"

Nicole cleared her throat. "I told you Martin didn't approve of us."

"Why not? He's not even Chad's dad. Why would he care?"

Nicole groaned. "I don't know. It's not like Priscilla's a real fan of me either."

"Now's not the time to worry about that. Besides, weren't you two working things out?"

"Yes."

Bianca crossed her legs underneath her table. "So you didn't get along with your in-laws. Welcome to the club." Bianca couldn't count the number of times she'd ask Malcolm to talk to his parents on her behalf. She sighed. "Think, Nicole. Who would want to get rid of Martin? What about last night? The argument with Richard?"

"Well..." Nicole paused. "Chad did tell me a few things. Before Richard and Judy merged their restaurant and bakery, he and Martin were business partners in real estate. Then Richard left to start his restaurant business. When he fell in love with Judy, it made sense to them to combine."

Bianca perked. "For how long were they business partners? Martin and Richard."

"A while," Nicole said. "Maybe ten years. Then Chad says Richard took his shares and left."

Bianca tapped her fingers to her lips. "Martin was pretty well off, so if Richard was a partner, why would he leave to be a caterer?"

"Chad thought the same thing, but Richard wanted to pursue his passion."

"A lot of hard work either way. Anything else?"

"Why are you asking?" Nicole asked. "Bianca, don't feel like you have to get involved."

Bianca twirled her spoon in her empty cup. It clinked in her ears. Justice was always worth fighting for and Bianca knew her friend was innocent.

"I can't stand the thought of innocent people..." She stopped.

"Your dad, huh?"

Bianca sighed. "Yeah." She stood to her feet. "I don't mind asking a few questions. It's not as if I'm going to the killer's house for coffee."

Nicole giggled, as if she needed the laugh. "I didn't intend for my wedding day to end like this."

"I wish it didn't have to be this way," Bianca said. She looked at the clock again. Almost eleven. "I need to get some sleep. You should too."

"I'm supposed to be on my honeymoon."

"How's Chad?"

"Worried about me. Anyway, thanks for listening. Good night, Bianca." She hung up.

Bianca held her phone to her chest for a moment, then decided to do a quick search on the internet. She typed in Martin's name. Real Estate Mogul worth over a million dollars. She saw no signs that Richard had ever been a business associate. Had Martin cut him off from the business once Richard had left?

She pulled her lips in. Why would a business mogul retire early to work in culinary? *Slow down.* That was the phrase Nicole used. Slow down from what? It wouldn't hurt to find out.

Reading further, she spotted a new name. Nora. The name popped up more than once with Martin's. Bianca's mouth dropped open at the various articles that appeared on screen. Based on the ones she skimmed through, Martin had been married to her before

Priscilla. His marriage to Nora had lasted for five years, and then he'd filed for divorce due to "irreconcilable differences."

Glancing at the clock one more time, Bianca knew she needed to go to bed. That would be difficult. The wheels were turning in her brain.

MONDAY MORNING, BIANCA'S eyes scanned the slanted displays of organic apples, oranges, melons, tomatoes, and colorful peppers. Since she had a taste for smoothies, she didn't forget to pick up some bananas and strawberries. Pushing her grocery cart farther along, she stopped in front of the meat section.

Plant-based beef? She wasn't sold on the idea until Nicole had talked her into eating a plant-based burger. To Bianca's surprise, it hadn't been half-bad. Picking up a packet, she added it to her cart. Nicole. How was she holding up?

Bianca couldn't get Martin's blood stained shirt out of her mind, nor Nicole's high-pitched screams. Who would do such a thing, and at a wedding, of all places? The wheels on her cart squeaked, but she pushed it down the organic food aisle. She didn't mind switching things up in her diet, as long as she could treat herself every now and then.

Though Bianca attempted to ignore her sensitive stomach, her mind raced with possibilities. Martin dead right after the reception. How long had he been dead? Poor Priscilla. She would check on her as soon as possible, but with the shock of losing her husband, Bianca had decided to give her some space.

Protein bars. She didn't see the brand she liked until she looked upward. Since when were they on the top shelf? Choosing to wear flats today, there was no way Bianca's short stature could reach the top. Her eyes scanned around her. No attendant in sight and no one on the organic aisle. It wasn't a popular as the soda aisle or the freezer section with the ice cream.

"Just great," Bianca mumbled. Reaching up, her finger barely grazed the top shelf, much less the box she wanted. She could step up on the bottom shelf as leverage, but hadn't she seen enough disasters from others who'd only made the boxes tumble to the floor? She tried again, a groan escaping her lips as she reached as high as she could.

Her hand was only met by a larger one that grabbed the box for her. Bianca froze for a moment, but then she turned her head. Detective Sims. He gave a faint smile, but her senses dulled at the woodsy scent of his cologne.

"Is this all you needed?" he asked.

Bianca couldn't think for a few seconds. He was so close, and his warm breath tickled her ear. Swallowing, she took the box from his hand. "Um... I think so. Thank you."

"Did you want another one? Or is one enough for you?" He gestured to the top shelf.

Bianca stepped to the side to give herself some space from him. How had she not seen him, much less heard him behind her? "One more, if you don't mind."

Detective Sims grabbed another box of her favorite protein bars. "Chocolate peanut butter?" He extended the box to her.

Bianca grabbed it, avoiding the touch of his fingers. "It's the only one I like so far. Some of these organic foods are an acquired taste."

He chuckled. "I know what you mean."

"Thank you again. For your help."

"You're welcome." He nodded his head and then stood in front of his own cart. "Have a good day."

"You too," she replied. As he walked past her, Bianca watched. Her eyebrows furrowed but then released. She had to know. "Detective?"

"Yes, Ms. Wallace?"

"Any progress with the murder case? I can't see Nicole doing something like this. Are you sure—"

He held up his hand to stop her. "Ms. Wallace, we're working on it. I know you want to help your friend. It's commendable, but I can't share details of this case with you."

"I understand, but you should've have seen her reaction. She was practically trembling."

"I understand, Ms. Wallace, but—"

"Martin wasn't the most likable guy in town, but I don't think Nicole is your murderer. What if there was someone else? What if Martin had some enemies you don't know about? He was an important businessman. Shrewd. Proud," Bianca said.

"Do you have any evidence to prove these things?"

"Not yet." Bianca folded her arms.

"Not *yet*? Are you intending to conduct your own investigation?" he asked. Was that a hint of humor in his eyes?

"I just don't want to see Nicole blamed for something she didn't do. It doesn't make sense to me. She couldn't wait to marry Chad, and this was the wedding of her dreams. Why would she throw it away like this by committing murder?" Bianca raised her eyebrows.

Detective Sims rubbed at his stubble-covered chin. "Your points may be valid, Ms. Wallace, but I deal with hard facts and evidence. So far, we have her bracelet. Though she hasn't been formerly charged, she is a suspect. We're questioning everyone who had contact with Martin right before his murder. We may have to talk to the witnesses more than once, including you."

Her chest heaved with a sigh. There was no gray area here. There was right or wrong, and while Bianca wanted the killer brought to justice, there had to be someone the police weren't looking into. "I understand."

"We'll keep in touch." Detective Sims gave her a nod.

Bianca's eyes drifted to his cart. "I do have one more question."

He sighed, as if annoyed, but he didn't say so. "Yes, Ms. Wallace."

"Do you only eat homemade vanilla flavored ice cream this early in the morning?" She pointed to his cart.

His eyes followed her hand, but then he faced her again with a smile. "This is for later after work. Besides, I like the simple things. Why?"

She shrugged. "No reason. I just wondered, but if you want to step out the box, I suggest chocolate chip cookie dough, mint chip, or cookies and cream."

His smile grew bigger. "Says the woman in the organic aisle."

"I indulge every now and then. I like to treat myself in between my balanced diet."

"So you're a risk taker?" he asked. Did he lean in closer?

The hairs on the back of Bianca's neck raised. This was ridiculous. She didn't even know the man, so why was her body reacting this way? Besides, there was no way she was ready to go down that road with another man.

Despite being divorced, she liked her single life. Sure, she felt the brunt of it during Christmas and New Year's, but the rest of the year, she was fine. Alyssa and her career were her priority.

"When I want to be." Was she flirting? "Have a good one, detective."

"You too, Ms. Wallace."

Bianca pushed her cart to the checkout line without looking back.

Chapter 8

Two days later, Bianca tapped her heeled shoe on the porch of Martin and Priscilla's mansion. She stared at the freshly cut lawn as she held a bouquet of yellow roses in hand. She hoped they brightened Priscilla's day. She'd been so distraught over Martin's murder.

Murder. Bianca still couldn't believe someone had killed him when they'd all been inside celebrating Nicole and Chad. Mandie greeted her like last time and invited her inside. This time her jet black hair was pulled back into a low ponytail.

Mandie extended her hands. "I can put those in water for you."

"Thank you." Bianca handed her the bouquet.

"Follow me." Mandie led her out of the open entry way and into the living room.

Once Bianca settled on the large sofa, she stared at the wall stencil pattern on the walls, the heavy maroon curtains framing the large windows, and the area rug underneath her feet.

"Bianca?" Priscilla had dressed in a plain white collared shirt and pinstriped pants. Her blonde bob cut hair shined. She hugged Bianca.

"I'm so sorry." She patted her back and drew back. Then Bianca pointed to the yellow roses on her wood coffee table, grateful that Mandie had put them in a vase.

Priscilla took her hand and sat next to her on the sofa. She held a handkerchief in her free hand. "I can't believe it."

Bianca sighed. "Me, neither. What's worse is the police suspect Nicole."

Priscilla dabbed her eyes. "The poor dear."

Bianca released her hand. The question burned in her mind. "Priscilla, do you have any idea who could have done this? Did you notice anything unusual with Martin?"

She shrugged. "After the rehearsal dinner, we didn't talk much that night. I was so embarrassed."

"Richard looked furious."

Priscilla's lips pressed together in a slight grimace.

Bianca tilted her head to the side. "Priscilla?"

"I talked to Richard that night before we left. He and Martin haven't been on good terms the last few years."

"Nicole told me something like that. Can I ask why?"

"Being former business partners doesn't mean they saw eye to eye. Richard had a motorcycle at one time. He had a terrible accident that almost took his life. By the time he recovered, he wanted to pursue his dream. I didn't know about his culinary skills."

"I take it Martin didn't care too much about his step-brother's passion." Bianca crossed her legs as she listened.

Priscilla wiped her nose but continued. "Martin is a businessman. His only passion is making money. Richard leaving the real estate company almost destroyed it. Richard dealt with the finances. Martin was the face of the company. He didn't enjoy having to replace him."

Bianca rubbed her lips together. Had there been so much bad blood between the step-brothers that Richard would kill him? Priscilla's story didn't give much of a reason for murder.

"I guess the storm didn't help, either." Priscilla sighed. "Judy's bakery wasn't doing well a few years ago. So Richard bridged his restaurant idea with hers. Then that terrible hurricane came through town two years ago. Remember?"

"I'll never forget it," Bianca said. It was the storm of the year.

"You know how it destroyed most of Edenville, their business included. Martin told me that Richard came to him for a loan, but Martin only agreed as long as he was a silent partner. Richard was desperate, and he took the deal despite Judy's objection."

Bianca blinked. Bingo. What if Martin had planned on taking over Richard and Judy's business? What if Richard had killed him to get rid of him? But how, without anyone at the wedding noticing?

The ringing from her purse caught her off guard. Bianca stood to her feet. "Can I use your bathroom?"

Priscilla pointed to the archway that opened to the hall. "Around the corner, and it's the first door on the left."

Bianca smiled as she walked down the hallway, only to spot black-and-white photos lining the walls. She saw what looked like a younger version of Priscilla. Then she noticed one with a newspaper clipping inside along with the picture captioned, "Breakout Broadway Star Priscilla Curry."

Pausing for a moment, Bianca stared at the framed newspaper clippings on the wall. Priscilla Lee, "The Bette Davis of Broadway."

Bette Davis? She read another clipping. The writer praised Priscilla for her emotional acting skills, calling her the "Queen of Tears."

Bianca didn't know how famous Priscilla had been on the stage. She'd have to ask her about her career later. She entered the bathroom and checked her phone. A text from her younger sister.

Call me

She called.

"Melanie?" Bianca said.

"I lost my key again. I need you to open the door."

Bianca groaned. "Mel, how many copies do I need to make?"

Her baby sister was a talented journalist, but she failed to keep up with her things, including her keys. "I know, but this time it wasn't my fault. You try writing an article on the health benefits of hiking and tell me how to keep up with all your belongings—"

"Okay, I'm on my way. You need to move out."

"Bianca!"

She giggled. "I'm kidding. I love having you and so does Alyssa."

"Getting used to our newest member?" she asked.

Casper. "I think so, but I'm thinking of charging him rent."

Melanie laughed.

A smile grew on Bianca's lips. "I have to go. I'm visiting with Priscilla."

"Something happen?" Melanie wondered.

Bianca swallowed. Of course her sister wouldn't know yet. When off on an assignment, her sister focused on her work only. "Martin. Her husband is... dead."

Melanie gasped. "What? How? When? I thought Nicole's wedding was this past weekend?"

"It was. That's when it happened," Bianca said.

"You're kidding?"

"I wish I was. I'll meet you soon and I'll tell you more then." Bianca hung up and returned to Priscilla in the living room. The maid was sitting a silver tray on the coffee table with a pitcher of iced tea.

"I brought your pills. The Digoxin, right?"

"Thank you, Mandie." Priscilla opened the prescription bottle.

"I have to go, Priscilla. My sister's back in town and lost her keys again."

Priscilla nodded. "Thank you for stopping by and for the flowers." Her voice cracked. "I appreciate it."

Bianca bent over and hugged her. "You're welcome. We're here for you." She waved goodbye to Mandie.

Stepping outside, she spotted a police car pulling up. Detective Sims stepped out of the car with another officer. He smiled when he saw her, but then his face slackened. Was he trying to remain professional while on duty? Bianca didn't dare ask.

"Ms. Wallace, I didn't expect to run into you," he said.

Bianca nodded at the other officer.

Lamar introduced his partner. "This is Detective Atkins."

Bianca shook his hand. Detective Sims then gestured for his partner to go ahead of him. Bianca walked the rest of the way to her car, and the detective followed.

"Is there a reason you're here?" he asked.

"Offering my condolences. Why?"

He shrugged. "Just checking. You seemed pretty intrigued by the case the last time we spoke."

Bianca faced him. "Would it hurt to be? I'm a concerned citizen. They're my friends."

"We're handling it, Ms. Wallace." He stared.

Bianca didn't move. He wasn't in a suit today. It was dark jeans with a leather jacket covering a gray collared shirt. She cleared her throat. "I'm sure you are, but that doesn't mean—"

"If you have valuable information, let us know."

Bianca wouldn't tell him what she'd learned from Priscilla. Detective Sims would probably tell her to stay out of it. Bianca would, once she found out the truth and cleared her friend's good name.

"I'll let you know if anything comes up." Her muscles tightened, but she wasn't keeping anything from him. It wasn't as if Priscilla had told her anything incriminating.

"Thank you, Ms. Wallace."

"Bianca." She corrected.

A smile grew on his face.

"What?" she asked.

"Nothing. I'll try my best to remember that."

"Though... I can appreciate the respect you're showing. We're just not that formal in Edenville."

"Thanks for letting me know." He bobbed his head, but his gaze directly met hers.

Bianca got lost for a moment in his gray eyes. Were those contacts? She didn't dare to ask. What surprised her all the more was her own breath catching in her throat. Swallowing, she collected her thoughts, knowing it was best to leave.

"Have a nice day, detective." She didn't intend for her voice to drop. Flirting with the new man in town was not in her schedule. Thankfully, all Detective Sims did was nod. Bianca started her car and headed out of the driveway.

The good thing about a small town was little to no traffic. Bianca pulled up to her farmhouse home, spotting her sister on the swing bench with her duffel bag next to her. Bianca cut the engine and hurried to the door.

Melanie shook her head. "I couldn't wait so I called Mom. Someone stabbed Martin?"

"Not here." Bianca opened the door, and they both walked inside. "Yes at Nicole's wedding."

"Who did it?" Melanie sat her duffel bag on the couch.

"I don't know." Bianca sat at her breakfast table, resting her hands on her thighs once she sat down.

"You're thinking. What is it?" Melanie asked, pointing at her.

"I saw Nicole's bracelet. The police think she's a suspect."

Melanie's mouth fell open. "Nicole? She couldn't have. The woman cries at those commercials showing abused animals."

"I know."

Melanie folded her arms. "This is terrible."

Bianca's mouth twisted. "Priscilla told me something while I was there. I think I can check it out without being too obvious."

Melanie shook her head. "You're not getting involved. Let the police handle this."

Bianca cocked her head to the side. "They didn't help Dad, did they?"

Her sister sighed.

"Sorry."

Melanie groaned.

"What? What's wrong now?"

"I'll go with you."

"You?" A smile built on Bianca's lips.

"If Mom finds out, at least I can tell her I tried to talk you out of it." Melanie adjusted her crossbody purse.

"Are you sure?"

"I'm sure. Let's go before Alyssa gets home from school. I told her I'd show her some pictures from my trip."

Bianca grabbed her keys and her sister followed her out the door.

BIANCA DIDN'T BREAK her stride, despite her sister trailing behind her. She filled her in on the details on the drive over. "You know you can stay in the car, right?"

Melanie gasped. "And leave you with a murderer? Mom would kill me."

Bianca paused. "Well, I don't need you second-guessing everything. I'm nervous enough as it is." Her muscles twitched, but she wouldn't leave until she talked with Richard.

Melanie touched her arm. "I just think we need a strategy. We can't just walk in and say, 'Hey, Richard, how are you? Did you kill your step-brother?'" Her sister cocked her head to the side.

A giggle escaped Bianca's lips. "I wasn't planning on saying that."

"What did they argue about?"

"All I heard was this loud crash. It got everyone's attention. Next thing I know, Richard tells Martin to get out. I think he said, 'We don't want you here.'"

Melanie bit her bottom lip. "You really think he did it? What kind of person does that to family?"

"I guess I don't have much to go on, but I won't know until I talk to him." She turned, but her sister stopped her again.

"I want you to know no matter how many times we disagree, I would never do that to you."

Bianca smiled. "Can we go?"

Melanie pulled out her phone.

"What are you doing?"

"Recording the conversation."

Bianca shook her head. "Not yet. I could be wrong."

The sisters walked inside R&J's Restaurant and Bakery. People murmured and talked as soon as they walked inside.

Judy greeted them with a faint smile. "Can I get you a table?" She grabbed laminated menus and handed them Bianca and Melanie. "Good to see you back, Melanie. How was your trip?"

Melanie bobbed her head. "Thank you. It went well. I uh... heard about Martin."

Judy's chin dropped.

"How are you holding up?" Bianca asked.

She lifted her gaze and forced a smile. "Still letting it sink I guess. Were you wanting a table or..."

Bianca said, "I think to-go would be best, but does Richard have any specials today?"

Judy gestured for them to follow her to the takeout area. "I'll also see if Richard has a moment. He's been meaning to call you."

What? Call Bianca? She sat on the wooden bench as Melanie lifted her menu to cover her face.

"He wants to talk to you?" Her sister whispered.

Bianca lifted her menu too. "I know. I wonder what it's about."

"Bianca?"

She lowered the menu to see Richard in his chef uniform. He nodded at Melanie.

"You mind?" He gestured to the corner of the room.

Melanie stood. "I'll take care of our order with Judy. You want the salmon?"

Bianca nodded and followed Richard.

"I was wondering... if we can have some more time with our payment."

Her design she did for their stargazing party. "Oh?" Not what she expected.

"Judy and I have been talking and with everything going on... we need more time," he said. Richard's hand curled around his husky mid-section. "Nothing's going on as planned."

Bianca only stared at him.

He gave a faint smile. "I'm sorry. I know you've been working with us already and I know you're running a business." Richard glanced around the area. "I know the feeling." His teeth bit down on his bottom lip for a moment, but he faced her again. "I can guarantee we'll pay what we owe."

The desperation in his voice could not be denied. "That's fine," Bianca said.

He released a deep breath. "Thank you." Then he folded his arms. "I hear you found Nicole's bracelet."

"It can't be all over town." Bianca only hoped the police didn't arrest her friend.

"I heard it this morning with our breakfast crew." His pupils appeared to dilate. "Nicole may need to think about getting a lawyer."

Bianca's mouth dropped. "What... How... Why?"

"I'm not saying she did it, but... Nicole and Martin have history." Richard blew out his cheeks.

"What do you mean?"

Richard ran a hand down his neck. He looked around to see if anyone was listening. "Nicole knew Martin before she met Chad. I only know because it was before I left the company. He was..."

"Was what?"

"Blackmailing her."

Bianca's breath hitched. Why hadn't Nicole told her that? They were friends. Bianca's muscles felt frozen. Was it possible that Nicole *had* killed Martin? But how? Bianca didn't recall her leaving the venue during the reception.

"Richard, are you sure?"

He bobbed his head.

"Why are you telling me?"

"Because I know you'll help her. She needs you."

"Does Chad know?"

"I think she was too ashamed to share the details. Martin was older than her, but..." He cleared his throat. "I think it would better if you asked her. I only wanted to give you a heads-up since I heard you found the bracelet."

"Have you talked to the police? You and Martin had a bad argument at the rehearsal. Did you see him after the wedding?"

Richard pressed his lips together, but he answered. "I didn't talk to him at the wedding or the reception. I wasn't planning on patching things up."

"You two didn't get along at all?"

Richard grimaced. "He was no brother of mine. We were in business together. The most we did every now and then was play golf. I knew I couldn't trust Martin with anything. Whoever did this must have hated him as much as I did." His nostrils flared.

Bianca didn't respond to Richard. Despite his information about Nicole, his body had stiffened when she'd asked about his own arguments with Martin. He'd hated him. *Hated* was a strong word and Bianca wondered if that hate was strong enough to kill.

"Anyway." Richard continued. His pale face softened somewhat. "Thanks again for giving us time on the payments."

"You're welcome." Then she looked at her sister at the counter as Judy handed Melanie a takeout bag.

"Thank you. I know this will be delicious." Melanie left a tip in the glass jar next to the register.

Bianca walked up to the counter, not too far behind Richard. He smiled at her sister.

"Enjoy your lunch." Then he focused on his wife.

"Did they find the butcher knife?" she asked.

Richard rubbed the back of his neck. "No, so I ordered a new one."

"Do you know how much quality knives cost? The set alone costed—" Judy asked.

"I know, but I'm not wasting time looking for it when I can get a new one. If it's gone, it's gone," he said. With a pinched expression, he marched to the kitchen.

"Excuse me," Judy said as she hurried after her husband.

Butcher knife? Richard was missing a butcher knife? Bianca walked beside her sister as she shuffled to the door. Melanie only bumped into a man they spotted washing the windows when they parked the car earlier.

"Excuse us," Melanie said.

"Sorry, I should have watched where I was going," he said, though he couldn't tear his eyes from Bianca's sister.

Bianca spotted the yellow towel that had fallen to the floor from his hand. She bent to retrieve it and handed it to him. "Here you go."

The man cleared his throat. His dark brown ringleted hair brushed the top of his broad shoulders. "Thank you."

Bianca led her sister back to the car. "Well, this just got interesting." She slid into the driver's seat after placing her bag in the backseat.

Melanie clicked her seatbelt on in the passenger seat. "What has? What did I miss? What did Richard say?"

Bianca started the car. "He says Martin was blackmailing Nicole."

"Why?"

"He said I should ask her, but from what it sounds like, Nicole and Martin were... involved."

Melanie's mouth fell open. "What? No way. How old is he?"

Bianca faced her sister. "You've dated older men before."

Melanie held up her hand. "The most I've dated is five years older. Nicole is in her thirties and Martin is over fifty."

"That surprised me too, but it happens."

"What else did Richard say?"

Bianca pulled out of the parking lot. "He hated Martin."

"Enough to kill him?"

She sighed. "I don't know, but did you hear him about the butcher knife?"

"He's a chef. I'm sure he misplaced it."

Bianca shook her head slightly. "The police didn't confirm it, but I honestly think Martin was stabbed."

Melanie gasped. "Wow."

Bianca wasn't sure, but had Richard killed Martin and was he pointing the blame on Nicole? He even went through the trouble of buying a new butcher knife. Did he not want the other one found because it was the murder weapon? Or perhaps he or someone on his staff lost it. It could be nothing and he was innocent, but why did it sound suspicious?

Chapter 9

Bianca pulled her car onto the wet concrete of Luther's Lather and Rinse Car Wash. Though she kept her car clean despite Casper's dog hair, she never wanted dirt to pile up on the outside where someone could write "Wash Me" on the window. Her nose wrinkled at the notion.

She approached the ticket booth with an attendant. Luther. The man owned the place, but he insisted on greeting the customers. Bianca let down her window.

"Well, aren't you the prettiest woman in Edenville," his raspy voice said.

"You say that all the time when my mother's not around." Bianca winked at him.

Bianca inhaled the smell of moist air and water as Luther's grin grew. She handed him her card to pay for the works. She didn't have to pick up Alyssa for another half hour, so she could get a few more errands done.

Everyone in town knew Luther had feelings for Bianca's mother, including her mother, but nothing had happened between them yet. Bianca would always miss her father, but she didn't see a problem with her mother dating again or even remarrying.

"Don't tell Ms. Deborah I said that. I wouldn't want her to get jealous."

"Sure about that?" Bianca raised her eyebrows.

He rubbed a hand down the back of his neck. Salt-and-pepper hair covered his head and face. For a man in his early sixties, Luther Burkes was quite handsome. Could Bianca do some matchmaking on her own again? It worked for Chad and Nicole.

"I'm sure. She didn't come by this week, so I didn't get to talk to her. Maybe in church, but with everything going on with this murder..." Luther handed Bianca her receipt.

"I'm still taken aback." Bianca folded the small piece of paper and slipped it inside her wallet.

"Can't trust people nowadays. Everybody's got an agenda."

Bianca's eyes looked ahead, past the high ceilings and fluorescent lighting. She spotted Judy motioning to the guy wiping down her white Honda. Judy folded her arms over her chest as she waited.

"You all right, Bianca?" Luther asked.

"Sure. I just saw Judy." She pointed ahead.

Luther looked in the same direction. "Yeah, she didn't seem in a good mood today."

"Really?"

Luther shook his head. "Woman drove in practically yelling at my workers. Claiming they didn't do a good job. I know my staff. They aim to deliver every time."

"Maybe she's having an off day."

"I'll give her that, considering the death in the family, but I've never seen anyone that ticked off because of water spots." He motioned for her to pull ahead. "I'll see you later."

"Want me to tell my mother you said *hello*?" She couldn't help but tease them. Her mother had said enough about her own personal life.

Luther winked at her but didn't reply. Bianca rolled up her window and pulled forward. She listened to the music blaring through the speakers, along with the gurgle of the draining system. Pressing the accelerator, she followed the guidance of the attendant, careful not to bump into the car ahead of her.

When he held his hand up, Bianca stopped. Waving to a few of the workers, she put the car in park. Grabbing her phone, she checked her emails as they washed her car.

"No!"

Bianca's head shot up to spot Judy once again yelling at another attendant. The way Judy's hands flung up in the air, Bianca's pulse quickened. She'd never seen Judy this upset before. Not over a car wash. Judy rarely lashed out at customers who complained to her at the bakery and restaurant.

Were she and Richard going through that much? Was that why he asked for an extension on their payment? Even when she'd talked to her a couple of days before, Judy hadn't seemed too out of sorts. What were the reasons for her outbursts?

Bianca watched despite the streaks of soap on her window. Judy, now on the phone, paced back and forth in a circle. The attendant drying her car shook his head, but he didn't respond to her.

Then her eyes shifted to see Luther walk over. Judy placed the phone to her chest as she talked to him. If Bianca knew Luther, he could manage the situation without it escalating any further.

Bianca tapped her thumb to her screen as she watched the interaction unfold. "I wonder what that's all about."

The suds on her car cascaded down as the water rinsed her car clean. Not much longer. Would she have a chance to talk to Judy before she left? Bianca thought hard about her conversation with Richard. What had sounded unusual? Biting her lower lip, she pondered.

The missing butcher knife was one clue, but Richard had been in the kitchen during the wedding. He'd even frequented the reception by walking around and greeting the guests, asking if they enjoyed their meals. When would he have had time to kill Martin?

There was the stargazing party. He hadn't wanted Martin there, and the Davises had left. Then the rehearsal dinner. The men had yelled at each other, gaining attention of all the guests. Bianca rubbed at her forehead.

Her eyes focused back on Judy. She appeared calmer. Luther even opened the door for her and she slid into the driver's seat of her car. Bianca didn't take her eyes off the exchange. Judy touched a hand to her chest. Her face had dropped. Was she apologizing for her outbursts?

When she extended her hand, Luther took it with a smile. Bianca breathed easier seeing Judy calmed down, but what had set her off in the first place? A knock to her window made her shriek. Bianca stared outside. The attendant gave her a thumbs up and motioned for her to pull forward.

Bianca smiled and mouthed, "Thank you." Putting her car in drive, she pulled ahead.

BIANCA, ALYSSA, AND Melanie pulled into the driveway of her mother's Cape Cod home. Dark green shutters, symmetrical shingles with a central door, multi-paned, and double-hung windows. Familiarity washed over Bianca, recalling the new memories that'd been made since her mother moved to Edenville, Texas, from Atlanta, Georgia, as a fresh start after her husband's death. Family dinners were usually on Sundays, but whenever Deborah Wallace cooked a grand meal, she invited her family over. Even on a Thursday evening.

"I wonder what Mom cooked tonight." Melanie unclicked her seatbelt.

"Enough for the whole neighborhood," Bianca said.

Mel bit her bottom lip. "I can't wait to dig in."

Bianca shook her head and cut the engine. Looking in the rearview mirror, Alyssa still had her phone in her hand. Was it the Kendrick boy who had her attention? "Alyssa, we're here."

How her daughter unclicked her seatbelt, stepped out the car with Casper in her free hand, and walked to her grandmother's front door without looking up, Bianca didn't know. Had she been the same as a teenager?

Bianca followed her along with her sister, and found her mother in her favorite place, the kitchen. The woman loved to cook, even to where she would donate homemade meals to the homeless shelter in town.

Bianca's eyes bugged at sight of chicken-fried steaks, mashed potatoes, and her mother's special green beans. "Mom, it's only us." She stared at the cooked food once more. "Why all this?

Her mother waved away her comment. "In case some neighbors stop by."

Bianca raised an eyebrow. "Like... Mr. Luther?"

Her mother didn't respond. She only turned her back. "Do you think this cake needs icing?"

Bianca looped her arm through her mother's. "Are you avoiding my question?"

"I think it needs frosting."

"Mom?"

Her mother eyeballed her. "He is a *friend* of mine."

"Just a friend?"

Her mother cleared her throat. "Enough about me, what about you?"

Bianca groaned. "Here we go."

"All this talk about my personal life, what about you?"

"I have Casper. Thanks to you."

Her mother's eyes widened. "You can't be serious? A pet can only do so much. At least your sister is dating."

Bianca walked to the kitchen island and rested her elbows on the butcher block countertop. "Mom, you're meddling again. I'm not Melanie. I'll get there when I want to. I'm just now getting to a point where I can say Malcolm's name without hating him."

Her mother pursed her lips. "Then you need to pray for me. I still can't believe he doesn't see Alyssa like he should."

Could her daughter hear this conversation? She was in the living room with Melanie playing with Casper, including her mother's dogs. Bianca shrugged. "I can't, either. He calls but his architect job keeps him pretty busy."

"What about that new detective? No, I'm not being nosy."

Bianca straightened, as if her mother had shocked her with a bolt of electricity. "What?"

"He's handsome. And those gray eyes... are very intriguing."

"I don't think so. Besides, I have—"

"Alyssa to think about." Her mother finished her sentence. "Alyssa will leave the house soon. You're a wonderful mother, but I don't want you to forget about you."

"What if I want nothing right now?"

Her mother winked at her. "I think you'll change your mind."

"Because of Lamar?"

Her mother touched a hand to her chest. "You know his first name?"

"I met him... before the murder."

Her mother wiped her hands with the dishtowel. "I still can't believe we have a killer in this town. We know Edenville for its friendliness."

"Among other things." Bianca tapped a finger to her chin. She couldn't get past Richard's words. What had Martin had to blackmail Nicole with? And why would he have cared to?

"Is the food ready?" Melanie asked. Jasper, her mother's Yorkie, trotted in behind her. His paws padded the hardwood kitchen floors.

"In a minute." Her mother smiled at her sister.

Melanie hugged her mother. "Smells good as always."

Her mother pointed to her. "You didn't give me the details of your trip. Nothing happened out there, did it?"

"Nothing I can't handle."

Alyssa followed into the kitchen, setting Casper down to the floor. Bianca's mother's other Yorkie, Jasper, barked. Why her mother had named her pets after the villainous characters in *101 Dalmatians*, she'd never know. Thank goodness they'd gotten used to Casper being with them the last few days. Bianca didn't waste time extending her hand to Alyssa. Her teen daughter's mouth dropped.

"You know the rules," she said.

"Mom, not tonight. Please? I promise I'll put it on silent."

"No phones during dinner."

Her teen groaned but handed her mother her phone. "Not fair."

Bianca set her phone along with her daughter's inside the small wicker basket on the table. Her mother's rules were no phones during dinner. Her mother wanted them to be present with the family, and though teenage Bianca had wanted to talk to her friends, her mother insisted her phone stay in the wicker basket. Teenager. Time had flown since 2005. Now at thirty-four, Bianca had carried the tradition to her own daughter.

Melanie held up her phone. "If there's a story and I miss it, you owe me." She set it inside the basket.

Bianca shook her head. Jordan's name flashed on her screen. She licked her lips. "Mom, I may need to take this?" She couldn't explain the tenseness in her stomach.

"No phones, Bianca," her mother said.

"But this has to do with murder," Melanie said. She then covered her mouth as if realizing her mistake.

Bianca's chest heaved.

"It's all over school," Alyssa said.

"To think there's a serial killer in a small town like this," Melanie said.

"Mel?" Bianca raised her eyebrows. "There's no serial killer." *Buzz. Buzz.* Bianca saw the screen on her phone light up in the basket. "Mom..."

"Bianca?" Her mother cocked her head to the side.

Bianca held up her two fingers. "Two minutes. I promise I'll be back." She hurried to the living room and answered the phone. It had to have been important, since Jordan had called a second time. "What's up?"

"Have you talked to the police?" Why did he sound worried?

"Jordan, what's wrong?"

"Tell me what you told the police." He sounded earnest. What did he know?

"Only what I saw. Martin didn't come back for a while and then we found his body inside the limousine."

"How's Nicole? Is she okay?"

"She's okay. The police only brought her in for questioning, but..."

"But what?" he asked.

"I found her bracelet near some blood at the scene. So far, they have made no arrests."

Silence. Was he processing what she was telling him? His disbelieving tone couldn't be denied. "That's impossible. I found her bracelet. I told the police that in my statement."

"You did?" Then what happened?

"Yeah. I went to find Nicole to give it to her before the wedding started. Priscilla was with her in the back room. I sat it on the table and wished Nicole good luck with Chad," Jordan said.

Did someone steal it? If Priscilla was there would she know? "Then how—"

"They can't do this."

"They? Jordan, what do you mean?"

"I don't know." He exhaled. "Who's doing this? They want to ruin her. I know it."

"Why? What do you know, Jordan?"

"Remember when you lost touch with Nicole for a while?"

Bianca sat on the arm of her mother's leather couch. "Yes?"

He sighed. "I don't know how she got mixed up with Martin, but he helped her out. I didn't understand, but she said they understood each other. She didn't know he was married. Priscilla didn't find out until later, but by the time Nicole realized she was seeing a married man, she called things off."

"What? Why didn't she tell me that?"

"Who wants people to know that? Not in Edenville." Was Jordan pacing? What was the rustling in the background?

"What are you doing, Jordan?"

"I can't let this happen."

"Who do you think is doing this? Is it only to get back at Nicole? For seeing Martin?"

"I don't know, but I wouldn't be surprised if Priscilla did it."

Bianca was taken aback. "I think that's farfetched, Jordan. Do you know how sensitive she is? Her heart trouble. She has her moments, but I don't think she's a killer. I doubt she has that in her."

"Then I don't know who else."

"What about Richard? The step-brother? One of his butcher knives is missing."

Jordan's breath hitched. "Butcher knife? So it's true what I read it in the paper?"

"Yes." Bianca read the most recent story on the *Edenville Gazette* paper's website.

"This just keeps getting worse," Jordan said. "I have to go. I'll talk to you later."

"Be safe." Bianca hung up, only to hear the doorbell ring. When she opened it, she blinked, spotting Mr. Luther Burkes. Not in his usual jumper, but in dress slacks and a dark blue collared dress shirt. He trimmed his beard and his smile grew.

His whiskey eyes gleamed. He held a pitcher of tea in his hands. "Hello, Bianca. Your mother invited me."

"Come in, Mr. Burkes." She stepped to the side and let him inside. Jasper and Horas trotted in the room. Casper followed, joining in their barks. Mr. Burkes smiled, but he picked up one foot as they ran around him. The pitcher in his hand shifted. Casper barked louder, standing on his hind legs. Jasper and Horas joined in the apparent fun, and Mr. Burkes tried to keep his grip, but the iced tea only spilled over. *Splash!*

Bianca gasped. The cold liquid drenched her shirt as she tried to help him. She inhaled and stared at her dog. Her mother chuckled along with her daughter. Melanie held back a snicker. When did they walk into the living room?

"You okay, Mom?" Alyssa asked, but her grin gave her away.

"Uh huh." She fingered at her soaked collar.

"Hello, Luther," her mother said. Then she looked at Bianca. "I have a shirt you can change into."

Bianca bobbed her head. She only blew through her cheeks as she made her way down the hall to her mother's bedroom. What were the joys of having a pet again?

Chapter 10

Sweat dripped down Bianca's neck as she squatted. Almost a week since Martin's murder. Trying to get back to somewhat normal routine, Bianca headed to the gym. Four times a week was her workout habit, and while she preferred exercising in the morning, coming in the early evening had become a habit as she'd switched up her regiment. Bianca hated cardio workouts—with a passion—but they did wonders for her health.

"Wow, these are killer." She gritted her teeth. Ten more seconds left on her timer. "One more." Standing straight, her leg muscles shook from the exertion. Bending over, she rubbed at her thighs. She took a needed break. Grabbing her water bottle, she gulped it, grateful for cold water rushing down her parched throat.

Exhaling, Bianca wiped her sweaty forehead. One hour sufficed for her workout. Time to head home. She gathered her towel and yoga mat, preparing to leave. Her phone rang. Noticing Alyssa's name on the screen, she answered.

"Yes, honey?"

"Are you on your way home yet?" Alyssa asked.

"In a few minutes. Why?" Bianca stuffed her towel inside her gym bag.

"Well... do you think I can order some takeout?"

"What do you have a taste for?" Bianca blocked out the music and sounds coming from TV sets. She passed the treadmills, stationary bikes, stair climbers, and elliptical machines. Then she headed out the building and to her car in the parking lot.

"Italian again?"

"Let's go for Mexican this time. You'll find the menus in the kitchen."

"Okay. Thanks, Mom." Alyssa hung up.

Bianca smiled to herself as she approached her car.

"Looking good."

A tenor voice startled her. She pivoted, spotting a man standing a few feet away from her. Broad chest, tattooed arms, and a bald head. A gym bag hung from his own arm. The way he licked his lips and his eyes traveled down her body, Bianca's fight or flight kicked in. She needed to get home—now.

Bianca responded. "Thank you. Have a good night."

"Why the rush?" he asked.

Wasn't there enough going on in Edenville? Possible stalker too? The last thing she wanted. Bianca didn't answer. Her mouth went dry.

"So that's it? Not even a—"

"I think the lady would like to be left alone."

Bianca knew that voice. She turned around to see Detective Sims in his athletic gear, standing between her and the man. His strong arms caught her attention in his sleeveless t-shirt, as she noticed his defined triceps. Her mouth flooded with moisture and she swallowed. This wasn't the time especially if things escalated between Detective Sims and this man. They wouldn't fight would they?

"What's it to you?" the man snarled.

"Go home now, or do you want to go to jail for assault?"

"What are you? A cop?" the man asked as he stepped closer to Detective Sims.

Bianca didn't say a word. She only watched the exchange.

Detective Sims gave a mirthless laugh. "Exactly."

A *tsk* sound escaped the man's lips. "Man, whatever." He stalked off to his car.

Bianca exhaled a breath she hadn't known she'd been holding.

Detective Sims faced her. His eyes softened.

"I could have taken him, you know," she said. "I know self-defense."

He chuckled. "I'm sure you could have, Ms. Wallace."

"But... thank you for your help."

"My pleasure. Are you all right?" he asked.

"I will be. Thank you again."

"You're welcome." He cleared his throat. "You come here often?"

Bianca laughed. "Well, that's a classic line."

He rubbed the back of his neck. "I mean... this is my first time working out here. I jog, but I try to switch it up."

"Me too. I'm here sometimes or I work out at home or the park." She folded her arms over her chest. The night air chilled her skin.

"Which is your favorite spot?" he asked.

She bit her bottom lip.

"What's that face for?"

She shook her head. "I don't have a favorite. To be honest, I don't enjoy working out. Especially cardio."

He threw his head back and laughed. "Okay, I wasn't expecting that."

Bianca shrugged. "I only do it to stay healthy, but if I had my way, I'd find another alternative. I've gotten used to it in the last few years. You?" She focused on his expression. He seemed much more relaxed. Was that why he hadn't left yet?

"I do it for my job, but I like to jog in the park. Gives me a chance to clear my head."

She smiled. "That is necessary in your line of work. Difficult, I'm sure."

"Yes."

"At least in my work, I've always been creative, so my job feels second nature to me. It doesn't feel like work."

"Graphic design, right?" He'd asked her profession when he'd questioned her on the night of the murder. He'd remembered?

"Right," she said. Her heart perked up. "I never imagined I would run my own company, but I love working for myself." The wind picked up again, and she rubbed at her arms. Though she enjoyed this side of him, she couldn't stay longer. Though deep down she wanted to. "I... um... need to get home and clean up. I'm having takeout with my teenage daughter."

"Teenager?"

She raised an eyebrow. "Surprised?"

"You just..." He eyed her from head to toe. "You don't look... I mean, you look..."

She raised a hand to stop him. "I think I get what you mean, so thank you. I married young, so she's sixteen."

"Sixteen. I remember those days. That age sounds so long ago now," he said.

"I know. Before I know it, she'll be graduating." She shrugged. "I'll be an empty nester."

"What about your... I mean?" He glanced at her hands.

Bianca rubbed at her bare left ring finger. "Divorced. Almost three years."

He bobbed his head. "Sorry to hear that."

Despite the sincerity she heard in his voice, the way his eyes lingered on her face made her belly flutter. Her lips parted at the tiny glimpse of hope she felt on the inside, but she shook her head. "Don't be. I have my daughter so I don't regret everything. You have kids?" She could stay longer if he wanted to.

Detective Sims shook his head. "No, not yet. I want them, so I'm hopeful."

Bianca smiled. "Maybe you will someday." She glanced at his bare left hand but refused to ask him.

He bobbed his head. "Well... I'm glad you're all right, Ms. Wallace. I'll let you get home to your daughter."

"Will you ever call me 'Bianca'?" she asked.

The corners of his mouth turned up. "You'll know when I do, Ms. Wallace."

Bianca licked her bottom lip. "Goodnight, detective."

"Goodnight, Ms. Wallace." He backed away from her car with a nod.

Bianca gave a slight wave to him and slid into the driver's seat of her car. Gripping the steering wheel, she ignored the tingles on her skin. One conversation.

That was all it had been. Nothing more. She wouldn't let her thoughts run wild.

Chapter 11

That evening Bianca exhaled. Her slouchy sweatshirt hung off her shoulders. After a relaxing bath, her muscles felt loose. Though her mirror appeared steamed, the hot bath had been worth it after squats, lunges, and her least favorite—burpees. Whoever had created that move must have had it out for her. Breathing in the steamy air, she smoothed the last of her lotion onto her hands and wrists.

Sniffing her wrist, she took in the tea tree scent. Not her favorite, but it was soothing. Wrapping her curls into a messy bun, Bianca walked out of her bathroom and into her bedroom. The restaurant, Mobile Aztec, would deliver her takeout meal any moment, but with a thirty-minute wait, she'd bathed and changed from her sweaty gym clothes.

She grabbed her phone from her nightstand and entered the hallway. Checking Alyssa's room, she spotted her shut door. Melanie was out on a date, so she wouldn't expect her back until later.

Was Alyssa finished with her homework? Leaning in, Bianca heard her daughter giggling. Shaking her head, she recalled her years as a teenage girl.

Everything she'd taken seriously at sixteen didn't carry the same weight to her as a woman in her thirties. Bianca tapped on her daughter's door.

"Yes?" Alyssa's voice didn't sound too annoyed.

Bianca opened the door. "Dinner will be here soon. Finished your homework yet?"

Alyssa sat on her bed, but her eyes diverted to her desk. Her notebooks covered it along with her open laptop. Bianca wondered how her daughter got any work done.

"Just taking a break," her daughter said. She pressed her phone to her chest.

"Is that Chloe?" Bianca asked, although her instincts told her otherwise.

Alyssa shook her head.

"I see."

"Mom, can we talk later? Please?" Alyssa tilted her head to the side with a pleading look.

"Sure. I'll call you when the takeout arrives." Bianca smiled to herself and closed the door. This was the phase that her mother had warned her about. Alyssa was becoming a young woman. Pacing down the hallway and into the living room, Bianca wondered when her baby girl had grown up.

Her smile grew at the memory of when the nurse had placed her newborn baby in her arms. Alyssa's high-pitched cries had filled the room, but the moment she'd rested her head on Bianca's chest, she'd calmed in her mother's arms.

Malcom had leaned over to kiss her along with baby Alyssa on the forehead. He had been so nervous to hold her, afraid he would break her. Bianca had assured him he wouldn't. The moment

Malcom's large hands had held his daughter, she'd had him wrapped around her little finger. Until the divorce.

Bianca plopped on the couch, only to hear the patting of paws on her hardwood floors. Casper reached up on his hind legs. Eyeing him and his wagging tail, she helped him up to sit with her.

"You're getting used to it here, aren't you?" she asked.

He didn't answer, not even with a bark.

A deep breath escaped her mouth just as her phone rang. Her lips parted at the name on the screen. Malcom? Her fingers curled, but she wouldn't let her emotions get the better of her. Though she had forgiven him, Bianca still felt a twinge in her chest.

She answered. "Malcom?"

"Hey, Bianca. How are you?" he asked. There was a time when his bass voice made her knees wobble. Now, it made her neck stiffen.

"I'm fine. You?"

"I'm okay. You got a minute?"

Not for him, but she wouldn't be rude. Besides, she had a boundary. No small talk. The only thing they shared was Alyssa. If Malcom asked about her personal life or if she didn't want to answer his questions, she ended the call. He knew that by now, although sometimes she wondered if he pushed her buttons on purpose.

"Sure." She hoped the conversation wouldn't last long.

"I wanted to ask about Alyssa. I thought about asking her to come and stay with me for the summer."

Bianca's eyebrows shot up. This was the most time he'd asked to spend with Alyssa since their split.

He continued. "I've been talking to her and—"

"You have? She didn't mention it."

Malcom sighed. "I know, Bianca. Look, I know I haven't done the best job at being a dad, especially since... Anyway, I want to change that."

Bianca poked a tongue into her cheek and inhaled a deep breath. "The entire summer?"

"I don't think it would hurt. There's a lot she can do here in California, and we can spend time together."

"How does your... wife feel about Alyssa coming?"

"She doesn't mind. Alyssa's more than welcome," Malcom said.

Bianca stood and paced the floor. "Malcom, I understand you want to make amends, but I don't want Alyssa disappointed. I'm not trying to bring up the past, but you don't have an excellent track record of keeping your word."

Silence.

Bianca tapped her foot on the floor. It was true. She didn't want to bring up the past, but Malcom's less-than-frequent calls only made Alyssa feel abandoned. Her talking to him baffled Bianca. They would have to have their own talk later.

"I know and I'm sorry."

What? He was sorry. The words had rarely left his mouth in the past. "You are?" she asked.

"I'm serious," he said. "I want to do better with Alyssa. She's my only child and I want to fix this."

Bianca heard the emotion in his voice, but she knew him. He'd had the same tone in his voice when she'd found out he had been unfaithful in the marriage. He had apologized then, but he'd still filed for divorce and left her to raise their daughter on her own.

"I'll need to talk to Alyssa first. I want to hear from her if she wants to," she said.

"No problem. No pressure, okay? I hope she comes. I think it'll be good for us. Thank you, Bianca." His voice picked up with a hint of excitement.

Her doorbell rang. "Sure. I have to go. There's someone at the door."

"Talk to you later." He hung up.

Bianca did the same, holding her phone close to her chest. Placing it on the coffee table, she answered her front door. A young boy, no older than twenty, smiled at her and handed her a takeout bag. Bianca tipped him with cash.

"Thank you, miss. Enjoy," he said with a wave.

"Have a good night." She closed the door, and carried the plastic bags to the dining table.

"Good. It's here." Alyssa walked in and joined her at the table. She sat in her seat and scanned the room. "Where's Aunt Mel?"

Bianca handed her daughter her Styrofoam plate. "Out on... a date."

"Oh, I see." Alyssa grinned. "Grandma must have set her up."

"No, this is someone she met on her own. Anyway..." She sat in the chair next to her daughter. "Your dad called."

Alyssa paused opening her plate. She didn't move at first, but she turned her head to face her mother. "He did?"

Bianca bobbed her head. "First, he said that you two have been talking, and that he wants you to spend the summer with him in California."

Alyssa blinked. "Really? He told me he had a surprise for me, but he wanted to talk to you first."

The rustle of plastic filled Bianca's ears as she pulled apart the knot to reach the plastic silverware. "I have only two questions."

"Yes, Mom?"

"Why didn't you tell me you've been talking to your dad?"

Alyssa tucked a loose curl behind her ear. "I didn't want you to get mad at me. I know how you feel about him."

"What makes you think—?"

"Mom, I know how much he hurt you. For a while... I hated him too. I would hear you cry in your room, or see the fake smiles you would put on for me. I didn't want him in my life since he left, but..."

Bianca felt jumbled in her midsection. "But what?"

"I still love him. He's my dad. I didn't tell you because I know you don't love each other anymore. I didn't want to disappoint you knowing that I still care about him, even though you... you..."

Bianca pulled her daughter into a tight embrace. She cradled the back of her head. "Sweetie, I don't want you to feel that way. I'm sorry if I made you think like this." Pulling back, she cupped Alyssa's face. "He is your father. That will never change. Do I still care about him? Not like I used to, but don't feel like you're in the middle of having to choose one of us over the other. No matter what, we'll always have something in common. We both love you."

Alyssa gave a faint smile. "Really?"

Bianca's hands fell from her daughter's face. "Always. I just... didn't want you to get hurt. I think your dad is still working through some things, but if you want to go, I won't stop you from seeing him."

Alyssa wrung her fingers together. "Well... I don't know. An entire summer?"

"It's not forever, you know."

"I know, but I'll miss you, Grandma, Aunt Mel, Casper, my friends." At the sound of the name, the dog trotted over and sat at Alyssa's feet. She bent over and scratched his back.

Bianca tilted her head to the side. "Forgetting someone?"

Alyssa straightened in her seat as her eyes widened. "Mom, please don't tell me you were listening to me on the phone?"

"No, I wouldn't do that, but you keep forgetting I used to be your age."

Alyssa's shoulders slumped. "I have a lot to think about."

"Yes, you do." Bianca took a bite from her chicken enchiladas, just as they heard a car pull up. Then the door to the garage opened. Melanie stepped inside and Casper barked at her arrival. Bianca eyed her sister's outfit of choice. A black jumpsuit accented with red pumps, a red belt around her waist, and Melanie never failed to wearing red lipstick. "Well, look at you."

"Aunt Mel, you look great," Alyssa said.

Melanie stepped out of her heels and picked them up. "Thank you." She spotted the takeout bag. "Yes! Takeout. Did you get me something?"

"Yes, but didn't you eat?" Bianca's forehead wrinkled.

Her sister sat at the table next to her. "Well... we had a picnic. He cooked." She shook her head with her eyes closed. "Didn't, um... I'd rather not."

Alyssa giggled.

Bianca nudged her shoulder. "Will you see him again?"

Melanie continued. "No, he's on his way to his ex-wife's house. She lives in Oklahoma. He's got a long drive."

"Wow." Alyssa blinked.

Was he related to the same man who'd been at her mother's matchmaking event? Bianca wouldn't ask her sister now. "How did that—?"

"That's the thing." Melanie held up her index finger as she made her point. "He said I reminded him of her. By the time he told me what had happened, I told him to go make it right."

Bianca choked. "What?"

"He might as well, since he wouldn't stop talking about her." Melanie rested her chin in her palm.

Alyssa covered her mouth to stifle her laugh.

"That is... something," Bianca said. "Are you okay?"

Her sister waved her question away and reached into the takeout bag. "Don't worry. I'm good."

Bianca nodded, but she couldn't resist. "So... what did he cook?"

Melanie eyeballed her and they burst into laughter.

Chapter 12

A memorial in Martin's honor, making it a week since his murder. Bianca adjusted the belt on her black knee-length dress. The funeral wouldn't take place until the police completed their investigation. A few police cars parked in front of the funeral home, but she doubted the killer would show.

A small crowd gathered outside. She didn't spot Nicole, Chad, or Priscilla yet, but she clutched to her purse, nodding. People she'd never met before crowded the front of the building. Bianca didn't know much about Martin's family, so out of town relatives attending proved logical. Where were Richard and Judy? Inside already?

Her mother, Melanie, and Alyssa exited the car to stand with her. Alyssa wrung her hands together. Her daughter didn't like memorials or funerals, but Bianca was glad Alyssa wanted to show her support.

"I never thought this would happen," Melanie said, her arm looped through Alyssa's.

"Saying goodbye is never easy." Bianca's mother swiped a finger under her eye. Was she crying?

"Mom?" Bianca wondered if this reminded her mother of losing her own husband.

Her mother waved her off. "I'm fine. We're here to give our condolences. Remember?"

Bianca wasn't quite convinced. If her mother wasn't up to it, they would leave. "Okay, but if you want to—"

"I wouldn't think of it. Let's go." Her mother assured her.

They bypassed some guests clasping wads of tissues. Bianca gave a slight wave to Ms. Ella, who owned the floral shop in town. Her large brim black hat covered her honey blonde hair, and she waved at Bianca.

Luther Burkes attended, and he didn't shy from waving either. Walt, the owner of the mechanic shop, bobbed his shaven head in acknowledgement. Bianca returned the gesture. She inhaled the fresh flowers as quiet weeping and sniffling flooded her ears. "Nice turnout."

"Can we sit in the back?" Alyssa asked.

Bianca nodded and found an empty wooden pew. Sitting, she adjusted despite the discomfort, while tapping her shoe on the thick carpet. Bianca glanced behind her, and since she sat on the end, she had a view of the aisle.

Her mother patted her hand. "I'm sure it's going to be lovely."

"I hope so."

Melanie leaned over to face her sister. She motioned her eyes toward the front, and Bianca saw Nicole, Chad, and Priscilla standing in the front. Richard and Judy were already seated. A large picture of Martin displayed for all to see. Bianca sighed. Priscilla's sad expression said it all.

"You want to wait until later to talk to them?" Melanie asked.

"There're too many people. I don't want to crowd them."

"I feel bad for them," Alyssa said.

"I think we should wait until later," Bianca's mother said. "We can talk later. Let's just show our support by being here for them."

"Okay." Bianca wanted to give the family space. She knew how it felt when her own father died. The smiles, hugs, and cards had been thoughtful, but she'd needed time to herself.

"You don't mind if I sit here, do you?"

Bianca's head jerked to see Detective Sims standing in the aisle next to her. "Um…"

"Of course, detective." Bianca's mother motioned for Melanie and Alyssa to slide down the pew.

"Thank you, Mrs. Wallace." He gave her a smile.

Hair lifted on the back of Bianca's neck. Forcing a smile, she slid down the pew so Detective Sims could sit next to her. "I didn't expect to see you here."

"Came to pay my respects to the family." He folded his strong hands in his lap.

Bianca eyed him. "You think the killer will be here too?"

His smile grew. "We'll make sure nothing goes wrong, Ms. Wallace. You'll be safe."

Bianca toyed with her watch to release her nervous tension. "I appreciate that."

"It's my job," he said.

"How do you like Edenville, detective?" Bianca's mother asked.

"It's growing on me. I like the close-knit feeling."

"Bianca said the same thing when she moved here. I moved here after my husband passed."

"My condolences," Detective Sims said.

"Thank you. I needed a fresh start." Bianca's mother touched her arm. "I assured her she would love it here too, despite her reservations. If you need someone to show you the best places in town, I'm sure Bianca would be more than happy to accommodate you."

"Mother." Bianca could have disappeared. The last place she wanted to be set up was at a memorial. "I'm sure Detective Sims can find his way around town."

"No harm in being neighborly, Bianca," her mother said, nudging her shoulder.

"Thank you, Mrs. Wallace. Believe it or not, your daughter has shown me a thing or two already." The corners of his mouth turned up as he stared at Bianca.

Her lips parted, but a high-pitched scream startled the room. Bianca stood, only to see Priscilla's hands reach for Martin's enlarged picture. "Oh, no. No!"

"Poor thing," her mother said.

"What can we do?" Melanie asked.

"Pray. Pray hard for this family." Bianca's mother took Melanie's hand.

Bianca didn't take her eyes off Priscilla, who allowed Chad and Richard to help her back to her seat. Then she spotted Judy, who gave her a tissue. Nicole sat next to her mother-in-law, with her head bowed.

"Wakes and funerals are never easy," Detective Sims said.

Memorials neither. "You're telling me." Bianca returned to her seat. The door opened and air rushed inside but quickly closed. Bianca saw Jordan. She hadn't thought he would show, but she knew his feelings for Nicole wouldn't keep him from supporting her. Bianca made eye contact with him and he gave a faint smile.

Then he proceeded down the aisle. When Nicole spotted him, she rose to her feet, but Priscilla rushed to stand first.

"Get him out!" she yelled.

Chad didn't hesitate. He marched over to Jordan. "It's best you leave. *Now*. I don't want a scene." The sternness in is voice apparent.

Nicole came up behind and touched her husband's arm. "Chad. Please?"

The murmurs between the guests increased in volume. Detective Sims stood. Would there be an altercation? Why wouldn't Priscilla want Jordan to attend? He'd done nothing wrong.

She pointed at him. "I can't believe you would show your face here. After everything you've done to this family."

"I only came to support Nicole," Jordan said as he took a few steps back.

"I bet you did." Chad snarled. "Looking for another way back into her life? Too late. She's my wife now. *Mine*."

"Get out! I don't want you here!" Priscilla motioned for him to leave.

Judy touched her sister-in-law's shoulder. "You're making a scene. I don't think—"

"I want him out! Now!" Priscilla returned to her seat as her voice broke in more tears.

Richard intervened and stepped closer. He said something to Jordan, and Bianca watched Detective Sims join the huddle. She didn't even see him get up, too engrossed in the melodrama ahead of her. Nicole pulled Chad back and to his seat. He snaked an arm around her shoulders. Who knew what they were saying to each other?

"I've never seen Ms. Priscilla act like that," Alyssa said.

"She's never had a problem with Jordan." Melanie covered her mouth with her hand.

"She's distraught. I'm sure she doesn't mean it, but he may need to leave. The stress is not good for her," Bianca's mother said.

Priscilla rested her head on Judy's shoulder as Detective Sims walked beside Jordan down the aisle to the doors.

"I'll be back." Bianca slipped out of her seat and stayed out of the detective's sight. Standing in the foyer, she cracked the door as she listened.

"You want to tell me what that was about?" Detective Sims asked Jordan.

Jordan folded his arms. "I came here for Nicole."

"Is there a reason Mrs. Davis acted that way? Is there something I should know? Chad seems to think—"

"I don't know what you're getting at, but I had nothing to do with Martin's death."

"I didn't say you did. Why would you assume that?" Detective Sims tilted his head to the side.

Jordan flung his arms in the air. "Okay, I didn't like the guy. Who did? I'm surprised this many people are here to pay their respects, but I did nothing. I only wanted to be here for Nicole."

Bianca's eyes shifted back and forth between the men.

Detective Sims stuffed his hands inside his pockets. "All right, but for now, your presence is causing a disturbance. I'm going to ask you to leave. You can reach out to Mrs. Lee in your own time."

A *tsk* sound escaped his lips. "This is dumb, man!" Jordan stalked off to the parking lot.

Bianca bit at her bottom lip. Why didn't Priscilla want him there? She could understand Chad's jealously by why Priscilla's sudden outburst?

"Lost, Ms. Wallace?"

Bianca shut her eyes but opened them. Detective Sims stood in the doorway, catching her snooping.

"I... um..." She straightened and adjusted her dress. "Just getting some air."

He chuckled. "Sure."

Chapter 13

Warm steam from a hot cup of herbal tea warmed Bianca's face. A repast at the Edenville Community Church immediately followed Martin's memorial, and she, along with Melanie, Alyssa, and her mother, sat at on folding chairs surrounded with Martin's relatives.

"I was hoping to have a word with Priscilla," her mother said, scanning the crowd.

"I'm sure she'll make her way around." Bianca sipped the warm liquid. She turned to her left and spotted Alyssa scrolling on her phone. She was grateful her daughter didn't gripe about staying too long.

Melanie bobbed her head. "I really didn't expect this many people."

"Melanie!" her mother said, taken aback.

Melanie shrugged. "What? Martin wasn't the... nicest man in the world."

Bianca couldn't have agreed more.

"I understand that, but we're here because someone killed him. Regardless of how we felt about him, it shows human decency to have compassion on our fellow man."

"Understood," Melanie said.

Bianca gave a faint smile. Crossing her legs, she noticed Detective Sims in the crowd. It surprised her he had stayed this long. Did he see anything unusual? Bianca had kept her eyes open during the entire memorial service. Outside the big-to-do about Jordan getting kicked out, nothing appeared out of the ordinary.

"Enjoying the view?" her mother asked.

Bianca choked on her tea.

"Mom?" Alyssa patted her back.

"I'm all right." Bianca touched a hand to her chest. She faced her own mother. "*Really*?"

"I only asked a simple question, although I noticed the subtle looks he gave you during the—"

"Mom, I don't think this is the time for your matchmaking."

Her mother dismissed her comment with a wave. "I'm always looking for opportunities to match make. People have met at..." She gestured to the crowd. "Memorials."

"Mom, who wants to tell that story?" Melanie asked. "'By the way, I met my husband at a memorial service right after they served the refreshments.'"

"It happens. I've done my research. People meet online. In grocery stores. Car accidents. I've even had a client tell me she met her ex-husband in an ambulance."

"Ex-husband?" Bianca tilted her head as she listened to her mother.

Her mother fiddled with the neckline of her black dress. "Well... it turns out she wasn't the only woman he'd met in an ambulance."

Melanie covered her mouth to stifle her giggle.

"The point is," her mother continued, "you never know where you might meet someone amazing. It never hurts to keep your eyes open."

Then Bianca spotted Priscilla's face in the crowd. She was coming toward them. While she hugged a few attendees with a faint smile, her face softened when she made eye contact with Bianca. She could only imagine what this woman was feeling.

"Some friendly faces." Priscilla opened her arms despite her red eyes.

Bianca stood to hug her, followed by her mother and sister. Alyssa even tore her gaze away from her phone long enough to hug Priscilla too.

"I can't tell you how glad I am you came." Priscilla wrung her hands together.

"We wouldn't miss it," Bianca said.

"How are you holding up?" her mother asked Priscilla.

"Sometimes it's like..." Priscilla's voice choked, but she finished. "It's like it's a nightmare, and I'm going to wake up and he's here." She shook her head. "He's not."

Bianca's mother pulled her into another embrace. Perhaps it was best for Chad and Nicole to take her home. Hadn't she been through enough without having to force a smile in front of Martin's family members?

As Bianca's eyes glanced the room, she couldn't help but focus her attention on Richard. Whoever he was talking to, he threw his head back laughing. All she could do was picture him on the night of the rehearsal dinner arguing with Martin. She wanted to give him the benefit of the doubt, but why did his presence send a slight chill through her?

"If you need anything, we're here for her." Her mother pulled back and held Priscilla's hands in hers.

"Thank you." Priscilla gave a faint smile. "Your support means more than you know." She turned her attention to Bianca. "Do you have a minute, dear?" She motioned for her to follow her.

Bianca followed Priscilla to a somewhat secluded corner.

Priscilla sniffled. "I haven't asked you about the... anniversary photos."

Bianca's lips parted. "Oh, Priscilla. I meant to get back with you." She pressed a hand to her forehead. The pictures were almost finished anyway.

Priscilla placed a hand on Bianca's shoulder. "No, I meant to follow up earlier, but then he..."

Bianca said, "I'll get right on that. I'm sure you'll want them now more than ever." Would she want Bianca's surprise? She wouldn't tell her yet, since another question burned in her mind.

"I do. Thank you, Bianca. This past week has thrown this town for a loop so I appreciate whatever you do." Her eyes glanced over at Detective Sims. "I wasn't expecting the police here though." She released a deep breath, regaining the color back in her cheeks.

"Can I ask you something?"

"Of course," Priscilla said.

"Did Jordan do something for you not to want him here?"

Priscilla shook her head. "I know he's your friend, but the way he pines over Nicole is too much. There are enough rumors around town and I don't want Chad in one with people wondering about Nicole and Jordan."

Not wanting a scandal? So far Bianca had heard nothing of that nature, but she didn't dispute with her. Nicole *had* had a history with Martin so she didn't blame Priscilla. "He said he found her bracelet. You were with Nicole?" Bianca had been in another room with the bridesmaids.

"I sat it on the table. Nicole was so nervous about her vows. I was trying to calm her down. Then the wedding planner came in and told us we were starting soon. I thought Nicole grabbed it." Priscilla's eyebrows squished together. "We were so busy that day. I think I may have left the door open when we left, but I told that to the police already."

Busy was an understatement for Nicole and Chad's wedding. If Priscilla put the bracelet on the table, who came up behind her then? Was someone else watching and snuck into the room?

Bianca bobbed her head as she noticed another woman walk through the door. Her face looked familiar. Though Bianca thought she had met everyone in Edenville, she didn't know this woman. Medium-length silky black hair rested on her shoulders underneath a large brim black hat. Her black dress fitted her slender frame, and judging by her chic style, Bianca wondered if she was a friend of Priscilla's. She appeared to be the same age, but had a square face and smooth skin. Slender in shape, and her black hat resembled Ms. Ella's large brim hat at the memorial.

"I think you have another guest." Bianca pointed toward the mysterious woman.

Priscilla stared toward her hand. "What is she doing here?" She groaned. "Give me a moment, will you?"

"Of course," Bianca said.

Priscilla pressed through the crowd and toward the door. Bianca returned to her family.

"Everything okay?" her mother wondered.

"Yes."

"Do you know her?" Melanie asked.

"I don't think so. She can't be a friend if Priscilla asked what she's doing here."

Bianca's eyes shifted to the sign that led to the restrooms. It wasn't too far from where the women stood. No harm in making a quick trip to the ladies' room. "I'll be back."

Bianca adjusted her purse on her shoulders as she paced to the ladies' room. She even refused to look in the direction as Detective Sims. He was a distraction from her mission. Mission? Not quite, but if it would help her friends, why not?

She stepped into the hallway of the restrooms but leaned against the wall as she listened. Despite the chatter and murmurs, she tuned into the conversation.

"What are you doing here, Nora?" Priscilla asked.

Bianca gasped. Nora. She'd seen her picture when she'd Googled Martin's business endeavors with Richard. Nora showed? Bianca didn't anticipate that.

"I came to see if it was true," Nora said.

"I think it's best you leave. He wouldn't have wanted you here anyway," Priscilla said.

"He may have left me for you, but that doesn't mean I can't offer my condolences. The man was my husband first."

"But he's my husband... *was* my husband," Priscilla said. "Nora, I think you should go before you cause a scene. This is a small town. I wouldn't want the rumors to start. Martin kept his private life private."

"Well..." Nora said. "We've come a long way, haven't we, Priscilla? We're having a civilized conversation."

Priscilla replied. "Time matures a person."

Nora spoke up. "You will keep me up to date on the investigation? Martin didn't deserve to die that way. Not even the world's worst husband deserves to die that way."

"I wouldn't dream of keeping this away from you," Priscilla said.

Bianca slipped into the women's restroom. Resting her hands on the counter, she pondered what she'd just heard. As she paced the vinyl floors, her heels clicked in the background. How long had Nora been in town? Had she come to the wedding with no one spotting her in the background?

She leaned against the counter and sighed. This case kept getting more and more complicated. She clutched her phone for a moment but decided to return to her family, before her mother sent someone looking for her. Exhaling a deep breath, she exited the restroom, only to bump into her sister.

Bianca held back a shriek. "Don't do that."

Melanie folded her arms. "Better me than Mom. Are you all right?"

Bianca shook her head.

Melanie touched her arm. "Are you sick? Do we need to leave? I can drive—"

"Martin had another wife."

Melanie's eyes bulged.

Bianca kept her voice low and stared behind her sister. Opening her mouth to continue, she thought better of it and pulled her sister into the ladies' room.

"Is it that bad?"

"There's a woman here that I saw Priscilla talking to. She was Martin's first wife. Nora," Bianca said.

Melanie's eyes got even bigger.

"Looks like he left her for Priscilla."

Her sister's mouth fell open. "So... Martin leaves this Nora woman for Priscilla. Why?"

"The better question is... How much of a grudge would she have held against Martin for leaving her?" Bianca raised an eyebrow. "I'm still suspicious of Richard though, especially with his butcher knife missing."

"Why show up now? Think about it. Would you attend Malcom's funeral and talk to his new wife?" Melanie covered her mouth. "Sorry."

Bianca's shoulders dropped. "I think I could be civil enough for Alyssa's sake, but infidelity is a powerful motive for murder."

"What are you going to do?"

"Not sure." She stuffed her phone inside her purse. "Let's get back out there before Mom sends a search party for both of us."

"Good point," Melanie said.

Chapter 14

Monday started a new week. Bianca erased her latest task from her dry erase board. Her computer chimed, alerting her of more emails. Wallace Designs was high in demand and Bianca loved the challenge of her job. Ever since she'd been a girl, her mother would catch her drawing pictures of trees, flowers, or the surrounding houses and buildings nearby. Her father had always told her she'd had a gift for art.

Though Bianca had wanted to study art overseas, marrying Malcom out of high school had changed her plans. Next thing she'd known, she'd been an expectant mother. She hadn't minded putting her dreams on hold for the time being. She'd had a new family to take care of, so when Malcom had filed divorce papers, he might as well have stabbed her in the chest.

Bianca's chest heaved with a sigh. That had been a long time ago. She'd healed and didn't mind being on her own. Closing her eyes for a cleansing breath, the color gray flashed in her mind.

Detective Sims. Rolling her shoulders back, she opened her new emails. It was best to focus on work. She inhaled the fragrant ocean breeze air from her freshener, but Casper soon disrupted her with his incessant barks.

Bianca caught him wagging his tail as he stood to the side of her office chair. "What now? You've eaten already." She couldn't say the same. The most she'd had for lunch had been a granola bar.

Casper only barked in response. Bianca leaned back in her chair. Glancing at the clock on her wall, it wouldn't hurt if she took a break to give her puppy a walk. Standing to her feet, she stretched her own hands over her head, feeling stiff from sitting so long.

Grabbing Casper's leash, Bianca locked the door behind them and they proceeded down the street. Then they continued to the nearby park. Casper didn't stop for a second. He must have been excited to get some fresh air.

Bianca settled on the bench. Unhooking his leash, she let her puppy roam the grounds. She inhaled the smell of fresh-cut grass mixed with pine needles. Rubbing her fingers together, she couldn't help but wonder again about Martin's death.

There was no way Nicole had killed him. The woman didn't have it in her, did she? Priscilla? Did she have the nerve to kill her own husband? Did she know about Martin's involvement with Nicole? What about Richard? He seemed to be going on with his life as if Martin's death didn't matter to him at all. Their argument had been intense for all to hear.

Bianca rubbed her head at the possibility, only to spot Chad running on the runner's trail. Did he usually run in the afternoon? He followed the path as it curved, and he headed in her direction.

"Chad?" She waved at him.

He didn't smile, but jogged to her on the bench. "How are you? Taking a lunch break?"

"Something like that." Bianca browsed the park for her dog, spotting that he was chasing after birds. A chuckle escaped her mouth. "Waiting for him."

Chad looked toward her dog. "Nice." He stopped running in place and wiped the sweat from his forehead.

Bianca couldn't help herself. "How are you? How's Nicole holding up?"

Chad blew out his cheeks. "We're supposed to be on our honeymoon in Italy, but we can't leave until all of this mess clears up."

Her heart sunk for them. "I'm so sorry."

Chad sat next to her, draping an arm on the back of the bench. "She said you talked to her before the memorial. Did she... tell you about her past with Martin?"

Bianca swallowed. What all had Nicole told Chad? "She... shared some things."

Chad's chin dropped to his chest. "She hated him, Bianca. I... can't say I blame her. I wasn't too keen on him marrying my mother, either."

Bianca didn't respond.

"I hate seeing my mother hurt like this," he said.

"Is that the reason you wanted Jordan to leave the memorial service?" she asked.

He looked past her and then behind him. When he faced her again, he cleared his throat. "I don't want him around Nicole. I tolerated it when we dated, but she's my wife. I don't want gossip around town."

Priscilla had been right. "But everyone knows they're best friends."

"Yeah, they're best friends, but it's not as if he hid his feelings. You and I both know, Bianca, this town will spread that around like wildfire. There are already rumors that I punched him at the memorial with Nicole screaming. I even heard the rumor that Nicole planned to leave me at the altar and run away with Jordan."

Bianca sighed.

He rubbed at his forehead. "Things aren't good with Nicole and me."

"This was a shock to everyone. I can't imagine how it's affecting you two."

Chad shook his head. "It's causing unnecessary tension. Have you... talked to Jordan?"

"Not today. He may need time to process getting thrown out publicly like that."

"It'll be better if he leaves town for good."

Bianca's lips parted. "What? Why? Chad I don't think he's a real threat to you. Nicole married you. She loves you."

Chad's fist clenched. "She kept telling me they were just friends, but I knew better. I saw the way he looked at her when he thought no one was looking. Martin did too."

"Martin?"

Chad ran a hand down his face. "Martin was blackmailing Nicole, and Jordan knew it. I know he would have done anything to protect her."

A sudden coldness hit Bianca's core. Jordan? Would he kill Martin on Nicole's behalf? Chad was right. The man would have done anything for Nicole, but he'd backed off. Right?

"Chad? You said that you hated Martin." She couldn't quite ask what she wanted to.

Chad sighed. "I know and I did. He had gambling debts, and I found out when I was working for him that he was laundering money from his own real estate company to pay them. He cheated people out of their money, Bianca. The man was awful, but I didn't kill him."

"Chad Lee?"

Bianca recognized Detective Atkins, with Detective Sims not too far behind him coming from the parking lot. Joggers and parents with young children watched as both officers walked over to where Chad and Bianca were sitting. Even a few dogs barked on leashes as they walked with their owners. Casper joined in the barking too, but Bianca picked him up and held him close. Why were the police here? Was Nicole alright?

"Officer? Is there a problem?" Chad asked.

"Chad Lee, we need you to come in for questioning for the murder Martin Davis," Detective Sims said.

Detective Atkins added. "If you would follow us to the police station, we'd appreciate your cooperation."

"For what?" Chad's stared back and for between both detectives.

Detective Atkins held up his phone. "Do you recognize this bag?"

Chad leaned in. "Yes. That's my gym bag."

Detective Atkins stuffed his phone back in his pocket. "We need you to clear some things up for us. A few questions and we'll let you go about your day." He gestured for Chad to follow him.

Had she heard this right? Chad?

"I'll see you later, Bianca," Chad said.

"Do you want me to call Nicole?" she asked.

"No, I'd rather she hear from me," he said.

Bianca watched as her friend's husband walked to a nearby police car with Detective Atkins as his escort. Detective Sims cleared his throat. He hadn't moved.

Bianca held Casper in one hand facing Detective Sims. "What's going on?"

Detective Sims said, "We're only bringing him in for questioning, Ms. Wallace.

"But why?"

"Ms. Wallace?"

She continued. "Don't forget I saw the body first. Maybe I can help. Something may jog my memory. Do you have a picture on your phone too?"

Detective Sims rubbed the back of his neck. "We found a bloody towel in his gym bag."

"Martin's blood?" she asked. But how?

"It's not official, but I'm sure when the results are in, it'll show it as Mr. Davis' blood."

How? Bianca thought back to when she was at the gym earlier this week. She didn't see Chad that day. "What about the butcher knife? Was it with the towel?" She caught herself as soon as she'd asked the question.

Did Detective Sims' eyes tighten around the corners? "We haven't located the knife yet, Ms. Wallace."

So much for calling her "Bianca." She nodded in response.

"Can I see the towel you're talking about?" she asked.

Detective Sims pulled out his phone to show her a photo. Bianca focused her eyes on the picture. The towel looked familiar. Hadn't she and Melanie seen something similar at... oh, no?

Bianca gasped.

"Ms. Wallace?" Detective Sims was observant.

"I... I recognize the towel."

"Okay good. From where?" he asked.

Bianca's skin tingled. It couldn't be, but who could deny it? "My sister and I stopped by Richard and Judy Long's restaurant and bakery last week before the memorial. One worker was cleaning the windows and he… had a towel similar to the one in the picture. It was golden, but not like a regular towel. I don't remember a pattern or a logo on it. Anyway he—"

"It's a microfiber towel. They're known for absorbency." Detective Sims sighed as he stuffed his phone back in his pocket. "Thank you, Ms. Wallace. I'll look into it."

With a final nod, Detective Sims walked away to join Detective Atkins. Chad a suspect. Bianca stared after them with Casper in her arms. Sitting back on the park bench, she released him, but kept the loop of his leash around her wrist. Then she reached for her phone in her purse. Bianca wouldn't tell Nicole about Chad leaving with the police since he wanted to tell her himself. Yet, she wanted to send a message of support.

Checking on you. I know it's been crazy but here if you need anything. Sent.

Chapter 15

Settling into the booths nestled against the wall, Bianca waited for Jordan at Edenville's diner, The Southern Quarter, for lunch. The sizzle sound of burgers made her mouth water, but today she'd decided on a Caesar salad. Then again, grilling meat and onions frying filled her nose. Despite the diner's specialty in southern cooking and town favorites, burgers and fries, they'd expanded their menu to include soups, salads, and even vegetarian choice meals.

Their double chocolate cake didn't sound too bad today. Bianca blinked. No, she would stay strong. She would treat herself over the weekend.

The bell dinged as a customer entered, but it wasn't Jordan. Bianca pulled her phone out of her purse. Ever since she'd found out about Martin's first marriage, she'd done more research on the internet. No kids together and after five years, he'd filed for divorce.

Digging into more of Nora's background, Bianca discovered she was the daughter of a well-known businessman who'd owned various oil rigs. After college, Nora had gotten into philanthropy work, volunteering at children's hospitals, as well as donating money to third-world countries.

Bianca even watched a recent YouTube video on the woman giving a speech to her most recent charity donation. She seemed pleasant, but had that changed when she'd been with Martin? Bianca knew all too well that looks could be deceiving. Like with Richard, but with Chad on the police's radar, she couldn't pinpoint why he would shift blame to Chad. What was the family dynamic to drive them to this? Did Richard have the man cleaning his windows follow Chad to the gym?

The bell dinged once more and she spotted Jordan. Another possible suspect. Chad painted him to be this man who would do anything for the woman he loved. Including killing the man who was blackmailing Nicole. Bianca's limbs should have shook with fear when he entered the diner, but he was her friend. She never felt unsafe with Jordan. Kindhearted. Charming. Sure, he had a temper, but he wouldn't kill. He scanned the room, but Bianca waved her hand in the air. He didn't waste time walking to her table.

"Hey." Jordan took off his jacket and sat across from her.

"Are you okay?" Bianca leaned in closer.

He wrung his hands together on the tabletop. "Getting there. Have you ordered yet?"

"Not yet," Bianca said.

"What can I get you both?" Harmony, the waitress approached them with her pen and small notepad. She had pulled her medium length platinum blonde hair into a pony tail. Despite the beads of sweat along her hairline, her makeup remained flawless on her ivory skin. "Sorry about the delay, but the lunch crowd is always like this."

Bianca's eyes scanned the diner as the chatter increased. The cutlery clinked on tables, scratching against plates. She turned to

Harmony. "That's okay, Harmony. I'll have water and a Caesar salad with the grilled chicken."

"Same for me, Harmony," Jordan said.

The waitress bobbed her head and took their plastic menus from their table.

Bianca waited until she was out of earshot. Then she focused on Jordan.

"I heard the police suspect Chad," he said.

"They brought him in for questioning. They found a bloody towel in his gym bag, but he hasn't been formally charged."

"This is getting worse by the day."

"Want to tell me why you were kicked out of Martin's memorial that day?" She hadn't seen him since, not even in church. When he'd texted that morning wanting to see her, Bianca had accepted. His altercation with Chad lingered in the back of her mind. Though she wanted to keep her eyes open, her heart great heavy considering Jordan was responsible for all of this.

"They didn't tell you?" he asked.

Bianca said, "I want to hear your side."

Jordan ran a hand down his face. "I wish I knew."

"You don't get along with Priscilla. Did you have a problem with Martin?"

"I never liked the guy. Nicole always gave him the benefit of the doubt despite their *history*. She blamed herself."

"That's how she is."

"Exactly, but back then, she didn't know how to set healthy boundaries. Martin took advantage of that."

There had to be more than that. Bianca leaned in again. "Jordan, what aren't you telling me? Why did you want to see me?"

He shook his head. "Looks like I've caused enough trouble already."

"But this can help Nicole. The police still suspect her. And Chad."

"Chad has enough money where he buy off a judge, lawyers, and the jury."

Bianca tilted her head at him. "What about Nicole? She's not in the clear yet."

His jaw clenched. "They can't prove anything."

She raised an eyebrow. "How do you know that? I still can't get past the bracelet."

"I found it, brought it to her, and sat it on the table." A smile grew on his face. "She looked incredible in her dress." His face fell. "Anyway, Priscilla answered the door. I wished Nicole good luck and left."

"Maybe Nicole misplaced it again. Priscilla said she'd been nervous about her vows. Perhaps the wedding jitters got the best of her. Then again, Priscilla did say the wedding planner came and they rushed out of there. She thinks she left the door open," Bianca said. Who would plant Nicole's bracelet at the crime scene?

"I guess it didn't help her if the police found it anyway." He cupped the back of his neck. "There's no way she could have done this, Bianca."

"How do you know?" she asked.

"I... was there."

"Where? At the murder?" Bianca's eyes shifted to make sure no one was listening.

Jordan folded his hands on the table and leaned in over the wooden table. "The rehearsal dinner."

"I didn't see you. I thought you said you weren't coming because of—"

"I know, but Nicole is still my best friend." He sighed. "I was going to leave, but I stopped by the men's room first. When I got into the hallway, I heard an argument."

"Between whom?"

"Martin and Richard. At first they were whispering, sort of, but I heard Richard asking Martin for more time."

"More time?" Time for what? Money? He did ask Bianca the same thing with his payment for her services. Bianca's fingers touched her parted lips. "What else?"

Jordan bit the inside of his cheek. "Richard had something in his hand. I couldn't see too close, but I think it was... a knife. That changed everything."

Bianca gasped.

Jordan continued. "Next thing I hear is Martin saying, 'Now calm down. Put the knife away and we'll talk about it nicely.' Then I head Richard's voice saying, 'No! We'll talk about this *now*.' He wouldn't put the knife down."

"That must have been the moment we all heard yelling. Something broke too." Bianca sat back in her chair.

"I slipped out the back. I figured it was best to leave anyway. I'm still... getting used to Nicole with someone else," Jordan said.

Bianca leaned in again and touched his hand. Even if Jordan didn't hear Richard actually threaten to kill Martin, a butcher knife in hand was threatening enough. Was that his intention? Was he in the middle of chopping something and happened to have the knife in his hand while talking to Martin? Did this argument start in the kitchen and then to the hallway for Jordan to hear?

Bianca covered her mouth with her free hand. "Have you told the police this?"

"As far as I know my story proves nothing. I didn't stick around to see what else happened. Like I said, it could be nothing. Maybe it's a coincidence."

"So... why didn't Priscilla act that way at the wedding?" Bianca then recalled how the woman practically turned her nose up at Jordan when he asked her to dance.

He continued. "She's never liked me no matter how much she pretends to be civil. Since Nicole and I were so close, I think she got into Chad's ear that I would steal her from him. I stepped aside once I saw how serious they were, but I did get into an altercation with Chad a while back. Only yelling so not a fight. Nicole wanted me at the wedding to bury the hatchet. I guess she convinced Priscilla."

"And?" Bianca asked.

"You know how Nicole would sleep on my couch sometimes when she was looking for an apartment?"

"Right." Bianca would have had her friend stay with her, but that was when she'd been with Malcom. He hadn't cared for anyone staying with them unless it was his own family members. Bianca rolled her eyes.

"Anyway, she told me to meet her with the rest of her things after she'd left my place. So I did. I ended up meeting her at an office building, which turned out to be Martin's building."

"She worked for him?" Bianca couldn't believe she didn't know this. She recalled the years of Nicole's job as a receptionist after graduate school, but not about Martin being her boss. Is that how this all started?

"That's how they met," Jordan said. "Anyway, Chad was there. You know how he is when it comes to her. Words were exchanged and next thing I know, Martin has security escort me off the premises. I was so angry and hurt over Nicole, I..."

Bianca did a double take. "You what?"

"I might have threatened to... kill him and Chad."

"What?" Her eyebrows shot up.

"That was a long time ago, Bianca. Chad and I have since been somewhat civil, but I never made amends with Martin. I don't know. I guess he told Priscilla and she probably thinks I had a hit out on him still."

"Is that what you told the police too?" she asked.

"Yes. I'm telling you they can't prove anything against me or Nicole."

Bianca ran her fingers through her hair. "What about Richard?"

"I wish I knew. Like I said before, I didn't stick around to hear."

"I wonder." Bianca tapped a finger to her full lips.

"What?"

Harmony returned. "Here you go. Enjoy your lunch." She placed two plates full of salad in front of both Jordan and Bianca. Once she'd served their water, Harmony left their table.

"What are you thinking, Bianca?" Jordan asked.

"If it was money he owed, do you know how much?"

"No."

"Are you free once we finish here?" Bianca grabbed her fork.

"I have some time. Why?"

"I think maybe we need to pay Richard a visit and see what we can find. I wonder if there's something in his books in his office." How much did he owe to Martin? $20,000? More than that maybe?

"He's not going to let us in his office, Bianca," Jordan said.

"No, but we can find a way inside."

Jordan narrowed his eyes at her. "Sounds like college all over again. Us sneaking off campus for a party."

"I'm a responsible adult now." She winked at him.

"Sure you are." Jordan took a bite from his salad.

CHOCOLATE SQUARES, macarons, and eclairs caught Bianca's eyes, but she would not order them. Jordan followed behind her as they entered R&J's Restaurant and Bakery. Her mouth watered at the smell of cinnamon, and judging by the small crowd, they had beaten the usual lunch rush. Customers chatted as they ate, but Bianca only focused on finding Judy.

Jordan cupped her elbow with his hand. "You see her yet?"

"Not yet." Bianca eyed the narrow hallway. She'd visited the bakery enough to know where the office was. Should she press her luck?

"Let's take a seat first." Jordan led her to a back table near the hallway.

Bianca folded her hands on the table once she sat.

"What are you thinking?" Jordan asked. He checked his watch. "I do have to get some work done."

The corners of her mouth quirked up. "How's the writing coming along?"

"I have two books I'm working on. It's going well so far."

"Will you ever write anything under your actual name?" she asked.

Jordan shook his head.

Bianca pursed her lips together as she ran her hand down her pant leg. Leaning over, she glanced down the hallway. "I'm thinking about slipping to the ladies' room."

Jordan looked behind her. "I think the office is the last door on the right." He turned and winked at her.

Bianca stood from her chair and walked down the hallway. Since she'd worn flats today, her heels didn't click on the floors, but when she came to the last door on the right, she noticed it was cracked. A small light shined from a lamp. When she peeked in, she saw no one.

Her stomach fluttered, but she stepped inside. Her eyes met a wooden desk covered with sticky notes, paper and pens, a desk phone, and a calculator. Bianca walked closer, bypassing a tall filing cabinet, and stared at the documents on the desk. More stacks of files and papers.

Reaching out, she opened a manila folder. A ledger. Richard and Judy didn't use an accounting software? Bianca raised her eyebrow as she read over the revenues. She didn't touch the receipts, but from the looks of it, their business was in a tight spot.

Not enough evidence. Spreading the papers further, Bianca spotted a piece of printed paper. A letter folded in half. Ignoring the hardness in her stomach, she opened it. Only speechless could describe her reaction.

Martin threatened to take over Richard and Judy's business? They owed $41,000. Bianca's gazed around the office. Forty-one thousand dollars, and they had until the end of this month to pay the money in full.

Was that a noise? Bianca jerked and folded the letter back in place. Stepping away from the desk, she headed for the door. Was there anyone there? Was Jordan coming to warn her? Bianca peeped her head out to see. No one. She looked ahead.

The ladies' room. There wasn't any more time to waste. Biting her lower lip, hoping she didn't get caught, Bianca dashed for the restroom, shutting the door behind her. She breathed easier once inside, rubbing the back of her neck.

Walking to face the mirror, she stared at her own reflection. Had someone seen her inside the office? How would she explain that?

Then Jordan's story replayed in her head. He'd seen Richard with a knife. Had it been the same butcher knife that had killed Martin? Bianca's hand scraped through her hair. When would this puzzle come together?

Okay. She had to remain calm. If what she'd thought she'd seen was true, Judy and Richard were having financial problems. Martin had helped with the funds, but it's possible he'd held the debt over their heads. What if Richard had gotten fed up? What if he'd killed Martin and covered it up by trying to pin the blame on Nicole?

That makes no sense. What did he have against Nicole? She thought they all got along. They'd even catered the engagement party, bridal shower, and the wedding reception. Bianca's shoulders dropped. This was getting her nowhere.

Stepping out of the ladies room, she ran into a hard chest, but before she could scream, a hand covered her mouth. Her eyes bulged. Jordan.

"Shh." He released his grip.

She punched his gut, but based on his toned stomach, she'd hardly hurt him. She kept her voice at a whisper. "Don't do that." She straightened her blouse. "What are you doing?"

"I came to check on you," he whispered back.

"Next time, text me." Her eyes shifted down the hallway back to the main dining area. "See anything?"

"No sign of Richard or Judy yet," Jordan said. "What did you find?"

"A motive. They owed Martin $41,000. They had until the end of this month to pay him or he was going to take over their business."

"*What*?" He still kept his voice to a whisper.

Bianca nodded. "I don't want to believe it, but..."

"But what?"

"It makes sense because of the money problems, but I don't see why Nicole is being blamed." Bianca didn't want to continue the conversation. Perhaps the noise she heard was someone listening. It was best to save this for later. "Come on." She looped her arm through his.

"Will you explain to me what's going on?" Jordan asked.

Bianca tilted her head to the side. "I will. For now, go home, and get your work done."

"You expect me to go to work and ignore what you just told me?" he asked.

"I don't think it's a good idea if you stay any longer. Now that I think about it, it'll probably be best if Judy and Richard didn't see you this soon after the... memorial outburst." Bianca gestured to the door.

Jordan opened his mouth as if to argue, but he didn't. Instead, he kissed her forehead. "I don't get what you're up to, just be careful."

"Okay." She motioned him to leave. He did.

Turning on her heels, Bianca made her way to the front counter. Judy. She must have been in the back. "Hey, Judy."

The redhead's eyes didn't beam as they usually did. "Bianca. I didn't see you come in. What can I get you?"

"An iced tea to go if you don't mind." She reached into her purse and grabbed some cash. "I didn't have time to talk to you during the memorial for Martin."

"I know." Judy pinched the skin at her throat as her forehead wrinkled. Circles under her eyes showed but it looked like she did her best to cover it with her makeup. "It was such a long day. I was so exhausted by the time we got home."

"I understand. How are you and Richard holding up?" she asked.

Judy scratched at her nose. "We're taking it one day at a time." Reaching into her back pocket, she took out a white envelope. "When I saw you were here, I grabbed this. It's only half of what we owe, but it's something. We'll have the rest of the money soon for our final payment for the invitations. Thank you again."

Bianca tilted her head to the side as she took the envelope. She put it inside her purse. "Of course. I didn't mind working with you on the payments." Especially now after seeing their $41,000 debt to Martin in their office. "But how are you two? Really with... everything?"

Judy looked around her and then back at Bianca. "The memorial didn't go as we planned. I didn't think Priscilla would act that way when Jordan showed up."

Might as well ask now. "Do you know why she did? I don't think I remember her having a problem with him before."

"Jordan never got along with Martin or Chad. I can't blame Chad since the whole town knew about Jordan's feelings for Nicole. Poor boy." Judy handed her a to-go Styrofoam cup.

Bianca handed her the cash. "You think Priscilla thought he would—"

"They all have tempers. I guess Priscilla didn't want to cause a scene, but her being so distraught over Martin, she probably overreacted more than usual."

Bianca tested the waters. "Business seems good for you and Richard though."

Judy dropped her head.

"Judy?" Bianca reached out her hand.

She shook her head. "It's nothing to worry about. It's been... tough, but we're getting back up on our feet."

"You weren't going to lose this place, were you?"

Her eyes focused on Bianca. "This is our dream and I won't let *anyone* hinder that."

Bianca's lips parted. The conviction in Judy's voice was undeniable. Was it possible that she...? No way. Holding up her cup, she gave a faint smile. "Thanks for the drink."

Judy extended her hand with Bianca's change, but Bianca shook her head.

"Keep it. Consider it a tip."

Judy bobbed her head with a smile. "Thank you. That's very generous of you, Bianca."

"You're welcome." How was she going to figure out this murder? Who was guilty and who was telling the truth?

Chapter 16

Plum or sunflower yellow? Bianca held both nail polishes in her hand. This was what she'd needed. A day at Nina's Spa and Nail salon. A chance to unwind from a full workload and investigating Martin's murder. Though no massage today in one of their private rooms, getting her nails done would suffice.

Nothing was adding up still, so Bianca dropped Casper off at her mother's house for a dog play day, while she treated herself. Steam wafted from her herbal tea on the side table next to her.

"Which would you like?" an attendant asked her. The woman's shaped eyebrows complemented her square face. Her kinky dark brown hair had been pulled into a high ponytail.

The summer hadn't quite arrived yet, but they were in spring. Yet Bianca loved wearing dark colors to complement her brown skin. "Let's go with the plum."

The attendant smiled, and Bianca took one last sip of her tea as the woman worked on her nails. She would check her emails when she returned home. Looking upward, she went over the list in her head. Answer emails. Pick up Casper from her mom's home. Pick up Alyssa from school.

Bianca hadn't told her daughter yet, but if she wanted to learn how to drive, she would give her some pointers and if Alyssa wanted to take lessons, Bianca would let her sign up. Her mother had told her that Alyssa could have her grandfather's restored Camaro once she received her license.

When her phone rang, she reached inside her purse in her lap. Thank goodness one of her hands was finished. Malcom? At least he was trying. While Bianca was still getting used to them co-parenting, she could appreciate his efforts despite his shortcomings before. Using her free hand, she answered.

"Hey," she said. No more, "Hey, babe" or "Hey, honey." Those days were over.

"Is this a bad time? I'm on break at work so I thought I'd call you," Malcom said.

"I'm on a break too. What's up?"

"I wanted to check back with you about Alyssa spending the summer here with me."

Bianca pondered the thought. Her daughter away from her for an entire summer? The most time they'd spend apart was her spending the night at her friend's or her grandmother's home.

"Bianca?"

"I'm still thinking about it," she said. "Have you called her?"

"Not yet." He sighed. "Look, I know it's a lot to ask, but I'm trying here. I want my daughter in my life."

Bianca bit back her response. It was another trigger for her. Where had this dedication been to Alyssa when he'd left them? He'd barely called Alyssa when he'd moved to California to be with his new wife. Now, he wanted Alyssa around.

She blew out her cheeks. She'd gone through this in therapy. When triggered, it only meant she needed another moment of healing. Bianca had already made peace with his decision. There was no sense in rehashing everything.

"Call Alyssa and if she wants to, it's okay with me." There, she had said it. "I'll find something to keep me occupied."

"Alyssa told me your mom gave you two a puppy," he said.

Bianca giggled. "Yes, Casper. He's growing on us, I guess."

"Thank you, Bianca. Thanks for agreeing to this."

"She's getting older, so I'm trying to get better at trusting her judgment," she said.

Malcom groaned. "We have a teenager."

"Don't remind me. I still can't get that baby girl is not a baby anymore." A *hmm* noise escaped her as she cleared her throat.

"Something on your mind?" Malcom asked.

"She hasn't said anything to me yet, but I know it's coming."

"What? Don't tell me she has a boyfriend. Who is he? Have you met him? How old is he? Where did she—?"

"Calm down, Dad." She grinned at his protectiveness taking over. "If she does, she'll tell you. I'm talking about her getting her driver's license."

"She's only sixteen."

"She's old enough, Malcom. Besides, this will teach her even more responsibility. My mom even has a car she's been wanting to give Alyssa. I think she's ready to take lessons now. Learning how to drive would help me too. My business is booming. Knowing that Alyssa can take herself places will lighten my load."

Malcom sighed.

"Still there?" Was he having another moment?

"Yes, I'm here. I don't like this, Bianca."

"What do you want her to do? Stay a little girl forever?"

He groaned. "I'll think about it. Maybe... a few lessons will be okay for now. Let her decide if she wants her license."

"I'll talk to her." Bianca's gaze lowered as the attendant finished her manicure. She pointed to the front desk. Bianca mouthed a "thank you" to her. She smiled and waved back.

"Good." Malcom continued. "Where did the time go? Wow, I sound old."

Bianca stood in her wedged sandals, grabbed her purse, and headed for the front desk. "Not that old."

"Thank you." He groaned again. "I have to get back to work, but tell Alyssa I'll call her if she doesn't call me."

"I will. Bye, Malcom."

"Bye."

He hung up. Despite the tenseness in her stomach, the conversation with Malcom hadn't been bad at all. Though he'd been paying child support consistently, that didn't replace quality time with his daughter. Perhaps things were getting better with time. He was reaching out more now than ever. Would they learn to be friends again?

For a time, they'd been best friends. They would stay up for hours on the phone. It didn't matter what the conversation had been about. She rubbed at the twinge in her chest. Perhaps that was what hurt the most. More than him leaving. More than him marrying another woman. Their friendship had died with their marriage.

Bianca paid the attendant and took her receipt. Would she find that with someone else? Was she willing to open up her heart that way again? Rolling her shoulders back, she thanked the receptionist and headed for the door.

Then Bianca paused. Nora. Her hand was on the door handle as she talked with another attendant. Perhaps she was in one of the private rooms for a massage. Was she leaving?

Bianca remained close behind as Nora said goodbye.

"I'm so sorry," she said to Bianca. "Here I am blocking the door."

"No problem." Bianca retrieved her keys from her purse.

"I think I know you. Your face looks familiar." Nora tapped her chin as she tried to remember. "I could have sworn..."

"I was at Martin Davis' memorial."

Nora raised her eyebrows. "You were?"

How would she play this? "Yeah, I think I saw you talking with Priscilla, his widow."

She and Nora walked into the semi-full parking lot.

Nora adjusted her purse. "She's... something."

Bianca didn't respond.

Nora paused her steps and turned to face her. "You two are friends?"

"I'm friends with her daughter-in-law. Nicole Lee." Could she ask Nora a question without being too obvious? Would Nora be defensive?

"I see." Nora cleared her throat. "Well, I hope things work out and whoever did this gets what they deserve."

"Were you close with Martin?" Bianca asked. She might as well keep her act up if it would get her the information she needed.

Nora raised an eyebrow, as if surprised. She huffed. "I was his wife before he left me for Priscilla." She shuffled her feet in the space she stood. "This was a mistake coming here. I don't know why I thought coming to pay my respects would bring me peace. It didn't."

"I hope I didn't upset you," Bianca said.

Nora pinched the bridge of her narrow nose. "You seem to care about this family. My advice to you? Leave them alone. Especially

Priscilla. She's nothing but trouble. She'll put on a smile one minute but turn on you in the next."

What? How would Nora know that? Was she only talking as a woman hurt and humiliated by her late former husband? How angry was she?

"I've said too much." Her thin lips pressed together for a moment. She toyed with the collar of her floral blouse. "Thank goodness I'm leaving town tonight. I can't stay here knowing that he..."

Bianca tilted her head, hoping she would finish.

Nora sighed. "I didn't get your name."

She extended her hand to hers. "Bianca Wallace."

Nora gripped her hand—tightly. "Stay clear, Bianca. Whoever did this to Martin will stop at *nothing*." She released her grip and marched to her car.

Had that been a warning? Who? That was the burning question. Who?

Chapter 17

"What is this? Thanksgiving dinner?" Bianca's eyes widened at the smoked turkey on her mother's kitchen island. Another Sunday meal after church that she couldn't wait to indulge in.

"I had it in the freezer and it needed to be cooked," her mother said.

Bianca bent over to smell it. "It's not freezer-burned, is it?"

Her mother eyed her. "No, it's a good turkey. Have a taste."

Bianca reached for a piece of meat from the breast of the bird. She said a silent prayer in case her mother was wrong about the freezer burn. One bite and a *hmm* escaped her throat. "Okay." Juicy. Flavorful.

"See." Her mother winked at her. "Grab the pan of cornbread dressing."

Jasper, Horas, and Casper ran into the kitchen. Horas stood on his hind legs, while the other two barked.

Bianca's mother gestured for them to go back to the living room. "Back. Go back."

Horas and Jasper obeyed, but Casper lingered. Bianca clapped her hands and he followed. Once he was out the kitchen, she returned to assist her mother.

"Mom." Bianca did as her mother asked and followed her to the dining area with the cornbread dressing. "Again, what's with the fancy meal?"

"We can't have one?" her mother asked.

"I just wondered." Bianca set the pan on the cloth-covered table.

Her mother tapped her fingers on the back of one of her wooden dining chairs. "I figured we could use a fancy meal. There's been a lot going on in town. I thought it would help get our mind off things."

Bianca cleared her throat and walked back to the kitchen.

Her mother trailed behind her. "What's that look for?"

Bianca didn't tell her mother about her personal investigation. She rolled her eyes as she faced the cabinets. One moment she'd had the answer, and the next, she couldn't tell who the culprit was. Perhaps her mother was right. They needed a break from it all. For now.

"Nothing. A lot on my mind."

Her mother grabbed a glass pitcher of iced tea from her stainless steel refrigerator. "Want to talk about it?"

Bianca could change the subject. "Well... Malcom called."

Her mother flinched. "Really?"

"Yes. He wants Alyssa to spend the summer with him."

Her mother placed the pitcher on the counter. "What did you say?"

"Alyssa is old enough to decide for herself. If she wants to go, I'm fine with it."

Her mother folded her arms. "I never thought I would hear you say that. After everything he's put you through."

Bianca leaned against the counter. "I know, but he's still her father. We're not together anymore, but Alyssa will always connect us. I can't change that."

Her mother gave a faint smile. "I'm proud of you. That can't be easy."

"It's difficult."

"Did I tell you I think you're an incredible mother?" Her mother's grin grew.

Bianca's limbs tingled with warmth. "Really?"

"Why does that surprise you?" Her mother raised an eyebrow as if taken aback by her reaction.

Bianca pinched the skin at her throat. "I guess I felt bad because... my marriage didn't last like yours and dad's."

Her mother's lips parted, but then she extended her arms. "Come here, girl."

Bianca didn't hesitate to hug her mother. Her mother patted her back and rocked her. Then she pulled back but placed her hands on her daughter's shoulders.

"I know I said you were too young, but sweetie, you were always beyond your years. You proved me wrong and I know you're capable of anything you put your mind to. It did not disappoint me. I just hated that you got hurt." Her mother's voice choked. "I never liked seeing you hurt."

"Mom." Bianca held back her own tears.

Her mother touched her cheek. "Just because it didn't work out with Malcom doesn't mean you can't experience love with someone else." She sighed. "I guess... that's why I've tried to work my matchmaking expertise with you. Not to force you, but I still want for you what I had with your father. Not perfect love, but unconditional love."

Bianca took her mother's hand. "I appreciate that, but can you let me find it in my own time? I keep telling you, I'm okay."

Her mother bobbed her head. "I'm getting better, but I can't help if I see an eligible bachelor whom I think will be perfect for you. But if—"

"Mom?"

Her mother held up her palms. "I promise no more matchmaking... unless I think he's perfect for you."

"You're not letting this go, are you?" Bianca shook her head.

Her mother's mouth twisted into a grin. "I will respect your wishes."

Bianca gave her mother two weeks. Her matchmaking skills couldn't go unused.

They both laughed.

"Okay, we got the cranberry sauce," Melanie said, toting in grocery bags with Alyssa by her side. Her sister pointed back and forth between Bianca and their mother. "Everything okay?"

"Perfect." Bianca's mother winked at her.

When the doorbell rang, the women turned their heads. The dogs barked as usual.

"I'll get it." Her mother walked to the door.

"I wonder," Melanie said.

"Wonder what?" Alyssa asked.

"What are you talking about?" Bianca asked.

Melanie wrapped both her arms around Bianca's and Alyssa's shoulders, forming a small huddle. "How much do you want to bet it's Mr. Luther Burkes?"

"Twenty dollars," Alyssa said, but her lips parted when she stared at her mother.

Bianca eyed her daughter. Then she faced her sister. "We don't know that. He only came one time."

"But we all know he's got a thing for Mom." Melanie added.

"All right, Grandma!" Alyssa said.

Bianca had to admit it was cute to see her mother and Luther together. Had he told her how he felt? So far, her mother had mentioned nothing else about them.

"Come on in." Her mother led Luther into the kitchen. "We were just getting ready to sit at the table."

Luther nodded his head in acknowledgement. "Nice to see you again, ladies."

"Hello," Melanie and Alyssa said together.

Bianca grinned. "Good to see you as well."

"Can you girls bring the rest of the food to the table?" Her mother then touched Luther's arm and led him to the dining room.

"All right now." Melanie's eyes followed them.

"Grandma's dating." Alyssa bobbed her head. "That's... different."

"You thought you were the only one?" Melanie commented, but then covered her mouth as if realizing her blunder.

"Aunt Mel!" Alyssa's eyes bugged as she made eye contact with her mother. "Mom, I was going to—"

"I figured things were getting cozy with *Kendrick*." Bianca folded her arms.

Alyssa cleared her throat. "I'm... going to join Grandma and Mr. Burkes." She grabbed the pitcher of iced tea.

Melanie bit her bottom lip. "Don't embarrass her too much."

"I'll talk to her when we get home. Let's see what's going on with Mom first."

"Is everybody hooking up in town?" Melanie asked.

"Are you?" Bianca tilted her head to the side.

Melanie's eyes scanned the room. "You know, I think I heard Mom call my name."

"Yeah, right." Bianca reached into her pocket for her phone. "Give me a minute. I need to make a quick call."

"Okay." Melanie exited the kitchen.

Bianca inched closer to the window and found Malcom's name. She was going to need specific dates so they could plan Alyssa's trip. The dial tone rang in her ear and she tapped her foot as she waited.

"Hello?" a woman said.

Bianca turned her phone to check the number. He couldn't have changed it in the last few days. "I'm calling for Malcom. This is Bianca."

"Oh, hi. He just stepped outside with the dog. This is Hope."

Hope. She should have known. She hadn't talked to Malcom's wife, not since the divorce had become final. Hope seemed nice, but how was her having an affair with her husband nice? Pressure increased as Bianca sucked in her cheeks to bite down. Almost three years since the betrayal, but she had to get used to her. If she's what Malcom wanted, she could have him.

"Hope, can you tell him I called? I wanted to get the dates for Alyssa's visit in the summer."

"Sure. No problem. I'm looking forward to having her," she said.

"Thanks. Bye." Bianca hung up. How was she supposed to end the conversation with her ex-husband's new wife? *Have a good day?* Bianca rubbed at her chest. Some days were better than others, but at least she didn't hate Malcolm anymore.

Snapping her fingers, she wanted to call Priscilla too before she forgot. Her shoulders drooped when she only got her voicemail. *Beep*.

"Hey Priscilla, I'm just checking on you. Let us know if you need anything. Also I'm sending you your anniversary photos in the mail so keep an eye out." She sighed. "No rush to call back. Take all the time you need." Bianca hung up.

Pressing her phone to her lips, Bianca decided to send Nicole a quick message too.

Hope you're okay. Here if you need me

Bianca's phone buzzed again, and she wondered if it was Nicole responding. Not this time. It was a text message from an unknown number. Bianca opened it.

STAY OUT OF IT!

A slight chill went through her body. What? Who'd sent this? The killer? A wrong number? Bianca put away her phone. Forcing her limbs to relax, she licked her lips.

"Bianca? Come on, let's eat." Her mother called out.

"Coming." Bianca stuffed her phone back into her pocket. Forcing a smile, she joined them at the table.

Chapter 18

After lacing up her sneakers, Bianca rolled her shoulders back. One perk of being an entrepreneur was she could switch up her schedule whenever she wanted. Once she dropped Alyssa off at school and mailed Priscilla her anniversary photos, Bianca went for a run. Hopefully the pictures would lift Priscilla's spirits. Bianca even added a personal note, reminding Priscilla she would be there for her.

Casper would have joined her in the park, but she'd left him with Melanie. Mel was not a morning person. Neither was Bianca, but after the disturbing message, perhaps a jog in the park would benefit her.

She hadn't replied to it. What was she supposed to say? She wouldn't stop until the killer was behind bars? Was it the killer? She'd received random texts before. Solicitors called all the time from unknown numbers, and while Bianca didn't care for them, it didn't make them murderers. Thankfully, that was the only message.

Blowing out her cheeks, she stretched her legs and arms. Was it all in her head? A slight heaviness took over her stomach. It was a threat. The police needed to know. That was what her mother would tell her.

Bianca's eyes widened. She wouldn't tell her mother. Melanie, perhaps, but not her mother. Running at a steady pace, she followed the trail in the park and jogged. Her huffs became more intense as her feet slapped against the dirt road.

Her heart rate increased. What if she was being followed? Sweat tickled her hairline, but she kept her pace as she ran. Bianca passed by the trees of various heights as she breathed in the morning humid air.

Then she detected another sound against the path. Was it another runner? She looked behind her shoulder to see a man in a dark jogging suit with a baseball cap. His face seemed familiar with his strong chin, broad chest, and towering in height. He had to be over six feet.

Bianca faced forward. There was no need to panic. She heard his huffs of breath. Would he pass her? Bianca didn't look behind her again. She didn't want him to think she was being suspicious. Then again, she was. He sounded closer as she heard the jarring of his feet against the pavement.

Bianca's instincts kicked in. She ran faster, praying that he changed courses or passed her altogether.

The man puffed. "Trying to get away from me?"

Bianca sprinted ahead. What was the plan? Trees lined them on both sides. He could kill her, hide her body, and no one would see. If she remembered the path, she would come upon the pond soon. Fewer trees and more visibility.

Did she scream? Why had she left her phone in the car? When the pond came into view, she sprinted ahead. The parking lot wouldn't be that much farther. Then she saw someone in the distance. Did she wave her arms? Yes.

Bianca waved her arms in the air. "Help! Help!"

A hand touched her back, which only made her run harder. She would be sore after this jog, but at least she would be alive. As she got closer to the person ahead of her, she recognized it as Detective Sims. Judging by his athletic attire, he'd come to work out too.

"Detective!" she shouted.

He didn't ask questions, but appeared to brace himself to catch the guy behind her. What Bianca didn't count on was the guy grabbing the hem of her jacket. He tugged, but then pushed her forward. Bianca tripped over her feet. She would fall into the pond.

It happened so fast, but she reached out for Detective Sims to break her fall. He went with her into the water. *Splash!* Cold water hit Bianca's face, but she felt hands around her waist and her body turned. She flailed her arms about her, looking for the bottom to push herself up. Thank goodness the pond wasn't that deep.

"Bianca! Bianca!"

She gasped for air and turned to sit in the water. Bianca rubbed her eyes despite the blurriness in her vision. "Wh-What?"

She felt firm hands on her shoulders. "Are you all right?"

Bianca coughed. She must have swallowed some water. Gross. "I-I'm..."

Detective Sims patted her back. "Take your time."

Blinking to see her surroundings, her head shifted to see the guy who'd pushed her. He was long gone. "Did he get away?"

"Yeah, but I've got an excellent memory."

"Why didn't you go after him? I would have been okay. Why didn't you catch him?" she asked.

Detective Sims motioned his hand to her left side. Bianca leaned in for a better look. A rock. A large rock.

"Oh," she said.

"I didn't want you to hit your head. I had to act quickly."

Bianca's chest heaved as she slowed her breathing. "Oh... thank you." She would've hated to be another victim.

"Do you know that guy?" he asked.

She shivered. "Can we get out of this pond first?"

He chuckled and extended his hands. Bianca took them as she stood to her feet. She was soaked from head to toe. Great.

"You sure you're okay?"

"I'll be fine." They stepped back onto the grass. She took off her jacket and wrung the water out onto the ground.

Detective Sims asked again. "Did you know that guy?"

"His face looked familiar, but I couldn't tell. I don't think he's from around here." Bianca draped her soaked jacket over her shoulder. "He was following me."

Detective Sims cocked his head to the side. "For how long?"

"A few minutes while I was running. I thought nothing of it. Then he said, 'Trying to get away from me?'"

"Did he say anything else?"

"No." She shook her head. "I wonder if..."

"Wonder what?" he asked.

Now was her opportunity. "I got a... text yesterday on my phone. I was at my mother's house. The message read, 'Stay out of it' in all caps."

Detective Sims pressed his hands against his temples. "You're just now telling me this?"

"You think there's a connection with Martin's—"

"Ms. Wallace," he said. They were back to that. "If you're in danger, the police need to know. Don't handle things on your own. Not something like this."

Her stomach clenched. "I should have come to you sooner."

"I need you to come to the station with me."

"Can I... Can I change clothes?"

He bobbed his head. Then he eyed her. "Are you sure you're all right?"

"A little shaken up, but it's nothing serious," she said.

"Good."

"Thank you."

He gave a faint smile. "I'm glad I was at the right place at the right time."

"You seem to be good at that." She stared into his eyes once more and her body temperature increased. "I mean... I'm grateful for your help and..." She pointed to the rock in the pond. "For saving me from a possible serious injury."

"You're welcome." He tugged at the hem of his soaked royal blue athletic shirt. It stuck to his skin and Bianca could see the defined muscles in his chest. "I need to change too. Meet me at the station and we can get your statement."

"I'll be there as soon as I can." A slight chill went through her. Bianca backed away, but Detective Sims only stepped forward. "What's wrong?"

"I'm walking you to your car. Just in case," he said.

Bianca turned to face the parking lot, and he walked beside her. "No Casper today?"

She grinned. He'd remembered her dog's name. "Not today, although he would have come in handy."

"I bet he would have."

"But... it's not like I didn't have help today." She glanced at him but looked away. She was flirting.

"I'm sure you would have handled yourself if I hadn't been here."

They approached her car. "Thank you for recognizing that."

He cleared his throat. "I'll see you later."

Bianca bobbed her head. When she shivered, she knew she needed to hurry and get home.

Chapter 19

"There you are," Melanie said, placing Casper on the floor.

Bianca's keys clicked against the front table. "Yeah."

"What happened to you?" Melanie looked past her and out the side window to the front door. "Did it rain? Why are you all wet?"

Bianca met her sister's gaze. Her heart palpitated. "I was jogging and..."

Melanie stepped closer. "And what?"

"Someone was chasing me."

"What?" Melanie's mouth dropped. "Did you call for help? Was anyone there with you? Did you call—"

Bianca rested her hands on her sister's shoulders and told her the story. Melanie followed as she paced to her bedroom.

"You sure didn't recognize the man?" Melanie asked, sitting on her bed.

"No." Bianca dug through her drawer for a change of clothes. "I know I've seen his face, but I couldn't remember."

"Thank God Detective Sims was there." Melanie stood to her feet and touched a hand to her back. "Are you sure you're okay?"

Bianca nodded and hugged her sister. "I'm sure." She sighed and pulled back. She needed a quick shower before leaving for the police station. "Not a word of this to anyone."

Her sister cocked her head to the side. "You think I would tell?" She held out her hand to Bianca with her pinky finger in the air.

Bianca locked her pinky with her sister's. "Thank you."

Melanie rubbed at her arms. "I'm working from home today so I can watch Casper."

"Thanks. I'll be back after meeting with Detective Sims. I'll be fine."

"Okay. I trust you. I'm glad you're okay." Melanie left her alone and closed the bedroom door.

"Me too." Bianca blew out her cheeks and walked into her bathroom. Resting her hands on the countertop, she released deep breaths. Her mind couldn't shake it. The slap of his feet behind her or the air that had rushed through her lungs as she'd panted for her next breath. Her back still tingled knowing he'd been that close to her.

What if Detective Sims hadn't been in the park? Would she have hit her head on the rock in the park? Her body floating face down in the water? Placing her hands on either side of her face, she cleared her worst fears out of her head. She needed to get to the police station.

A hot shower washed away the residue from the pond, along with the smell of wet earth against her skin. Facing the mirror again, she kept her natural curls intact instead of using her flat iron. Grabbing a hair tie and headband, she settled for a slightly messy bun.

Changing into a blouse and her dark jeans, she slipped her feet into her flats and grabbed her purse, along with her phone. Bianca headed out the door and to her car. The drive to the police station wasn't long at all, and when she pulled into the parking lot, she exhaled.

Once inside, she gave her name to the front desk. Then she took a seat. Phones rang. Doors buzzed. Keys jingled. Bianca did her best to keep her knee from bobbing up and down. How was someone supposed to act in a police station? The mix of cleaning products and coffee filled her nose.

"Ms. Wallace?" Detective Sims walked over to her.

She stood to her feet. "I'm here."

"Come with me." He gestured for her to follow him.

Bianca did. When they came to a room with a plain table, she sat in the hard plastic chair. Detective Sims closed the door.

He sat across from her. "Are you all right?"

"I think so." She fiddled with the strap of her purse.

He reached for a pad of paper along with a pen. "Ready?"

Bianca bobbed her head.

"Do you usually jog in the morning in the park?"

She shook her head. "I switch up my workouts, so sometimes I go to the park or the gym, or I'll work out at home."

He made a note. "What time did you arrive today?"

"It was after I dropped my daughter off at school... 8:15 this morning."

"When did you notice someone was following you?"

"I'm not sure, but I took the trail in the park. That was when I heard footsteps. I thought nothing of it, but when I heard his voice, I ran faster."

"Can you describe his voice?" Detective Sims made more notes on his notepad.

Bianca stared at the table as she tried to recall the stranger's voice. "Creepy, but I guess it was... low and deep. He was running, so I could tell he was panting."

"Anything else you can think of?"

Bianca tucked a loose curl behind her ear. "I could tell he had an athletic build. I didn't look too long, but he looked tall. At least six feet. Tanned skin with dark brown hair."

"Anything specific? To help us narrow that down?"

She shook her head. "No." A *tsk* sound escaped her mouth. "I'm sorry."

"Don't be sorry. It happened so fast." He tapped the pen on the table. "I've been trying to remember too. I remember his hair almost came to his shoulders."

Bianca snapped her fingers. "Yes, it did."

Detective Sims wrote on his notepad. "Okay. We're getting somewhere." He faced her. "If you remember anything, let me know. Sometimes details come back to us later, after the shock wears off."

"Shock, huh?"

He laced his fingers together. "It happens. We go into survival mode in situations like this, so we forget details. Sometimes we remember and other times we block them out."

"Well... I'll let you know if I remember anything." She licked her lips. "Detective, have you made any progress with Martin's murder case?"

"Do you remember something else?" he asked.

She took her phone out of her purse. Bianca pulled up the anonymous message. "This is what I told you about earlier. I think someone is following me. First this and now the man in the park today."

He exhaled.

"I didn't want to panic and bring something to the police for nothing."

Detective Sims tapped his fingers on the table. "Anything else?"

"No, that's it." She felt a tickle in her nose. Was she going to sneeze? Not now. Covering her mouth, she prepared herself. Nothing. Thank goodness.

"Are you okay?"

"Yes." She sniffled. "I'm all right."

He didn't look convinced, but he didn't reply. He stared at the message again on her phone. "For them to send this, have you been asking questions in town?"

Bianca adjusted in her seat.

"Ms. Wallace, I'm sure you mean well. You seem like a woman who cares about her family and friends, but I can't have you butting in." He held up her phone to her. "This is nothing to play around with."

"I know."

"Do you?" He raised an eyebrow.

"Everything I've done has been to help."

He leaned over the table. She ignored the smell of his woodsy cologne. "And it's my job to protect the citizens in this town."

"Thank you."

His face softened. "You're welcome."

"Can you... trace that number?" She wanted a change of subject, to ignore her tingling skin.

He stared at her phone. "It depends. It could be from a burner phone. Or the person could be using an untraceable phone app."

"They have apps for that?" she asked.

"You'd be surprised, Ms. Wallace." He handed her back her phone. "If you receive another message, let us know right away. Don't keep this to yourself."

"I won't." She locked her phone and put it back inside her purse. "I do think... it may be connected to Martin's murder."

He parted his lips to speak, but she held up her hand.

"But I will lie low." That was until another clue came.

Detective Sims narrowed his eyes at her. "Why am I having a hard time believing that you will?"

A grin grew on her face. "That sounds like a trust issue, detective."

"Can I trust you, Ms. Wallace?"

She leaned in closer to the table. "That's something only you can answer." She draped her purse back onto her shoulder. "If that's all you need, I have to get to work."

He cleared his throat and rose from his seat. "That's it." He walked over and opened the door for her.

Bianca stood and headed for the door. She smiled to herself as she exited the building. She'd been doing that a lot since she'd met Detective Sims.

Chapter 20

Later that day, squinting her eyes, Bianca wondered if she'd used too much royal blue for the furniture business logo they had hired her to create. Rubbing her head, she pondered another approach. Though the company had requested blue, did it have to be royal blue? Opening her color chart in her software program, she searched for a lighter shade.

Sky blue. Perfect. Making the adjustment, she pieced her design together. Merging the company letters, she… *Achoo!* Bianca grabbed several tissues. She wasn't getting sick. Not today.

A cup of hot tea would remedy her. She had a slight chill from her fall in the pond, but it wasn't as bad as it could have been. Passing through the living room, she caught Casper asleep in his dog bed. Bianca smiled and proceeded to the kitchen and grabbed her favorite mug from her cabinet.

She checked her watch on her wrist. It was after three o'clock already? Alyssa would be home soon with Chloe. Melanie was helping their mother with another matchmaking event downtown since she had some time off. Bianca opened her refrigerator and stared. What did she cook for dinner?

Spotting some leftover salmon, she decided she could work around that with some vegetables and some mashed potatoes.

Alyssa's favorite. Filling her teakettle with water, she placed it on the stovetop to boil. Before she knew, the kettle whistled. Perfect. Not too hot, and the heat warmed her chilled hands. Her spoon clicked the sides of her cup as she stirred in the honey.

Bianca rested her chin in her palm for a moment. She couldn't get Detective Sims' words out of her mind. Whoever had sent her the message wasn't playing games. Her mind flashed back to Nicole's wedding day. When wasn't she having flashbacks?

Martin had been stabbed to death. Her heart raced inside her chest as the man's voice from the park rang in her mind. Where did she know him from? She shut her eyes. Had he been at the wedding?

Bianca's mouth dropped. The driver. He reminded her of the limo driver at the wedding. Were they the same person? She didn't know but it was worth a shot. Grabbing her cell phone, she called the police station.

"Edenville Police Department," the woman said.

"This is Bianca Wallace. I need to speak to Detective Lamar Sims, please."

"I'm sorry, he's left for the day. Is it an emergency?"

"Well..." Was it? If it was Martin's killer, than yes. How could Bianca be sure? "I just have some important information for him. I can call back later."

She didn't give the woman a chance to answer. Bianca hung up. She sipped her tea. What would the motive for her stalker have been? A record? Had he hated Martin too and had a grudge against him?

Was Priscilla aware? Bianca adjusted in her seat. This case was getting crazier by the minute. When her phone rang, she shrieked and her body jerked. Casper barked at her outburst and headed for the door.

"Calm down." She grabbed her phone, seeing Malcom's name on her screen. She exhaled. "Hey."

"Hey. Sorry I'm just getting back with you. I had some work to catch up on at the office."

"Not a problem."

"Hope said you needed dates?" he asked.

"Yeah, I wanted to know the dates so I can plan her trip. Get flight details together."

"Sure. One second."

She heard a tapping noise in the background. Bianca took another sip this time, thankful for the warm liquid. She sniffled.

"You okay?"

Bianca swallowed. She wouldn't tell her ex-husband about her sleuthing. "I'm fine. Just a runny nose."

"Okay, well, take care of that in case it gets worse," he said.

"I will." Along with everything else getting worse around here. No need to mention that to Malcom.

"Okay, I'm thinking... The first week of June. School starts back for her mid-August, right?"

"Right."

"So I think that'll give us plenty of time to hang out. Will that work?"

That only gave Bianca about a month left with her daughter. "That's fine with me. She should be home soon, so you can call and tell her."

"Teaching her how to drive yet?"

"Not yet. She's riding home with her friend Chloe."

"What about that boy she's crushing on?" Malcom asked. The protectiveness in his voice returned.

Bianca grinned. "Ask her, Malcom."

"I can't handle this."

Bianca giggled.

"Laugh. I'm tempted to lock her in her room when she gets here."

Bianca raised an eyebrow. "You have a room prepared for her already?"

"We're working on it."

We. Him and Hope. Would that ever register in Bianca's brain? "That's nice." She heard keys jiggling outside the door. "I think that's her now. You can call her now."

"Sure thing. Thanks. Talk to you later."

Bianca hung up, only to feel something warm at her feet. Casper stretched across her feet, but when the door opened, he sprinted to Alyssa.

"Casper!" Her daughter held out her arms. The puppy jumped into her arms. "Hi, Mom."

"Hi, sweetie. Hi, Chloe."

"Hi, Ms. Wallace." Chloe waved just as Casper jumped into her arms. She giggled and patted his head.

"Honey." Bianca gestured at her daughter. "Your dad's going to be calling you about dates for your visit this summer."

"I can't believe you're going. Awesome!" Chloe bounced on her toes.

"I need a new wardrobe," Alyssa said.

Bianca shook her head as the chatter of teenagers faded down the hallway. She hoped and prayed Alyssa enjoyed her time with her dad. This wasn't the way she'd pictured raising her daughter, but she would make the best of her situation.

Finishing the last of her tea, Bianca moseyed to the sink and washed her cup. Dinner. That was something she needed to start. Taking out the salmon to heat in the oven, she grabbed three bags of frozen vegetables.

Ding dong.

She turned her head. Who was at the front door? Bianca hurried to answer but paused. Was it the man from the park? Had he followed her... no, he wouldn't have rung the doorbell, only to hope for her to be careless enough to answer it.

Looking through the peephole, she noticed Detective Sims. Had the receptionist told him she had called? After opening the door, he greeted her with a faint smile and a plastic bag in his hand.

"Ms. Wallace," he said.

"Detective, what are you doing here? I called the station, but I was told you left for the day already." She folded her arms over her chest.

He extended the bag to her. "I thought you could use this. I made a stop by the store."

Bianca took the bag, only to notice something warm inside. Looking inside, she saw a container of chicken noodle soup. She grinned. He'd brought her soup. "You did this for me?"

"I couldn't take the chance of you getting sick." He stuffed his hands inside his pockets.

"That's sweet. Thank you."

"You're feeling okay overall?"

"I had some tea and some over-the-counter medicine. I can take it if I need it."

His smile grew. "Good." His chest heaved a sigh. "Well... that's all. I won't keep you."

She snapped her fingers. "Wait. I called the station for a reason. The man at the park. I think I remember him."

He inched closer. His eyebrows rose with apparent curiosity. "From where?"

"The wedding. I think he was the limo driver for Chad and Nicole. He favors him at least."

Detective Sims rubbed at his stubble-covered chin. "We did question him that night. He said he was inside during the murder. I think Mrs. Long vouched for him with his alibi."

"Judy?"

He bobbed his head. "That's what she said. But I can look into it again. In case we missed something."

"Does he have a record?"

He eyeballed her.

"Off the record if... you don't mind sharing."

"I can't."

"Oh."

"Keep an eye out, all right? Call if you remember anything else. We'll bring him in for questioning about where he was during your attack."

Good. Bianca held up the bag in her hand. "Thank you for the soup. You don't need any, do you?"

He chuckled. "No, Ms. Wallace, but thank you."

"You're welcome."

He backed away from her porch. "Have a good evening."

"You too." Bianca watched him turn his back, and she closed the door. Locking it, she rested against it. She didn't straighten until she heard a clearing throat.

Alyssa and Chloe.

Her daughter folded her arms over her chest. "Who was that, Mom?"

Bianca narrowed her eyes at her daughter. "Never mind that. Since you're so interested, why don't you both help with dinner and help peel the potatoes?" Bianca had expected a groan or the rolling of the eyes, but Alyssa's smile only grew bigger.

"Sure thing, Mom." Was that a smirk?

Bianca pointed to the kitchen. "Get to peeling. Thank you."

The girls whispered as they walked side by side to the kitchen. Casper trotted behind them. Bianca held on to her container of soup, ignoring the goosebumps sliding along the back of her neck.

Chapter 21

Loud, thumping music rang in Bianca's ears. A nightclub. Her sister had managed to talk her into coming to a nightclub. Adjusting the strap on her spaghetti plum dress, she wondered if anyone would notice her slip out the back door.

"Give me another reason we're here?" she asked Melanie.

"To unwind a little. You're either working or researching into Martin's murder. I think you need a break."

"But a club, sis? I'm not in college." Bianca's eyes scanned the room. From his booth, the DJ announced R&B 90s Throwback over the speakers and the crowd cheered as the former hits played from Toni Braxton, Brandy, En Vogue, 112, and many more. An area of small tables and stools weren't filled, and judging by her high heels, Bianca would need a seat soon.

"This place has a good mix. Who knows?" She nudged her sister's shoulder. "You may meet a nice guy. Regardless, we're here to have fun." They found an empty table and sat.

Bianca crossed her legs and rubbed at her ankle. Her flats were in the car. "Now you sound like Mom." She narrowed her eyes at her sister. "Did she put you up to this?"

Melanie raised her hands as if in a surrendered gesture. "You know I wouldn't do that to you. Unless..."

"Unless what?"

"Alyssa told me you had a visitor the other night." Her sister eyeballed her, while resting her chin in her palm.

Bianca's mouth dropped. "Okay."

"You won't tell me? This is me you're talking to." Melanie pressed a hand to her chest.

"There's nothing to tell. It was... only Detective Sims. He brought some soup over my house." Despite having dinner in progress, Bianca did taste the soup. Delicious. Good choice by the detective. Not all store brand soups were created equally.

Melanie tilted her head to the side. "Why?"

Bianca stared at the table. "He was... just being nice, I guess."

"He saves your life and you think he brought soup over because he's being *nice*?"

"Why wouldn't he? I'm not reading into anything. Sometimes soup is just soup."

"I can do a little detective work of my own." She perked in her chair. "Maybe I can ask around town about his story. Is he married? In a relationship?"

"Don't you dare!" Bianca readjusted in her seat.

Melanie's grin grew. "Why not? Don't you think it's time you met someone amazing?"

"I meet new men all the time. Hello?" She raised her hands and gestured at the surrounding crowd.

"Okay, I get it, but I think there's something to this."

"I say there isn't." Not quite, but a part of her wanted it to be. As of yet, Bianca didn't know what to do with her attraction to Detective Sims. She'd been out of the dating game for a while.

Her sister's look turned serious. "Just promise me one thing."

"What's that?"

"If you meet someone who's worthwhile, will you at least give it a chance?"

Bianca inhaled the perfume in the air mixed with cologne. Give someone a chance. Could it be that Detective Sims was being more than nice? She'd caught his stares a few times, but he'd said nothing. Nothing was clear, and Bianca didn't want to build a fantasy in her head based on assumptions.

The question she needed to answer was: Did she even like him? He was a skilled detective. Thoughtful. Caring. Even considerate when he brought soup to her house. When his gray eyes flashed in her mind, her nerves fired all at once. The attraction was apparent, and for him to be the first man she'd taken serious interest in since her divorce, she pondered her feelings. Then again, her father had been a cop. Rubbing her palm over her chest, did she want to get involved?

Bianca's memories flooded of the nights her mom would wait up for her father during his night shifts. She'd never forget waking up in the middle of the night for drink of water, only to find her mother sitting on the couch. Bianca didn't say a word. She only poured herself a glass of cold water and went to bed.

"I see you're thinking about it." Melanie smiled. "Promise?"

Bianca bobbed her head. "Okay, *if* being the keyword. I'll give it a chance."

Her sister clapped her hands.

"Having fun?"

Bianca raised her chin. "Jordan? What are you doing here?"

Dark jeans hugged his waist and he wore a dark polo shirt. His face lit up when he smiled. He pulled up a chair and sat between the ladies. "Just hanging out. I'm guessing you two had the same idea?"

"Getting some sister bonding in," Melanie said. Then she stood to her feet. "What do you want to drink, sis?"

"Give me a soda," Bianca said.

Melanie disappeared into the crowd, leaving Jordan alone with Bianca.

"How have you been?" she asked.

"Okay. What about you? Anything more come from our visit to the bakery?"

Bianca shook her head. "I wish I could say everything makes sense, but I think I'm missing something."

"Like what?" Jordan draped an arm over the back of her chair.

She filled him in on the latest developments, including her dive in the pond.

"What?" Jordan's eyes widened.

"I know."

"Have you seen the guy since then?"

Bianca shook her head. "Do you remember seeing the driver at the wedding?"

Jordan rubbed at his chin. "I think so. I saw him talk to Priscilla a few times. Though they hired a wedding planner, Priscilla offered to help with the plans too. I guess she was trying to show Chad she could accept Nicole."

"So she would know the driver." Could Bianca ask Priscilla about the man without seeming too suspicious?

"Here we go." Melanie set two glasses on the table.

Jordan cleared his throat. "Want to dance, Melanie?"

Her head jerked toward him, but then she grinned. "Sure. That's if you can keep up."

Jordan held out his hand. "We'll have to see, won't we?"

Bianca did a double take. Her sister took Jordan's hand, and they pressed their way through the crowd. While she had a moment to herself, Bianca pulled out her phone. She sent a text to Priscilla.

Sorry if too late, but quick question. Do you know the name of the limo company you hired for the wedding? My mom has a red carpet match making theme event coming up.

Sent. Bianca bit her bottom lip. It wasn't a complete lie since her mother had another matchmaking event on the calendar. One lucky matched couple would get a limo ride as part of their date. Bianca's eyes drifted to the dancefloor. She smiled as she watched Melanie dance close with Jordan.

Buzz. Buzz.

Priscilla: *How exciting! Maxwell's Limousine Service. I recommend them.*

Any chance we can request the same driver?

Long shot, but she asked.

Priscilla: *Not sure. I would call and ask.*

Do you remember his name?

Priscilla: *Not off-hand. I think it starts with a P?*

That was no help.

Thanks! Have a good night.

Priscilla: *You're welcome. You too! I did get your voicemail but I've been busy. Thanks. Can't wait to see the photos!*

Great!

Bianca opened a browser on her phone to look up Maxwell's Limousine Service. Home page. Rates. FAQ section. Services. Nothing about their drivers.

Her chest heaved a sigh just as Melanie and Jordan returned to their table and sat down. "Have fun?" she asked.

"He's not too bad." Melanie winked.

Jordan chuckled for a moment, but his face dropped.

Bianca looked behind her, but there wasn't anyone she recognized in the crowd. She faced Jordan. "Are you okay?"

Despite the low lighting in the club, his face looked flushed. He cleared his throat. "I'm fine." He stood to his feet. "I need to head home. You ladies enjoy your night." Jordan didn't say another word. He left.

Melanie sipped her drink. "I hope it's nothing serious."

"Me, neither." Bianca watched as he disappeared into the crowd. What had changed? What had he seen? Or better yet, whom?

ALYSSA RELEASED FAST, panicked breaths as she shifted the car into park. Bianca wasn't too far behind her, but at least they were in an empty parking lot instead of her daughter driving on the highway. Hairs lifted on the back of her head, and she patted her daughter's shoulder.

"Not... too bad," she said.

Alyssa eyeballed her. "Really, Mom?"

"You'll get better. Trust me, once you learn, you'll never forget."

Alyssa's hands dropped from the steering wheel. "I know I said I wanted to drive, but this is... scary."

Bianca listened to the wind fluttering a plastic bag against a bush. "I told you: Don't grow up too fast."

Alyssa bobbed her head. "Are you sure you don't mind me spending the summer with Dad?"

Bianca smiled at her daughter. "I'll find something to do. Just call me when you can and let me know how you're doing."

Alyssa grimaced. "I guess I would feel better if... *she* weren't there."

"Hope?"

Her daughter nodded.

"I've always taught you to respect adults. Hope is no different." If only her stomach didn't turn at her own comment.

"You respect her? She—"

Bianca held up her hand. "Alyssa, if you want to ask your father, I've told you before to ask him, but I'm not here to bash him or his new wife with you."

Alyssa's chin dropped to her chest. "I'm sorry. I just wish things hadn't ended the way they had."

Bianca took her daughter's hand. "I know. Me too."

Her daughter released a deep sigh. "I'll try to make the best of it. For you."

She shook her head. "No, do it for you. Your father and I are adults. He'll be fine. I'll be fine."

Alyssa squeezed her hand. "Okay."

Bianca released her daughter's hand and gestured to the steering wheel. "Want to try again?"

Alyssa blew out her cheeks. Putting the car in reverse, she backed out of the parking space.

"Easy on the brakes," Bianca said.

Alyssa drove down the lot. Bianca checked the odometer. Twenty-five miles per hour.

"You can go faster," she said.

"How much?" Alyssa asked.

"Try thirty miles."

Alyssa did.

"Okay, now thirty-five."

Alyssa sped up some more.

"Good. Keep your hands steady. Now try forty." The engine hummed. "Now slow down without jerking the brakes."

"Mom?" Alyssa sounded panicked again.

"You can do it." She had to. Or they would drive in the grass. "Careful."

Alyssa was, and despite the slight jerk at the end, at least Bianca didn't have to worry about whiplash later.

"Good." She beamed at her baby girl. Bianca must have blinked because her little girl who used to draw stars on construction paper was driving. "I told you it gets better."

Her daughter blew out her cheeks again. "You think we can call it a day? I've had enough time behind the wheel."

They switched places, and Bianca settled into the driver's seat. She saw Alyssa playing with her phone, but when she put it to her ear, Bianca looked straight ahead.

"Hey, Dad," Alyssa said. "Yeah, first driving lesson with Mom. No." She laughed. "No, I didn't run over anybody."

Bianca held back a snicker.

"No, I'm not driving in your neighborhood." Alyssa giggled.

Bianca took a deep breath, savoring the moment.

"Okay." Alyssa continued. "I'll let you know. Love you too." She hung up.

Bianca turned into their neighborhood, only to see another car behind them. A white Honda. She thought nothing of it. There were plenty of people in her neighborhood. Then again, her stomach quivered at the thought of the man in the park.

She hadn't told Alyssa, but she had already taught her daughter to be watchful of new people. The car followed her onto her street. Bianca swallowed. She hoped it was her imagination.

She had to protect Alyssa. No one would hurt her daughter. "Can you go take out the leftovers for dinner?"

"Sure." Alyssa grabbed her backpack. As soon as Bianca pulled into the garage, Alyssa didn't waste time getting out.

Bianca cut the engine, stepped out the car, and grabbed her phone. She noticed the car following her had parked in front of her neighbor's house two blocks down. The only person she knew with a white Honda was... Judy? Why would she be following her? Bianca took her phone out to take a picture, but the engine ignited. The car sped down the street.

Bianca sprinted to the edge of her driveway, snapping pictures, but when she looked at them, her pictures were blurred. As far as she could tell, Judy wasn't driving. Who else had the same car as her?

"Snap." Bianca groaned. Did she call the police? No one threatened her or Alyssa. She hadn't seen the man that chased her in the park recently either. Did Detective Sims catch him and hadn't had time to tell her yet?

Bianca headed back to her house and let down the garage door. She locked the door behind her as she entered her home. Then she set her house alarm.

Chapter 22

"That's cute, honey." Bianca tilted her head to the side as Alyssa modeled a mustard solid blouse.

Alyssa faced the full-length mirror. "Are you sure?"

Bianca took a picture of her daughter. She loved their mother-daughter shopping trips, but she invited Nicole to join them so they could talk. Nicole said next time. With everything going on, Bianca understood her friend taking space if she needed to.

"Mom?"

Bianca blinked. "Sorry. What did you say?"

"The blouse. Are you sure you like it?" Alyssa asked. She tugged at the hem as she faced the mirror again. "I just don't..."

"Just don't what?" Bianca inched closer.

Alyssa's lips twisted. "Not all the girls are dressing like this at school."

Bianca folded her arms. "How are they dressing?"

Alyssa bit her bottom lip. "They... show a little more."

"Let me guess..." Bianca bobbed her head. "Is this about Kendrick? Is there another girl who's eyeing him who wears less than you do?"

Alyssa's eyes bugged. "How did you know?"

"I've been your age, sweetie. The same thing happened to me with your father." She ignored the dull ache inside her chest.

"Wow." Alyssa tucked her dark brown curls behind her ears. "Well, what do I do?"

"Is he dating her?"

"I don't think so."

"Whom does he pay attention to? You or this other girl?"

"When he's with me, he focuses on me. I just don't know what he's doing when I'm not around. We're getting to know each other..."

"But?" This was the most Alyssa had shared with her about a crush.

"I don't want him to get bored with me and leave. I don't want to end up like..." Alyssa caught herself. She covered her mouth as she stared at her mother.

Bianca motioned for her daughter to sit in a nearby plastic chair. She sat next to her.

"Is that what you think happened? Your dad got bored and left me?"

Alyssa wrung her hands together. "I don't know. He never told me why. I asked, but he never explained."

"Ask him again if you need to. It's his place to tell you his reasons for leaving." She paused and took her daughter's hand. "For me, it was a hard decision. It was heartbreaking. Marriage takes work, and sometimes one person will fight for love while the other wants to walk away. I didn't force your father to stay." Bianca focused her eyes on Alyssa. "If a man doesn't see your value, that's on him. You're a prize."

"But how do I stand out? The other girls are—"

"Don't worry about the other girls. You're you. Be yourself and love yourself the way you are. A man who cares for you will see that and love you too."

Alyssa nodded. Her eyebrows drew together. "Did Dad see your value?"

Bianca gave a faint smile. "I think he did the best he could." That was the best answer she could give without thinking the worst of Malcom. Her phone buzzed inside her purse. Bianca spotted Jordan's name. Where had he been? She motioned for Alyssa to return to the dressing room. "If that's what you want, you have enough money. I'll meet you at the front of the store."

Alyssa nodded and Bianca paced to the front doors.

"Jordan?"

"Bianca? Can you talk?" Did his voice sound shaky?

Bianca stared outside. The light from the sunset peaked through the store window. Then she decided to take the call outside, standing a few inches away from the front doors. "Jordan, where are you? Are you all right?"

"I'm at a convenience store. Why? How's Nicole? I can't reach her. She—"

"Slow down." She shuffled her feet as she waited for Alyssa. "I can't either. Nicole hasn't gotten back with me so I'm giving her some space. Do you know anything? I know you still—"

"Nicole has a good heart, but she made some desperate choices," Jordan said.

Bianca chose her next words carefully. "Jordan, I know you would do anything for her."

"Forget that. Think about it, Bianca." He exhaled a deep breath. "I didn't tell you this. Priscilla knew about Nicole and

Martin. Nicole told me she talked to her about it once she and Chad started to get serious."

Bianca's lips parted. Her heart went out to Priscilla. Bianca knew what it felt like to be caught between her husband and another woman.

"What's your point, Jordan?" She'd have to talk to Nicole about this one for sure. As long as they'd been friends, why didn't she bring this up?

"I think Priscilla has more to do with this. Plus I think I'm being followed."

"Priscilla? Why? She's too..."

"Too what?"

"The woman has the poise of Grace Kelly. I can't see her causing all of this mess."

"Didn't you watch *Dial M for Murder*?" Jordan asked.

"That was self-defense in that film and you know it. Why do you think you're being followed?"

"Since we met up at the Richard and Judy's place. It looks like Judy's car. I'm going to the police again. Bianca, I'm telling you, something's not right about all of this. Nicole said they hashed it out, but I don't think Priscilla's forgiven her. Plus when I went to see—" *Clank!*

Bianca flinched. "Jordan?" What happened? "Jordan? Jordan, are you okay? Jordan!"

COLORFUL LIGHTS FROM police cars and an ambulance flashed as Bianca pulled into the parking lot of the convenience store after she'd dropped off Alyssa at home. Though her daughter noticed her change in demeanor and repeatedly twisting at her right earring, Bianca assured her daughter not to worry. She'd called Jordan multiple times, but he hadn't answered. Bianca had called the police. She'd scrunched her face and then released it, trying to remain calm as she'd explained what had happened to the dispatcher.

Cutting the engine, Bianca stepped out of the car. She saw Jordan's car, but no Jordan.

"Jordan?" she called out. Despite the yellow tape urging caution, Bianca stepped closer. Her mouth dropped at the sight of his charcoal sedan. She spotted a pair of shoes still on the feet of a body sticking out from the side of the vehicle. "Jordan!"

"Ms. Wallace." Detective Sims. Of course he was here. What surprised Bianca was him reaching out to keep her at bay, his hands on her arms.

"What happened?" she asked. "I was just on the phone with him."

Detective Sims led her to the front of the convenience store. "When did you last talk to him?"

She shrugged, clasping her hands together. "It was... maybe almost thirty minutes ago. I was shopping with my daughter and he called."

Detective Sims wrote on his notepad. "Do you know who might have done this?"

Bianca's eyes widened. "Are you saying he was attacked?"

He sighed. "Someone struck him on the head. The EMTs are working on him now."

"Struck with what? I heard like a clanking type of noise."

Detective Sims looked over his shoulder, but he faced Bianca again. "We found a golf club next to him. The attacker struck and left right afterward."

"Have you checked the security cameras? Did you ask the workers inside if they saw anything? Have you—"

"Ms. Wallace, we're doing everything we can to sort this out. There's a killer on the loose. I don't need you snooping around and asking people questions. Let us do our job."

Bianca raised an eyebrow. "Snooping?"

"For the lack of a better term, yes." He stared her down, but Bianca didn't flinch.

She opened her mouth to give him the rebuttal of his life, but she stopped. Bianca stared ahead. A golf club. Someone had hit Jordan in the head with a golf club. "Richard."

"Ms. Wallace?"

Bianca blinked. "Richard Long." She ran a jerky hand through her hair. Did he involve Judy in this? "Martin's step-brother. I remember him saying that he would play golf with Martin now and then."

"He told you that?" he asked.

She bobbed her head. "He also told me that... he hated Martin, especially after Richard left the real estate business to run a restaurant and bakery with his wife."

Detective Sims ran a hand down his face with his free hand. "Anything else you can think of?"

Bianca pinched the skin at her throat. "Jordan did mention Priscilla. Nicole's mother-in-law. He said that she..."

"She what?" Detective Sims asked. "Go on."

"Only that she may have had something against her husband." Bianca didn't want to overstep her bounds. Yet this was a murder investigation. Boundaries no longer existed, apparently. "And... he said the car following him resembled Judy's. Richard's wife."

"I'll look into it. We also know about Richard playing golf with Martin, and Judy reported her car stolen this week. We're more aware than you think." He focused his eyes on her. "Now, will you do me a favor?" He used his free hand to cup her elbow. He led Bianca to her car.

"Is he going to be okay?" she asked as she looked behind her shoulder. "Judy's car stolen? Who would do that? What about the man from the park? Have you found—"

"I'll let you know when I have more information. Please, Ms. Wallace. Go home."

Her eyes bored into him. Was that concern in his voice? Why wouldn't there be? She was a civilian, and he'd sworn to protect people like her from crime.

"But I think I saw the car."

He jerked, taking out his notepad again. "When?"

"Yesterday. It was in my neighborhood. It followed me, but I wasn't sure. At least I think it was Judy's car. I'm sure she's not the only one that drives it in town. I tried to take pictures, but they were too blurry." She rubbed at her eyebrow. "What is going on?"

"We're working on it. Right now, go home to your daughter. Lock your doors and call next time." He cocked his head to the side for emphasis.

Bianca nodded. Then she looked over again to the place where Jordan was. "He's my friend."

"I understand that, but you're not doing anyone a favor by interfering."

She folded her arms. "Didn't I give you valuable information?"

"You did."

"So?"

He chuckled. "So I thank you, and now I would like for you to return home."

Bianca didn't smile. "That's all?"

"That's enough."

Bianca's nostrils flared as she bit the inside of her cheek. She unlocked her car and slid into the driver's side. Detective Sims backed away as she started her engine. Bianca let down the window. "Detective?"

He stepped closer. "Yes, Ms. Wallace?"

"You will let me know if he's okay. Please?" Her voice trembled. Jordan... attacked like this?

Detective Sims gave her a faint smile. He reached into his pocket and handed her a business card. "Here's my card with my cell phone number. Call me and I'll make sure you're informed about his condition. I'll also let you know if we find the guy that attacked you in the park."

"Thank you." She let up the window as he gave her a final nod. Bianca pulled out of the parking lot but didn't hesitate to look in her rearview mirror. Richard had attacked Jordan?

The evidence pointed to him. He'd told her himself he hated Martin, and being $41,000 in debt to him too? Bianca drove home in silence, wondering how she would piece together this puzzle.

BIANCA EYED THE ROWS of tables and booths filled with local seasonal produce. Bundles of beets, carrots, asparagus, and bags of potatoes. She heard the hum of people socializing and breathed in the fresh herbs, citrus fruits, and ripening berries.

"Can you believe that?" Melanie asked.

Bianca blinked. "What?"

"Are you even listening?" her sister asked.

"Sure."

Melanie paused in her tracks. "What is it? You've been acting funny since we got here."

"I'm just... worried about Jordan." He was still in the hospital healing from a head injury. At least the doctor said he was going to pull through it all.

Melanie's eyes softened. "I still can't believe somebody attacked him. Who would do something like that?"

"I'm trying to figure it out."

"Why?" Her sister exhaled. "I was okay going to Richard's restaurant, but this is getting too dangerous, sis. The text message? The park? Whoever this person is, is on to you."

"I know." Bianca couldn't dismiss the obvious.

"Then why don't—"

Bianca pulled at her sister's sleeve to get her to follow her behind the jars of honey and beeswax.

Melanie whispered. "What are you doing?" She ducked beside her sister.

Bianca pointed ahead and her sister followed her gesture to see Richard. He stood beside the herbs, talking with the attendant behind the table. "I don't want him to see us."

"Why not?"

Bianca pursed her lips together. "I think attacked Jordan in the head with a golf club. When I talked to him last, he said that he played golf with Martin."

"Lots of people play golf in town." Melanie pointed out.

Bianca shook her head. "I wonder if he's dragging Judy into this. She reported her car stolen."

"This doesn't make sense."

"I know. It's completely twisted." Bianca added.

"Are we hiding back here forever or is he leaving?" Melanie asked.

Bianca watched Richard wave at the attendant as he walked away. Was that all he'd needed?

"Looking for something?"

Bianca shrieked along with her sister. Pivoting, she spotted Priscilla. A black-and-white scarf decorated her neck, covering her quarter-length black dress. White gloves covered her hands, favoring the ones she'd worn to Chad and Nicole's wedding. Priscilla never failed to dress her best.

Pressing a hand to her chest, Bianca said, "Not really. Nice to see you."

Priscilla covered her mouth as if to stifle a laugh. "I couldn't help myself. Forgive me for startling the both of you."

Melanie rubbed at her shoulder. "No harm done. I'm going to browse the jams and jellies for Mom. I'll meet you at the car."

Bianca nodded her head as her sister left her alone with Priscilla.

The older woman gave her a soft smile. "I heard about Jordan. How are you holding up?"

Bianca folded her arms across her chest. "I'm still trying to wrap my head around it. I hope the police catch whoever did this. Too many people are getting hurt."

"I agree. Who would do something so horrible?" Priscilla shrugged.

This was a change in her attitude about him since Martin's memorial. Perhaps Priscilla didn't mean to overreact as she did. Bianca pulled her lips in. She needed to know one thing. "Did Martin ever mention his relationship with Richard?"

"Martin didn't tell me everything. Even during our family gatherings, he and Richard kept it to small talk. I don't think they were ever close." Her chin dropped. "I was so worried when they brought Chad in for questioning."

"I was there when it happened."

"He's only trying to protect Nicole, but my son's not a killer. He and Martin didn't get along, but my son always respected my marriage," Priscilla said. She looked away but continued. "I suppose Nicole told you about her past with Martin."

"She mentioned 'a few things," she said.

"Martin and I... separated for a time. That's when he met Nicole. He confessed everything to me when we got back together. I didn't know what to think, but I knew I loved him." Her bottom lip trembled.

"Priscilla?" Bianca cocked her head to the side.

Priscilla covered her mouth, as if she'd said too much. "Oh, Bianca. I didn't mean to dump our family problems on you, and I don't blame Nicole. I fell for Martin's charms too." She took out a handkerchief and wiped at her nose. Then her lips parted, and she pressed a hand to her chest.

She wasn't having a spell, was she? "Are you okay? Do you need your—?"

Priscilla dug into her purse and pulled out a prescription bottle. "Good. Can't go anywhere without these."

"What kind are they?" She recalled seeing them at her house but forgot the name. Were they the same ones her father would take when she was a child?

"Digoxin." Priscilla shook the bottle, causing the pills to rattle inside. "A lifesaver."

Bianca's father's recent heart medication before he passed had been Xarelto. "Do you need to take one now? Can I get you some water?"

"Don't worry about me." She exhaled. "Thank you. I try not to get overwhelmed, but... I can't help it."

"I understand." She snapped her fingers. "I almost forgot. I had a surprise for you and Martin but with everything going on—"

"I understand. I saw the photos." Her lips quirked into a soft smile. "They're amazing. Too bad he... didn't get to see them."

Bianca's heart sunk. "I... made a video of you two. I thought it would be a nice touch to the pictures for your anniversary. You're welcome to come by and get it anytime."

"You're a gem, Bianca." Priscilla's eyes beamed, though they still shined with fresh tears. "I'll let you know for sure."

Bianca's heart went out to her. "Can we give you a ride home?"

Priscilla shook her head. "I have a driver today, so I'll be fine." She touched a hand to Bianca's shoulder. "I didn't mean any harm. I would hate to think the worst of Nicole, or even Richard. We can only hope the police resolve all of this mess."

Bianca agreed.

Priscilla hugged her. "I'll talk to you later. Have a good one."

"You too." Bianca nodded as Priscilla walked away. She headed to her car, where her sister was waiting. She tried to put the upsetting information out of her mind, and even with Martin dead, she couldn't believe how he had treated his own wife.

Pausing in her tracks, Bianca's brain recalled her own anger when she'd discovered Malcom's infidelity. She'd thrown a coffee mug against the wall. It had shattered to pieces on impact and the shards had scraped the hardwood floors.

She had been numb, and while she had worked toward forgiveness in the last couple of years, it didn't change what his decision had done to their family. Bianca shook her head and cupped her cheeks. This wasn't about her, although the scenario had brought up her triggers. This was about Martin's killer, the serial attacker, and finding out who it was.

Chapter 23

Bianca opened her car door to find Melanie gulping from Bianca's extra water bottle.

"What took you so long?" Melanie asked. She screwed the cap back on.

Bianca locked the door, started the engine, and fastened her seatbelt. "Priscilla. I think she needed a moment."

"I can't imagine what's she's going through."

Bianca pulled out of the parking lot. She held on to the steering wheel and turned onto the main road back to Edenville. "I can't stop thinking about Richard."

"You really think he did it?" Melanie asked.

Bianca's eyes widened. "Remember the summer bash he and Judy held on their yacht a couple of years ago?"

Melanie popped a mint in her mouth. "Yeah, it was the best. I don't know why he and Judy stopped hosting them. Everyone in town loved their parties on their yacht."

"But their finances have changed. He went to Martin for a loan out of desperation. He regretted it since Martin held it over his head." A $41,000 debt would worry almost anyone.

"That sucks."

"I know. Maybe it wasn't a good idea to duck out on Richard today." Bianca switched lanes. "Maybe we can stop by his restaurant and talk to him about Judy's stolen car."

"I don't know. Haven't enough people gotten hurt already? What if he is the killer? I don't want to be next on his list." Melanie's forehead wrinkled.

As they approached the bridge leading them back to Edenville, Bianca switched lanes again. A white Honda repeated her move. She hadn't noticed it before, but they edged closer, tailgating her. Bianca swallowed just as Melanie's phone rang.

"It's Mom." Her sister answered. "Hey, Mom. We're on our way back."

"Did you get the strawberry jams?" their mother asked through the speakerphone.

"Yes, we did," Melanie said.

Bianca shifted her eyes between the rearview mirror and her side mirror. She switched to the middle lane. Was it her imagination? No. The car followed again. Who was driving it? Her lips parted. Sweat surfaced on her palms, but she didn't want to panic with her mother listening.

"Mom?" Bianca said. "Do you mind picking up Alyssa up from school today? We're stuck in traffic and I don't know when it'll let up."

Melanie's eyes widened at the obvious lie, but Bianca mouthed, "We're being followed." Melanie gasped but covered her mouth.

"Sure, sweetie. No problem. I can probably get more info for you on that boy she's crushing on. I know young love when I see it," her mother said.

Bianca answered. "Sure thing, Mom."

"Talk to you later." Melanie's voice sounded shaky, but their mother didn't seem to pick on it. She hung up.

"Don't panic," Bianca said.

"We're being followed and you don't want me to panic?" Melanie clutched to her seatbelt.

"See if you can tell whose driving."

Melanie leaned over to the side mirror. "I can't. What are we going to do, B?"

Bianca released a deep breath. They weren't that far from town. "Grab my purse and call Detective Sims. He's in my contacts. Put him on speakerphone."

Melanie's hands fumbled, but she did it. Bianca pressed on the gas to speed up.

"They're speeding up too," Melanie said. She didn't take her eyes off the side mirror while holding Bianca's phone in her hand.

He answered. "Lamar Sims."

"It's Bianca Wallace, Detective. I'm being followed. I'm about five miles outside of Edenville. We're crossing over the bridge, leaving the Farmer's Market."

"What kind of car?"

"A white Honda," her sister said, running a free hand down her pant leg.

"Which way are you traveling?" he asked.

"Um..." Bianca bit her bottom lip. "The farmer's market is west out of town, so we're traveling back eastward on Highway Four."

"We have someone patrolling the welcome sign for speeders. I'll let them know you're coming in. I'm on my way."

"You're not hanging up, are you?" Bianca didn't want to be at the mercy of a killer if the police didn't make it in time.

"I'm staying on the line," Detective Sims said.

"Bianca!" Melanie clutched to her seatbelt.

The Honda got closer. Bianca's speed odometer rose to seventy miles per hour.

"Tell me what's going on?" Detective Sims asked.

"They're gaining on us!" Melanie yelled.

"Don't panic. Help is on the way," he said.

Bianca gripped the steering wheel, hoping that help would come soon. As she approached the back of an eighteen-wheeler, she switched lanes again to pass him. The Honda attempted to follow, but another car blew its horn. Bianca didn't stop as she shifted her eyes between the mirrors.

The engine of her car roared. Her heart pounded. Her mouth went dry.

"Stay with me," Detective Sims said on speaker.

"Are they going to hit us?" Melanie clutched tighter to her seatbelt.

Bianca passed another car with no problem, and she switched lanes again. Just a little longer. There would be help, but that didn't stop her palms from sweating. Yet she didn't lose her grip on the steering wheel.

"I see the police, Bianca. Thank God!" Melanie pointed ahead.

Bianca breathed easier but didn't slow down. It wasn't over yet. The sirens blared in her ears, and she heard tires screeching.

"They're turning around." Melanie looked behind them.

Bianca watched in the rearview mirror as the Honda made a dangerous U-turn. The car burned rubber, with smoke resulting from the sharp turn. Horns honked at it, but it didn't stop. Two police cars chased after it, and Bianca prayed they caught the perpetrator. That had been another close call.

BIANCA SAT NEXT TO her sister on the hood of her car. With one arm draped around her shoulders, Melanie wrapped an arm around Bianca's waist. Thank goodness her heart palpitations had subsided. At least they weren't hurt. What would have happened if the chase had gone further?

Detective Sims walked over to them. "How are we doing, ladies?"

Melanie didn't answer, and Bianca hoped she wasn't too shaken up. Her sister had had her share of scares as a traveling journalist, but nothing too life-threatening.

Bianca sighed. "We're fine."

"I feel like slashing tires," Melanie said.

Bianca jerked, holding back her own chuckle. Melanie showing violence? Bianca would love to see her sister in combat. Sometimes in school she and her sister had stood up against school bullies bothering other children. Going up against a killer? Out of their element.

She shook her head at her sister. "I don't think so."

"Ms. Wallace, we're doing everything we can to find the person driving the car," Detective Sims said.

"You mean you haven't caught the bum? That's the best you guys can do? Tell us you're—"

Bianca stopped her. "Sis, they're doing their job."

Melanie used her free hand and wrung her fingers through her curls. "I'm sorry. I'm just not used to be tailgated by someone who probably *stabbed* Martin Davis." Her phone rang inside her pocket. She groaned. "It's Mom. What am I supposed to tell her?"

Bianca's stomach roiled. "Tell her we're on our way. Something came up. Don't talk too long, either."

Melanie's free hand clutched her necklace. "Lying?"

"We're not lying. We'll tell her later. I don't want to worry her now. Not with Alyssa with her."

Melanie bit her lip. Forcing a smile, she answered the phone, stepping away from Bianca and Detective Sims.

"Anything else you can think of about the driver? You weren't able to see who was driving?" he asked.

Bianca shook her head. "No."

He made a note.

"When will they catch him? Did they get the license plate?"

"Yes and it's registered under Judy's name so it's her stolen vehicle she reported." When his cell rang, he answered, holding up his index finger to Bianca. "Yeah?" He groaned. "Alright. Head back here." He hung up and focused his eyes on her once again. "Looks like our driver took a back street and got away from us. They found the car abandoned on the side of the road, so we'll inform Mrs. Long. We will find him."

Bianca folded her arms over her chest. "Did he get away on foot or someone picked him up in another car?"

"We don't know yet." Detective Sims stepped closer. "Ms. Wallace, would you like an escort home? I can follow you or have someone do it."

"That would only make things worse for my mother." Her chest heaved and she groaned. "Yes. An escort would be helpful but please don't make it obvious. I don't want to worry my daughter either.

Detective Sims said, "We'll use discretion."

Bianca rubbed the back of her head. "I'm trying to remember if I saw anyone suspicious when we were at the farmer's market."

"Did you?"

She shrugged. "I saw Richard Long and Priscilla Davis. Nothing more. I left after talking with Priscilla. Melanie was waiting in the car."

He made another note. "Priscilla Davis. I can only assume you asked her some questions."

Bianca tilted her head to the side. "No, she shared some things with me about Nicole. Then she had a minor episode with her heart."

"Heart problems again?"

"She's fine. She had her medication with her. I saw the same thing with my dad." Too bad it had killed him.

"Since we're on the subject..." He paused. Detective Sims shut his eyes as if it pained him to ask the next question. "Was there anything important you discussed?"

"No. I'm sure you've already questioned Nicole and looked into her past with Martin."

He bobbed his head.

"Then that's all."

"So you can promise me you're done asking questions? You'll let us handle things from now on?" he asked.

"How about Jordan's attacker?" she asked.

"We know the owner of the golf club."

Bianca perked up. "Who? Did you catch the guy?" Was it Richard's? Would he confirm that for her?

"I can't tell you that, Ms. Wallace."

"Of course you can't." She rolled her eyes. She hadn't visited Jordan in the hospital yet. Bianca wanted to give him time to rest.

Perhaps he'd seen who'd hit him. He'd been trying to tell her something over the phone, claiming Priscilla had it out for Nicole.

"Okay," Melanie said, returning to stand with her sister. "I told Mom we're on our way home."

"Did she ask questions?" Bianca asked.

"Only if we were hungry. She has leftovers if we want them." Melanie looked at her sister and Detective Sims. "I miss something?"

"They haven't caught the driver," Bianca said.

"Great." Melanie sighed. "Is that all you need, detective?"

"That's all," he said.

"I'll be in the car." Melanie made her way to the car and slid inside the passenger's seat.

"I'll have someone follow you home and monitor your house." He added. "With discretion."

Bianca's eyes met his. This was part of his job, right? It wouldn't help if anything happened to her or her sister. Yet his strong eye contact and the way he watched her lips as she talked sent a shifting feeling near her heart.

She blinked, trailing her fingers along the collar of her shirt. "Thank you."

He cleared his own throat. "Then... um... be safe going home."

"I will." She lingered for a moment as he stared. His pupils dilated and she scraped her own fingers through her hair.

"Ms. Wallace?" He tilted his head to the side.

Bianca cleared her throat. "Yes. I'm fine. Thank you again." She returned to her car.

Chapter 24

That evening, Bianca closed her laptop. What a day. Being chased by a killer. She couldn't wait for this case to be over. A *hmm* escaped her throat. She couldn't give up now. Her dad hadn't raised a quitter.

No. She would finish this. Bianca didn't want her or Jordan's attacker to get away, nor did she want Nicole or Chad in trouble. These were more than her friends.

They were a part of her community. If she learned one thing about Edenville, the town saw themselves as family. Bianca hadn't thought she would enjoy small town life, but Edenville embraced her during the most troublesome time of her life. Her divorce. When her mother raved about the community of Edenville, Bianca couldn't resist moving to the small town, especially to be close to her mother again. Even when Melanie broke off her engagement with her fiancé, Bianca offered her home to her sister.

Casper barked, making her body jerk. She eyeballed him, but he only wagged his tail and barked again. Bianca groaned.

He stood on his hind legs, pawing at her leg. Bianca looked outside. "What?" Did he want to walk? Go outside?

She would have woken up Alyssa, but Bianca only exhaled and walked to her front door. Casper trotted behind her. Opening the door, her puppy headed to the bushes. So he'd had an emergency.

Bianca folded her arms. "Okay. I'm sorry I got annoyed."

"Hi Bianca."

She didn't recognize the raspy and scary-sounding voice. Oh no. At this time of night, who was this? Casper barked. On impulse, Bianca turned on her heels and kicked her foot high, landing between her attacker's legs.

Casper barked louder, and she grabbed him. Next thing to do was run inside. Did the cop watching her house see this? Was he coming?

"Bianca! Wait!" The man cleared his throat.

Wait. She knew that voice. Turning back with Casper in hand, she saw Richard on her front lawn. He bent over with his hands on his knees. He exhaled.

"Richard? What are you doing?" she asked.

He held up a hand. "I didn't mean to scare you. I had a frog in my throat." He cleared his throat a second time. "I only came to bring the final payment for the invitations." In his other hand, he held up an envelope.

"Everything okay, Ms. Wallace?" Detective Atkins stood at the edge of her driveway. Dressed in dark jeans and a gray hoodie, the street light shined on him.

She waved back with a smile. "Everything's fine."

He bobbed his head and walked back down the street. She didn't see his police car, so she was glad he stayed incognito.

Bianca could kick herself. Focusing back on Richard, she took the envelope. "Judy did mention it. I'm so sorry. Are you okay? I didn't know what else to do."

"I'll be fine." He was still hunched over.

"Why didn't you call?" she asked.

He shook his head, blowing out his cheeks. "I did but I got your voicemail. I left you a message saying I was coming over with the money. I didn't want to wait. When I got here, I saw you outside."

Was she that distracted with her dog that she didn't hear a car pull up? Bianca cradled Casper who had calmed. "I did leave my cell phone inside." She scrunched her nose. "Sorry again."

He straightened to stand despite his shaky legs. He stepped on to her porch. "It's okay. At least this is one less thing for me to worry about."

"What do you mean?" she asked. She didn't close the gap between them. He was still on her list of suspects.

"Everything's been a mess since Martin's death. Thank goodness the police found Judy's car today. No one's acting like themselves. The police questioning Chad and.... I don't know. Maybe you can talk to him better than me."

"Why?" She kept what she knew about Judy's stolen car to herself.

Richard sighed. "Chad worked for our real estate company for a time. He and Martin didn't get along. Martin didn't give me the details, but when he fired Chad, he blacklisted him. Chad ended up starting his own real estate company because Martin made sure he couldn't get a job anywhere else."

"So you think Chad wanted vengeance?" Enough to kill? The possibility was there, but the police had only brought him in for questioning. Even Bianca still couldn't connect the microfiber towel to Chad despite it being found in his gym bag.

"Or Nicole convinced him to. I know she's your friend, but I'm telling you, Bianca, Martin obsessed over her, and Chad knew it. Between Martin harassing her and almost ruining Chad's career, I wouldn't blame him for... killing him."

"He ruined most of your life too." Bianca pointed out. "But you... didn't kill him?" He wasn't in the clear with her yet.

Richard shook his head. "I couldn't do that to Judy. I love my life with her too much."

Bianca couldn't help but ask. "What about Jordan? Someone attacked him with a golf club. I remember you telling me you and Martin—"

"What? Attack Jordan? Why would I do that?"

"The police say someone hit him in the head with a golf club."

Richard rubbed at his chin. "I haven't played for the last few weeks. I'm still missing my hybrid."

"Your what?" Bianca didn't play golf, so how would she know?

Richard gave a faint smile. "There are different clubs in golf. The hybrid helps to get through the grass and make contact with the ball."

Bianca nodded. "And you're missing yours?"

Richard bobbed his head.

"Did Martin borrow it?"

"No, we never borrowed each other's clubs. Even when we would bring Judy and Priscilla along, we all had our own golf clubs."

Bianca raised an eyebrow. "Priscilla and Judy would go with you?"

"Sometimes. Why?"

"I just can't see chic Priscilla on a golf course." If she did, it would surprise Bianca. The woman had her own style.

"She came when she could." Richard's shoulders drooped. "I need to go. I'm sorry I scared you."

"No problem, Richard."

He smiled and then stepped down her porch. He stalked off to his car. Bianca carried Casper inside, locking the door behind her.

THE NEXT DAY, BIANCA'S heels clacked on the vinyl floor as she entered Jordan's hospital room. She inhaled the smell of latex mixed with hand sanitizer. Sitting in the visitor's chair, she reached for Jordan's hand. An IV stuck in his arm, and a bandage covered his head. At least he was breathing.

Tapping her foot on the floor, Bianca willed herself not to worry. This was Jordan. He'd played basketball and football in college, and he had been the toughest player she'd ever seen. Unlike most of the players, who'd been cocky, he'd remained a gentleman.

Bianca couldn't figure why Nicole didn't love him back. Yet Jordan respected her wish to remain friends. To her, it sounded like a sad romance novel.

She heard Jordan exhale. His hand twitched in hers. The doctor said he would make a full recovery, despite the concussion he'd suffered. A few scratches and purplish bruises covered his face, evidence of his fall to the hard concrete.

"Jordan?" Bianca scooted closer to him. She didn't want him to strain to hear her. He needed his rest. She wouldn't stay long.

"B... Bianca?" His voice sounded hoarse, but his eyes fluttered open.

"I'm here." She clasped his hand tighter. "You're okay."

He exhaled. Though he opened his mouth to talk, Bianca held up her hand.

"I only came to check on you. The doctor says you're going to be all right."

"Somebody... hit me," he said.

"I know. I heard it."

"What? Who? Do you know?" Jordan asked.

Bianca shook her head. While she was hoping he could tell her who attacked him, she wanted him well first.

"Bette Davis."

Bianca raised an eyebrow. "What?" What did a former Hollywood star have to do with anything? She sighed. The doctor had mentioned Jordan's disorientation.

"Nicole..." He closed his eyes.

"She's fine. The police are working on it. Don't worry."

Jordan tightened his grip on her hand. "B... Bianca."

"Shh, get some rest. I'll come back to check on you soon." Her phone pinged. "I got to go." Raising to her feet, she planted a soft kiss on his cheek.

Jordan must have dozed off again, because his grip loosened on her hand. Bianca backed up, hearing the click of her heels once more. Checking the time, she realized she had to pick up Alyssa from school and Casper from her mother's house.

Exiting the automated doors, she ran into Nicole. Her friend's arms crossed over her chest. Her eyes looked red.

Bianca cleared her throat. Despite her disappointment in her friend not confiding in her, she hugged Nicole. "I've called and texted."

Her friend nodded once they broke their embrace. "I'm sorry. I needed some time. This is all so... overwhelming."

"How's Chad?" she asked.

"Trying to forget being questioned by the police." Nicole shrugged. "Who would put a towel with Martin's blood in his gym bag?"

"Does he go to the gym often?" Bianca asked.

"A few times a week if not jogging in the park, but he locks up his things."

Did someone pick the lock without him noticing? Did Chad know she was here? "I have to say, I didn't expect to see you here." Bianca's skin prickled. Nicole's secrets were catching up with her. One person was dead. Jordan was fighting for his life. Bianca had been chased and attacked.

"I had to see him. Is he okay? I heard he woke up." Nicole's eyebrows wrinkled.

"He's awake, but he needs to rest." Bianca tapped her foot on the concrete.

Nicole didn't speak for a moment. She pressed a hand to her cheek as she closed her eyes. Her eyes shined with more unshed tears. She sniffled. "I can't imagine what you think of me. Martin and... me."

Bianca paced to her car with Nicole at her heels. "We've been friends since college. You never told me any of this."

Nicole ran her fingers through her loose, blonde curls. "I'm not proud of it. What was I supposed to say, Bianca? I dated an older man for money? I know it was wrong, but I didn't know what else to do." She lowered her head. "I was in a horrible place financially, and I didn't see the harm in him helping me at the time. Eventually I did, but when I called things off, Martin wouldn't let me go. He was blackmailing me! He threatened to expose me."

"So instead you endanger the lives of Jordan, my sister, me, and who knows who else." Bianca's eyes bored into her friend. "Did you have anything to do with Martin's—?"

Her eyebrows shot up. "I'm not a killer! I know I'm being set up. The police are watching our every move. Priscilla gives me suspicious looks, probably wishing I'd never married her son."

"Can you blame her? Since you have a past with her husband?"

"No, but once I started seeing Chad, she came to accept our relationship."

"She never tried to convince Chad otherwise?"

Nicole shook her head. "If she did, he didn't tell me." She rubbed at her arms. "I thought things were getting better."

"And Jordan? He would do anything for you."

"He wouldn't kill for me if that's what you mean," she said.

Bianca stared at her friend. What a mess this all was. "I don't know what I can do to help anymore."

Nicole's lips parted, as if she remembered something.

"What?" Bianca asked.

"When Jordan told me how he felt about me, I don't know why, but I confided in Martin. He told me that Jordan wasn't good enough for me. It slipped out when I told Jordan I only saw him as a friend. The words came out in the heat of the moment. I didn't know his feelings for me were that deep. He's my best friend, but I never saw him that way. He—"

Bianca raised a hand to stop her. "Wait a minute. You told Jordan what Martin said?"

"I know it was stupid, but I was young, Bianca."

"And Jordan?"

"He lost it."

Bianca spread her fingers out in a fan against her breastbone. It made little sense for Jordan to kill Martin. Then again, he'd fight anyone who disrespected Nicole. He even argued with Chad when he'd found out about their relationship. Jordan had only backed off when Nicole asked him to.

Had he lost his temper after finding out about the blackmail? Had his aggression and hatred boiled over and he'd killed Martin to protect Nicole? Then Bianca recalled how Jordan had disappeared after their dance together. He didn't return to the reception. Had Bianca missed the clues? Had she been so blinded by friendship, she'd failed to see what was in front of her?

Then again, if he'd killed Martin, who'd attacked Jordan? An accomplice? Had his head injury all been a setup?

"Bianca?" Nicole tilted her head and touched a hand to her arm.

She gave her friend another quick hug. She wouldn't worry Nicole with her theories. "The police will find out who did this." Unless she beat them to it. Then she gestured to the hospital building. "Go see Jordan."

Nicole gave a faint smile and then walked inside. Bianca proceeded to her car, and slid into the driver's seat. Connecting her phone to her Bluetooth, her cell phone rung with Alyssa's ringtone.

"I'm on my way."

"Mom, can I spend the night at Chloe's tonight?"

Bianca turned the corner once the traffic light turned green. "It's a school night."

"I know, but we have a history exam tomorrow and since we're studying together, I wanted to ask."

Perhaps it was a good idea. With Alyssa at a friend's house, Bianca wouldn't have to worry about anyone following her daughter. Not after the car chase and Richard's impromptu visit. Well, in that case she forgot to answer her phone. Yet, she didn't know what was coming next.

"When will you be home?" she asked.

"I'll be home this time tomorrow," Alyssa said.

"Her parents will be there?"

"Yes, Mom."

"Will it be just you two studying or is this a group thing?" Bianca asked, recalling her antics as a teenager. Turning on the Main Street in Edenville, she bypassed the mom-and-pop restaurants.

"There may be a few others stopping by. Please, Mom?"

"As long as the parents are there." Knowing Chloe's parents, Bianca had little to worry about with Alyssa. "I'll pick you up tomorrow. You have what you need? Did you pack in advance?"

No response.

"You forget I was a teenager, sweetie."

"It's like you know my every move," Alyssa said.

Bianca giggled. "I'm your mother, remember that. Love you."

"Love you too, Mom." She hung up with a squeal.

Bianca laughed as she stopped in front of another traffic light. Resting her arm on the console, she looked out the passenger door window. She spotted Priscilla walking out of the town's specialty gift shop. Bianca almost rolled down the window to speak but widened her eyes when she saw Priscilla run her hand down her driver's face and further to his chest. She even leaned in closer but then threw her head back laughing. For a grieving widow, was she hitting on her driver? Then his hand caressed her waist. How much younger was he than her, anyway?

Bianca gasped. The driver. His face. When her phone rang, she looked at the number on her screen. Connecting her phone to her Bluetooth, she answered.

"I have something for you." Detective Sims. "A name of the man in the park who attacked you."

"Who?" She pulled forward as the light turned green.

"Luis Mineo. Age 34. Looks like he's been working for the Davis family as a driver for the last six months. He favors the driver from the wedding too."

"So these are two different men?"

"Looks like it. The limo driver from the wedding no longer works for the company. He skipped town since then. We brought in Luis for questioning. I'm sending you a picture of him to identify him."

Bianca's phone buzzed. Putting Detective Sims on speaker, she opened the photo. "That's him."

"Thank you. I hate to ask you to come back to the station to identify him in person, but I need you too."

The last thing she wanted to do. "Okay. I can come now if that works."

"Perfect. Once you do that, we can charge him with assault at least, if not attempted murder," he said.

Bianca's skin prickled. "Detective?"

"Yes?"

"There's a man with Pricilla Davis and... he looks familiar," Bianca said.

Chapter 25

Bianca eyed the parking lot filled with vehicles and golfers. Carts buzzed along the fairway and she adjusted the cap on her head. Stepping into the parking lot, she sighed as she plotted her strategy in her head.

Since this week was mild with work, Bianca didn't see the harm in checking out the golf course. Perhaps someone here knew Martin. Had he come often to play with Richard? Tugging the skin at her neck, Bianca shivered when she thought of how Richard had come up from behind her at her home. She had to stay alert. As she approached the front door of the clubhouse, she froze in her tracks. Detective Sims.

She breathed in the fresh-mown grass. Swallowing, Bianca adjusted her purse strap on her shoulder. Detective Sims raised an eyebrow and gave her a glassy stare. Was she getting under his skin?

He stopped in front of her. "Ms. Wallace. You're here."

"Nice to see you again, detective." She folded her arms over her chest.

"How are you?" he asked.

"Doing better. Any news on Jordan's attacker?" She pointed to the clubhouse behind him. "Any leads?"

"Is there a reason you're so invested in this case?"

"Nicole is my friend."

"I understand that, but why get involved?" he asked.

Bianca rubbed at her neck. "I don't like good people being blamed when I know they're innocent."

He gave a faint smile. "That's noble of you, Ms. Wallace, but I can't afford another civilian getting hurt. You've come too close. More than once already."

Bianca licked her lips as she pondered his words.

The corners of his own mouth turned up. "Is there a reason you're here?"

She shrugged. "Maybe I came to play."

He chuckled. "You golf?"

"Some women do."

He laughed harder, and Bianca's lips parted to respond, but then she spotted a car on the far end of the parking lot pulling off. A white Honda.

"You're kidding?" She sprinted to her car.

"Ms. Wallace?" Detective Sims trailed behind her.

"That's the car. The car from the chase!" She slid into the driver's seat. Didn't Judy get her car back? That was the news around town. Was it her driving this time? Someone else with the same model?

Detective Sims motioned for her to let down the window.

"What?" She started her car.

"I don't need you tailing them. We'll handle it."

"I'm not letting this go, detective."

He groaned and walked in front of her car. Her eyes followed him, and when he came to the passenger side, she unlocked it. He slid inside and pointed for her to go.

Bianca's vehicle hummed as she drove down the road. Detective Sims got on the phone.

"So far, they're heading west on Farming road. I'll keep you posted. Bye." He hung up.

"Requesting backup?" she asked.

"No." He released a mirthless laugh. "Are you always this stubborn?"

"I'd like to say *persistent*. Determined. Strong-willed."

"If you say so."

She sighed as both of her hands gripped the wheel. "My dad was a police officer. One of the best cops I knew, but... he was mistaken for a shooter while off duty. They accused him of murder. He died in prison since his heart condition worsened. He never... got the chance to prove his innocence and come home."

Detective Sims released a deep breath. "Sorry to hear that."

"What about you?" she asked. "Why did you get into the police force?"

"I grew up in a single parent home. My mom worked two, sometimes three jobs at a time. I didn't plan on getting involved in gangs, but I did. Next thing I know, I'm fighting a guy from another gang with a knife."

Bianca stiffened in her seat as she followed the Honda through a green light. Detective Sims in a gang? He didn't seem like the type, nor did he possess the bad boy appeal. Yet Bianca listened, not wanting to judge him by his past.

"Did you..." How did she ask him if he'd killed someone?

"No, but the guy came close to dying," he said.

Bianca breathed easier.

"But it made me realize I was on the wrong road. It was ruled as self-defense for me, but it was a wakeup call to change. So I did.

Graduated high school. Joined the police academy and I've been on the right side of the law ever since." He straightened in his seat. "Turn left here."

Bianca did as the Honda pulled into the parking lot of a cheap motel and parked. Her eyebrows furrowed. A cheap motel?

"Park in the back." Detective Sims motioned her to a spot to park.

Bianca eyeballed the external staircases and the seedy characters coming in and out of the building. Putting her car in park, she stared along with Detective Sims to see who got out of the Honda. A red-headed woman. Judy.

"Judy?"

"Interesting." Detective Sims said.

Bianca's body heat rose. Was she in on this? This case had just gotten even more complicated. She'd never suspected Judy, but protecting Richard was a good enough motive.

Judy paced to the double story building with dirty bricks and peeling paint. Outside on the first floor, she knocked on the door. Bianca focused her eyes. Who would open the door? She couldn't see since Judy went inside the room.

Taking out her phone, Bianca opened her camera and zoomed in. "Nothing. The curtains are closed."

Then Detective Sims leaned over to see. Bianca cleared her throat as the heat from his body penetrated her skin. His cologne tickled her nose, but she only turned her phone for him to see. Bianca ignored the quivers in her stomach.

"We already have Luis Mineo in custody for attacking you," he said.

It was a good thing she'd identified him the other day. Judy exited the room with an envelope. She stuffed it inside her purse.

What was in it? Money? Bianca clutched the back of her neck. Is that how Judy got the money to pay her? Then they watched Judy get back into her car.

Bianca sighed. "It looks like she got what she wanted." She bit her bottom lip as the wheels turned in her brain. "I wonder if Richard knows about Judy taking money." She turned to Detective Sims, resting her arm on the console. Maybe—"

Detective Sims held up a hand.

Bianca turned and put her car in drive to follow Judy. "What now?"

"See where she goes." He rested his hand against her dashboard.

Bianca didn't drive too close, but she did her best not to lose her. With one car between them, she turned to keep following. She shook her head. "If Judy was taking money... it makes sense."

Detective Sims didn't hear her last comment. He tapped the dashboard. "Let's head back."

"I thought you said—"

"Change of plans, Ms. Wallace. I'm asking you to go home."

She kept her eyes on the road. "If it weren't for me, you wouldn't be here."

"I only came here to do my job, while keeping an eye on you."

"An eye on me?"

He continued. "I took an oath to protect and serve. You're not making it easy for me."

Bianca headed for the clubhouse. "I'm only here to help Nicole and Chad."

"I could charge you with obstruction of justice."

She sighed, biting back her sarcastic remark.

His tone softened. "I'm not saying you haven't been an asset in *some* scenarios, but—"

"I get it. I'm not trying to cause trouble or make things worse."

Detective Sims said, "I was beginning to think you liked messing with me."

Bianca couldn't help but rattle him. "I have more important things to do."

He chuckled. "I don't think I've met anyone like you, Ms. Wallace."

She smiled. "And you never will again, detective."

Chapter 26

Detective Sims didn't make conversation on the way back. With his faced glued to his phone, Bianca didn't dare look to see what was on his screen. Instead, she kept her eyes on the road. When she came to a red light, she recalled Alyssa's shriek when she'd practiced parallel parking in the parking lot. Bianca giggled.

"What's funny?" Detective Sims asked.

"Nothing." She covered her mouth with one hand, and her snickers persisted.

"Nothing, huh?"

She waved it off but answered. "Sorry, I'm teaching my daughter how to drive. It's... interesting. She reminds me of me when I learned."

"How so?" He wanted to know?

Bianca's foot switched to the accelerator from the brake pedal when the light turned green. "Parallel parking. She doesn't quite get it. I didn't, either. I'm surprised I passed that part of the test."

"Even till this day you still can't?" he asked.

"Only when I have to, but it's rare unless I'm downtown. Even then, it takes a few tries."

Detective Sims chuckled.

She glanced at him for a moment but then faced the road again. "Okay, laugh."

"No, I was thinking about when I learned to drive. I ran over my mother's rose garden."

"What?" she asked.

He bobbed his head. "Yeah, I thought she was going to disown me for a moment. She worked so hard in that garden."

"I guess we have that in common."

"I guess so."

From her peripheral vision, she could see him staring. She didn't dare look. "How would you rate your driving now?"

"Let's just say... no one's gotten away from me in a police chase."

Bianca said, "Maybe you should have been driving that day."

"That part is over. We got him."

She trusted his word. His integrity was evident. Pulling into the parking lot filled with parked cars and trucks, she spotted his police car and parked beside it.

"Here we are," she said.

He unclicked his seatbelt. "Thank you. I appreciate it."

"You're welcome." She ran her hands down her pant legs. "Can I ask something? As a concerned friend?"

His eyebrows drew together, but his face softened. "Sure."

"What's going on with Chad?" she asked.

"No concrete evidence to prove anything," he said.

"And Jordan's attacker?"

Detective Sims offered a small smile. "All we have is him collapsing to the ground. With the angle of the security camera, the attacker was out of view. Until Jordan's better to talk, he can't give us a statement."

Bianca's chest heaved with a sigh. "Thank you."

He bobbed his head. "Make sure you get home safe."

She smiled. "I will."

The door clicked when he shut it and her eyes followed him walking to his car. Bianca grabbed her phone to check her messages, only to see a text from Nicole. How did she not hear her phone buzz?

Nicole: *Thank you for your support in all of this. I want this to be over.*

Bianca touched a hand to her chest. Then she typed her reply. *How are you? Chad? Priscilla?*

Nicole: *So far, Chad's fine. I'm trying not to worry about Jordan. I think Priscilla's the only one holding it together.*

Bianca recalled her own mother's attitude when her father had died. Her strength had never wavered for her daughters and she'd worked to take care of them. Next thing Bianca had known, her mother had started her own matchmaking business. Her reasoning, "I want people to find what I had with your father."

I hope she's taking it easy.

Nicole: *Me too. Also, no rush on our thank you photos. Chad and I want to wait until this is resolved to send them*

Bianca didn't blame her. She would keep the pictures saved. While she thought about asking her about the young man she'd seen with Priscilla, her eyes spotted Richard exiting the country club.

Have to go. I'll talk to you later. Let me know if you need anything.

Nicole: *Thanks. I will. Talk soon!*

Bianca cut the engine to her car and sprinted to the front door. Would her plan work?

"Bianca?" Richard said once he saw her.

Bingo. She pivoted to face him. "Richard? Hi! Nice to see you in the daylight."

He ran a hand down his neck. "Haha yes it is. What are you doing here? You play golf now?"

Bianca bit at her bottom lip. "I'm not any good, but my dad was a fan so…"

Richard bobbed his head. Thank goodness her answer sufficed.

Her next question was worth a shot. "How are you and Judy? With, you know, everything going on?"

He gestured for her to walk with him. "So far, we're doing fine. She's been on edge, but I can't blame her."

"Is… Judy at the bakery by chance? I may want some cinnamon buns to take home."

Richard checked his watch. "She should be. It's getting close to our peak hours. I only came here to unwind." Then he walked to his truck and loaded his golf clubs. "Will you be stopping by the bakery later?" His phone buzzed, and he retrieved it from his pocket. "One second."

Bianca nodded. "Sure."

Richard's eyes widened as his fingers typed away on his phone. "Looks like Judy needs me at the bakery." He raised his chin and looked at Bianca. "See you later."

"I hope so. If not, I'll come by sometime next week."

"Have a good one," he said.

She replied. "You too."

Then he slid into his driver's seat. The engine roared when he started it, and he backed out of his parking space. Left alone in the parking lot, Bianca tapped her foot on the concrete.

Buzz, buzz.

Bianca stared at her phone in her hand. She knew this number.

She answered. "Hello?"

"Are you home as promised, Ms. Wallace?"

Detective Sims?

She placed her hand on her hip. "I promised that?"

"You agreed to get home safe."

She marched back to her car. "I ran into... a friend, so I stopped and said *hello*."

"A friend?"

"Richard Long. Judy's husband. He says she was at the bakery. I don't think he knows about her trip to the motel."

Detective Sims sighed.

Her mouth twisted. "I know. Go home."

"What else do you know?"

Her eyebrows raised. "Nothing more, I promise."

Chapter 27

Friday night. Pacing outside of Alyssa's room, Bianca inhaled and exhaled. Her daughter's first date. Correction. Group date. Apparently, a group of kids from her school were throwing another party, but her daughter couldn't wait to get home to tell her that Kendrick, her crush, had asked her to go with him. Alyssa had practically squealed and bounced on her toes.

Malcom wanted to run a background check on the boy. Bianca had talked him out of it. Still, Malcom had her swear to take a picture of the boy on her phone, in case he tried something with their daughter.

"Mom!" Alyssa yelled through her door.

"Yes?" Bianca could hear her rattled nerves in her daughter's wavering voice.

Alyssa's door opened with a whoosh. "What do you think? Too much?"

Bianca stared at her daughter's fitted floral blouse and dark blue jeans. "I like it."

"Ugh." Alyssa stalked back inside her room and to her closet.

Bianca followed her. "I don't think you have much time, sweetie. Didn't he say six-thirty?"

Alyssa's gray shirt flew out the closet along with another jean jacket. "I don't know which one."

Bianca stopped her daughter and placed her hand on her shoulders. "First, breathe."

Alyssa exhaled.

"Second." Bianca inspected her daughter's makeup. "Is that a plum color on your lips?"

"Too much?"

Bianca bobbed her head. "I'd go with a lighter lip color. Sometimes less is more."

Alyssa sat in front of her mirror, and with a tissue, she wiped her lips clean of her plum lip color. Then she held up another color. "Pink?"

Bianca tilted her head. "I think that'll work." She walked behind her daughter. Leaning over, she kissed the top of her head. "Don't worry. Just be yourself and have fun. Not *too* much fun." She raised an eyebrow.

"I know, Mom." Alyssa smiled. When the doorbell rang, she wrung her hands together. "Mom, please don't grill him with questions."

"If I don't, your father will. Choose."

Alyssa's shoulders drooped.

Bianca rubbed her back and headed to the front door. "I won't embarrass you." When she opened the door, she saw an athletic-looking teenage boy, round faced, brown skin, with small mole on his left cheek. Bianca could have sworn she saw sweat glistening along his hairline, but she didn't want to put him on the spot. "You must be Kendrick?"

He bobbed his head and extended his hand. "Yes. Ma'am."

So far, so good. She motioned for him to come in. He followed her to the living room.

Kendrick sat on the couch, running his hands down his pant legs. Casper trotted over and sniffed the hem of his jeans. When the boy reached down to pet him, Casper licked his hand.

A *hmm* escaped Bianca's mouth. She sat across from him on her loveseat. "You have his approval. Alyssa should be ready soon."

"I don't mind waiting." His tenor voice tremored, but he cleared his throat.

"Mind if I take a picture of you two before you leave?" Bianca waved her phone. "Her father lives in California."

Kendrick nodded. "Sure, no problem."

"And don't forget her curfew is eleven-thirty."

"She told me," he said. "Thank you. I really like Alyssa." His eyes bulged. "Probably shouldn't say that right now."

Bianca chuckled. "Don't worry. I won't tell her. Besides, I think she'll appreciate that coming from you."

He smiled.

"I'm here," Alyssa said. When her eyes locked with Kendrick's, her grin grew. "Hi."

He stood to his feet. "Hi, Alyssa. You look great." He inched closer to her.

Bianca didn't know whether to bask in her daughter's first date or laugh at her old teenage self. Had she been that wrapped up in Malcom on their first date? Bianca looked upward. Yes.

"Don't forget. I need a picture." She opened her camera.

"Mom?" Alyssa groaned.

"It's no problem," Kendrick said. "It's cool."

Alyssa faced him. "You sure?"

He bobbed his head and draped an arm over her shoulders.

Bianca inwardly winced but snapped the photos. Man, was her daughter almost grown. "Perfect. Have a good time."

Kendrick extended his hand to Alyssa and headed for the door. "Thank you, Ms. Wallace."

"Bye, Mom." Alyssa added.

Bianca followed them outside and waited on the porch until Kendrick pulled out of the driveway. She ignored her eyes filling with tears and waved goodbye as they drove off. The pitter-patter of Casper's paws made her look downward.

"What?" She dabbed her eyes. "I'm not crying. Not really."

He wagged his tail, looking unconvinced.

"Stop judging me." She marched inside and he followed. Bianca's breathing slowed as more memories of the past flooded her thoughts. She blinked.

Everyone in her life had moved on. Malcom had remarried. Her mother had started her own business. Alyssa was repairing her relationship with her father. Bianca paced to her bedroom.

Sitting on her bed, a shallow sigh escaped her lips. It wasn't too late. She could change her life. That's what she had been doing, except in her personal life. Even at the nightclub, all Bianca did was think more about Martin's murder.

Stalking to her closet, she chose one of her dressier outfits. No shame in taking herself out. Choosing a mint green blouse, black-and-white pants, and her heeled boots, Bianca dressed quickly.

Buzz, buzz.

She picked up her phone. Malcom.

Did she leave?

Bianca texted him the pictures she'd taken of Kendrick and Alyssa.

See for yourself.

She touched up her makeup and pulled her hair back into a low ponytail

Malcom: *I can't deal with this.*

Me, neither lol

He didn't message her back, so she could only assume Malcom was still processing his baby girl out on her first date. Casper barked and Bianca bit at her bottom lip.

"She left already? I was on an important call." Melanie came from the hallway. "I was hoping to see her date before they left."

"She's gone."

A *tsk* escaped her sister's lips. "Okay. Did Mom call you?"

"She called Alyssa earlier," she said.

A grin escaped Melanie's lips. "Well I have an article to finish."

"When are you leaving for work again?"

"At the end of the month so I have some time off," Melanie said.

Bianca walked past her sister. "I'll be back."

Melanie teased her. "You have a date too?" She headed back to her room.

Bianca's mouth hung open but didn't reply. Then she looked down at Casper. "You want to come?"

He wagged his tail.

"Fine." They headed out the door and to her car. The drive to downtown Edenville was short, and Bianca didn't have to worry about parking. She hooked Casper's leash and the two of them walked.

Bianca listened to the occasional honk of a horn, while taking the in the spices and food cooking at nearby restaurants. She stared at the few buildings that lit at night, and pausing at a crosswalk, she tapped her foot.

The light changed, signaling her to walk forward. Casper took the lead, and she grinned, but warmth spread through her body when she spotted Detective Sims.

He wasn't in his usual police attire or his gym clothes. Dark jeans and a dark polo shirt were his attire for the evening. Was he out on the town too? Bianca swallowed.

When he saw her coming toward him, he stuffed his hands inside his pockets. He gave a crisp nod.

"Detective," Bianca said.

"Ms. Wallace." He bent to pet Casper, who stood on his hind legs. After a few scratches behind the dog's ears, he straightened to his feet. "You out for a walk too?"

"More like trying not to spy on my daughter." She covered her hand with her mouth as soon as the words left her. "I didn't mean—"

He chuckled. "I guess if I had more information, I'd understand."

"Her first date is tonight. She's out with some friends and the boy she likes." She walked forward, and to her surprise, Detective Sims walked beside her.

"So you're keeping yourself occupied?" he asked.

"Right."

"How's that working for you?"

"It's... not." She stopped in her tracks. "Anyway, enjoying the fresh air after a hard day at work?"

He chuckled. "Something like that."

"Don't worry. I'm not asking you about the case. Tonight's my night off from sleuthing."

Did he inch closer? "I can't tell you how relieved I am to hear you say that."

Bianca's breath quickened. Casper tugged her toward the street. "I should, um... get going. It's getting... late." Why did she sound like a bumbling teenager? She backed to the curb, thankful she didn't fall to her face.

Detective Sims waved. "Have a good night."

"You too." Bianca turned to walk, only for her body to jerk. She looked down. She wiggled her right foot, but it didn't budge. Had she caught her heel in a utility hole? Great. Her heel caught in the cover of a sewage hole.

"Ms. Wallace?" Detective Sims walked over.

"I got it." She wiggled and yanked, but nothing. Not her favorite boots. Why did this have to happen now?

"I think you need some help." He bent down, touching a hand to her ankle.

Bianca's eyes wandered about. Were there people watching?

"Pull on three?" he suggested.

She forced a smile, wishing she could disappear from the embarrassment.

Detective Sims secured his hands around her ankle. "One. Two. Three."

Pop. Bianca's heel was free from the sewage hole, but boy, was this something she didn't want to spread around Edenville.

"The heel's a little scuffed, but I think you're all right. You don't feel any pain in your ankle, do you?" he asked.

She put weight on her right foot. So far, so good. "I'm fine." She had to get home. Her free hand curled around her middle. Where was her car? She needed to get back to her car.

"Goodnight, Ms. Wallace," Detective Sims said.

Bianca waved with her back to him. What a night. It couldn't get any worse.

Chapter 28

That Sunday afternoon, Bianca, Alyssa, Melanie, along with Casper joined her mother for their family dinner. "I don't want you anywhere near this case." Deborah Wallace pointed to her daughter. "I can't believe you're just now telling me about that car chase."

Melanie shrunk back in her chair. Bianca knew her sister hadn't intended for the information to slip out, but once it had, their mother touched a hand to her chest. Her brow wrinkled.

Bianca twirled the spaghetti, hearing the scrape of cutlery on her plate. How long had her mother been lecturing her? At least five minutes. She sat next to her sister, who nibbled on a breadstick. How did they go from talking about Alyssa's first date to Melanie slipping up about the car chase?

Bianca watched her mother pour a glass of tea. "I don't care. I want my daughters safe."

"We are," Melanie said.

Bianca breathed in the garlic that wafted off the tomato sauce. Too bad her appetite wasn't there.

Melanie reached for her mother's hand. "Mom, we know you're worried, but there's no need to be."

"That is scary." Alyssa added.

Bianca squeezed her daughter's hand.

Then Bianca's mother continued. "How do I know this idiot won't come after you again? I've already lost..."

Bianca felt a twinge in her heart. Her father. She stood from her seat and walked over to her mother. Leaning over, she wrapped her arms around her mother's shoulders. "Mom, nothing bad is going to happen to us."

Her mother patted her arm. "I know you, sweetie. You don't give up. You get that from your father."

"That's a good thing, right?" She straightened to see her mother's face.

Her mother turned in her chair and raised an eyebrow. "I'm serious, Bianca."

"Mom, don't worry. We'll both be careful." Melanie then played a song on her phone.

Bianca's grin grew, noticing the tune. A favorite of her dad's. The Temptations' "Since I Lost My Baby." She took her mother's hand, pulling her to her feet. "Come on. It's tradition."

Her mother shook her head as her daughters danced to the classic song. Then her eyes beamed as she shimmied her shoulders. They all laughed.

These were the moments that mattered the most. She would be careful. Nothing would harm her or her family again. Bianca had made a promise to herself to do just that when her dad had died and she'd reminded herself of that after Malcom's infidelity. She would take care of her own.

The ladies moved side to side, grooving to the song. Even Casper, Jasper, and Horas barked along. Bianca snapped her fingers as she twisted and turned to the music. It wasn't until her phone rang on the table that she stopped dancing.

Melanie continued with her mother. Bianca covered one ear to hear.

"No phones, Bianca." Her mother reminded her.

"It's Chad, Mom. It could be important." She answered. "Hello?" she said.

"Bianca?"

"Chad?"

"The police officially arrested Nicole. They found the murder weapon. Plus a witness came forward saying that she was missing during the time Martin was murdered."

"What? No. You were with her—"

"We were greeting guests, drinking, dancing, and talking with friends and family. Perhaps she slipped away and I didn't notice." He groaned. "I can't remember, Bianca. I've been going back and forth in my head trying to remember, but I can't."

At least Bianca didn't drop the phone, but she stood still. Chad's frustration was evident in his voice.

He continued. "I'm following them now to the police station. She could use your support. I... can't believe it."

Bianca pressed a hand to her forehead. "Yes, of course. I'll come." She hung up. Her heartbeat raced as a sudden coldness hit her core.

"Bianca?" Melanie came and stood next to her.

"They arrested Nicole. They found her prints on the murder weapon."

"What?" her mother asked. "That makes no sense at all. She didn't leave the reception."

"A witness said she did." Bianca grabbed her purse. Then she faced her sister. "Can you take Casper home?"

Melanie bobbed her head.

Bianca hugged Alyssa. "Chloe's meeting you here, right?"

Her daughter shook her head. "Maybe I should stay, Mom. You—"

"No. Go and have fun." She assured her daughter.

"You sure you don't want me to go with you?" Melanie asked.

"No, I'll just meet you at the house." She turned to her mother and hugged her too. "I'll be careful. I promise."

Bianca headed out the door to her car. Nicole arrested for killing Martin? With one hand on the wheel, Bianca processed all that had happened, trying to connect all the dots.

Nicole had a motive. Blackmail. But why ruin her life? She and Chad had been starting a new one together. Why would she have thrown it all away?

Bianca groaned. This puzzle was too much, but she wouldn't fail. Pulling into the parking lot of the police station, she parked close to the entrance. Cutting the engine, she spotted Chad talking to Detective Sims. Chad's head hung low as he pressed a hand to his forehead.

Bianca exited her car and sprinted to join them. "Detective. Chad?"

Chad's expression looked pained. "Thanks for coming."

She nodded. "Of course. What's the charge?"

"Murder in the first degree." Chad rubbed his face.

"What?" Bianca's mouth dropped open. "You're kidding? This is Nicole we're talking about."

Detective Sims said, "We have the weapon, her prints, and a witness. She could have killed him and came back to the reception in no time at all."

"It's a mistake!" Chad barked. "My wife's not a killer!"

Bianca touched his arm.

Detective Sims handed Chad a plastic bag. "These are the belongings she had when we arrested her. I am sorry, but I'm doing my job. We work with the facts and evidence." Without another word, he stepped back inside the precinct.

Bianca walked alongside Chad. "Did you talk to her?"

"Not long enough. She's so scared."

"But I'm sure you post bail?"

He bobbed his head.

Bianca heaved a deep sigh. "I'm so sorry." Turning away, a pain increased in the back of her throat. It was her father all over again. Someone she cared about was in jail for no reason. She'd failed her father, and she'd failed Nicole. Drawing her shoulders up, she tucked her elbows to her side. Not wanting to upset her stomach, she exhaled to calm herself.

"What are you going to do?" she asked.

"Find the best lawyer. My wife will not spend the rest of her life in prison." As he opened the plastic bag, a *tsk* sound escaped his lips.

"What?" Bianca leaned in closer to see the contents inside.

He pulled out a manila folder. "Our wedding pictures. She wanted you to have a few copies." He handed them to her.

Bianca took the folder. "Chad, I wish I—"

"I know, Bianca." He blew out his cheeks. "I'm going to go home. There's nothing I can do for her standing in the parking lot."

She bobbed her head. Stepping back, she paced to her own car. Bianca clasped the folder to her chest.

Chapter 29

Bianca's keys clicked when she threw them inside the bowl on her foyer table. The floorboards creaked underneath her feet, and she plopped on her sofa. How had she beat Melanie home? Her heart ached for her friend sitting in jail.

Murder. Nicole? How would she explain it? Removing her jacket and placing it over the arm of the couch, Bianca took the manila folder in her hand. Perhaps the wedding pictures would cheer her up.

Undoing the clasp, Bianca reclined in her seat and held up the photos to look at them one by one. Nicole and Chad looked so happy during their first dance. She felt a twinge in her chest. She couldn't imagine what Chad was going through.

Making a quick trip to her home office, Bianca retrieved her own laptop. Since she'd downloaded the photos she'd taken from the rehearsal and reception, perhaps they could shed some light. How? If only she knew. When did Nicole go missing?

"We're home," Melanie said.

"In the living room." Bianca crossed her legs at the ankles on her coffee table.

Casper trotted inside with Melanie, but when she unclasped his leash, he made himself comfortable in his dog bed. Bianca couldn't help but smile.

"What's that?" Melanie sat next to her.

"Nicole and Chad's wedding pictures." Bianca paused. Then she repeated what Detective Sims told Chad. "The police found the murder weapon... with her fingerprints."

"I don't get it," Melanie said.

"I know." Bianca thumbed through more pictures. Smiles were everywhere. How had a beautiful day turned into a nightmare for the bride and groom? "I wish there were something I could do."

"Bianca?"

"I should stay out of it, but... I can't."

Melanie pointed out. "Maybe you don't know her the way you think you do, sis. People change. Nicole is not the same person you met in college. She even kept some secrets from you."

Bianca faced her sister. "I know, but that doesn't make her a murderer. I can't put my finger on it, but I know something's wrong." Picking up another picture, she caught Richard in one of them. With his arms crossed, he appeared to be looking at the crowd. "I still don't know about him."

"Richard?" Melanie leaned in closer to study the photo.

"He had a lot to lose."

Melanie then focused on Bianca's laptop screen. "Aw, this is cute with Nicole and Chad."

Bianca smiled and admired the happy couple embracing. Hands were in the surrounding air, so the guests must have been applauding. As Bianca focused her eyes, she saw someone in the background, closer to the back of the ballroom, whose hands weren't in the air.

"Is that Priscilla?" Bianca pointed to the person in the picture. The she zoomed in further.

Melanie looked to where she was pointing. "I think so. I recognize her haircut. Looks like a champagne glass in her hand too."

Bianca's eyebrows rose. Champagne? "She's drinking?"

"Yeah, didn't you have a glass? It's a wedding."

Bianca shook her head. "She shouldn't have been drinking with her condition, Mel. Priscilla is on heart medication. I don't think it mixes well with alcohol. She's had enough of her spells to know that. She even refused at the rehearsal so why at the reception?" She gasped.

"What?" Her sister asked.

"What if she didn't take it? What if she faked her spell? Mom said she took Priscilla to the ladies room. She said she *had* her pills with her. Mom didn't say she *took* them." Bianca snapped her fingers before opening a new browser and typing on her laptop.

Melanie shrugged. "Maybe she didn't have that much to drink."

The wheels in Bianca's mind turned further. Priscilla's expression looked... questionable, especially toward Nicole. Her eyes bored into the woman. Though she appeared pleasant in a few photos, her tight expression said one thing—hate.

Typing Digoxin into Google, Bianca read the recommendations. DO NOT MIX WITH ALCOHOL. Bianca pointed to her screen and read aloud. "See? 'Taking alcohol with digoxin will decrease the amount of the drug in your bloodstream, which may cause abnormalities.' Priscilla called the pills her *lifesaver*. I don't think she took them that day."

"What are you thinking?" Melanie asked.

Bianca wrung her hands together. "I don't know."

"You've got that look. What is it?"

"I don't know, but I'm going to figure it out. I have a hunch, but it's a long shot."

Melanie shot to her feet. "No chance. No way. You know Mom's already worried."

"Mel, this is about helping Nicole. You and I both know she's not a killer.

Her sister folded her arms. She sat back down. "I *don't* know, sis."

Bianca moved closer and placed her hands on her sister's shoulders. "Remember when Mom was working with lawyers to prove Dad's innocence? We all knew he didn't do the crime they accused him of. I hate that he died in prison before he had time to prove his story."

Melanie's features softened. She hugged her sister. "Me too."

"If only we had more time." Pulling back from their embrace, Bianca gave a faint smile.

Melanie asked. "Are you sure about this?"

Bianca wrung her fingers together. "We just have to prove it. If only I knew *how*."

"Where would we even start?" Melanie asked.

Ding Dong.

Both ladies shrieked.

Melanie pressed her hand to her chest as Casper barked. "Who is that?"

Bianca grabbed her phone again. She had a text from Priscilla.

On my way to pick up the video

That was almost twenty minutes ago. Bianca didn't hear her phone buzz. She blew out her cheeks and faced her sister. "Take Casper with you to my office. It's Priscilla outside." She would wait to call Detective Sims about her theory since he seemed so open-and-shut about the case.

BIANCA'S OWN PALMS sweated. Her scalp prickled. She opened her front door to find Priscilla standing in her finest pant suit. White gloves included. Did the woman ever dress casual? The night breeze chilled Bianca's skin as she inhaled her flowering plants. Priscilla's eyes gleamed and Bianca invited her inside.

"Did you get my text? I didn't get your response," she said.

"I did. I just didn't see it until I heard the doorbell." Bianca ushered her into her living room.

Priscilla shook her head. "Is this a bad time?" She eyed her computer. "It looks like you're working."

"No, please sit. Take your jacket off." Bianca kept her breathing steady as best she could.

"Thank you." She slid her black jacket off her shoulders. "I won't stay long," Priscilla said, taking off her gloves one finger at a time. "Thank you so much, dear for the surprise. I insist on paying for it. A bonus." She laid her jacket and gloves along the shoulder of Bianca's couch. She took a seat in a nearby chair.

Bianca held up her hand in objection. "I wouldn't dream of it. It was a surprise so no extra charge."

"You're too kind." Priscilla's lips turned up into a smile, but then she rubbed at her arms. "I guess I caught a chill."

"Want some tea? I can put a kettle on to boil while I get the video," Bianca said.

"Perfect." Priscilla replied.

Bianca walked over to her kitchen. She wouldn't ask Priscilla about the man who was caressing her at the gift shop. "How are you really doing?"

Priscilla followed. "It's been… tough, but I'm taking it one day at a time. Chad told me about Nicole."

Bianca lit her stove. "I was there. He's so distraught."

Priscilla bobbed her head.

Bianca cleared her throat. "Give me a minute and I'll get the CD for you."

"Take your time," Priscilla said. She reached inside her purse and busied herself on her phone.

Bianca gave a faint smile as she turned to walk, but she paused at her couch. Eyeing Priscilla's gloves, there was a small stain on the edge of the thumb area. Was that glove for her right hand? Had it been there all this time?

Reaching into her back pocket, Bianca grabbed her phone and took a quick picture. Looking behind her, Priscilla's head was still down. Bianca quickly stuffed her phone back into her pocket.

"Everything okay?" Priscilla asked.

Bianca's chest heaved. "Yes." She grabbed the wedding pictures off her coffee table along with her laptop. "Just taking these back to my office. I'll be back."

Proceeding down the hallway, Bianca exhaled. Her stomach quivered. Her office door was closed, and when she opened it, Melanie shot to her feet. Casper sat in the corner.

"Well?" her sister asked.

Bianca hurried to her desk and placed her laptop and pictures down. After grabbing the disk sitting on the corner, she faced her sister. "You have your phone?"

Melanie reached in her back pocket for it. "Yes."

Bianca took hers out and sent the picture of Priscilla's glove. Melanie opened her phone and zoomed in.

She gasped. "Bianca?"

"I think that's dried blood."

"What are we going to do?" Melanie asked.

"Send this picture to Detective Sims. Keep an ear close to the door. I didn't tell Priscilla anyone was here with me, so thank goodness your car is in the garage. If anything goes wrong, call him."

"Bianca?"

"Call him, Mel." She pleaded with her sister.

"Be *careful*," Melanie said.

Bianca left her sister along with Casper in her office, closing the door behind her.

BIANCA FORCED A SMILE as she found Priscilla in her kitchen with her phone still in hand. Did she take a phone call? Bianca's heart pounded, but she wouldn't give herself away. If her suspicions proved true, there could be no slip-ups. "Everything okay?"

Priscilla nodded. Though her eyebrows squished together, she grinned. "I believe so. I was checking on Chad again." She placed her phone on Bianca's bar countertop, with her purse lying next to it.

Bianca tilted her head. "I can't imagine what he's going through with Nicole in jail."

Priscilla shrugged. "I guess he's chosen to make the best of it."

"Oh? He was pretty upset when I was with him." Bianca played her part, hoping it would work.

Priscilla raised her hand as if taking an oath. "I'll be the first to admit I didn't care for Nicole, but Chad loved her. Who was I to tell my son not to marry her?"

"He loves her. I can tell." Bianca stood in front of her bar.

Priscilla nodded. "I know, but I think even he's realized that she's... not the right fit for him. He may want an annulment. The scandal of all of this is too much for our family." She released a deep breath. "I think it may be for the best too."

Bianca raised an eyebrow. "Chad? Him leave Nicole? Now?"

Priscilla brushed it off with a wave of her hand. "I'm not surprised." She spotted the disk in Bianca's hand. "Is that it?"

She handed it to her. "Yes. I hope you enjoy."

Priscilla's eyes glowed. "Thank you." She stuffed it inside her purse. "Anyway, I could tell it was coming with Chad and Nicole. A mother knows these things." The teakettle whistled and Bianca walked past her to turn off the burner. Retrieving a cup form her cabinet, she poured the hot water inside it.

Bianca cleared her throat. "Do you think he'll go through with it? What if he changes his mind?"

"He won't." Priscilla snapped.

Bianca didn't flinch. She placed the kettle back on her stovetop.

Priscilla's eyes widened as if she'd caught her outburst. She touched a hand to her chest. "I mean, after everything she's put this family through, Chad deserves better than her." Her face tightened but she forced a smile. Walking back over to the couch, she grabbed her jacket and gloves.

"One sip for the road?" Bianca handed her the cup after adding a tea bag with some honey. "Wouldn't want you to catch cold."

Priscilla finished putting on her gloves. "You're a gem Bianca." She cupped her drink and took a sip. "Chamomile. I love it. Thank you."

Bianca nodded in response. With her hands so close to her face, Bianca's eyes zeroed in on Priscilla's white gloves again. The stain *was* on her right thumb. Did Priscilla not know?

"Can I ask you something?" Bianca focused back on her face.

"Sure."

"Do you really think that... Chad deserves better than Nicole?"

Priscilla snickered. "A mother knows what's best for her child. I won't let her ruin him the way she ruined..." She stopped.

Bianca's lips parted. "Martin?"

Priscilla didn't reply. Her eyes bored into Bianca's.

Bianca's mouth went dry. "You hate her that much, don't you?"

Priscilla pulled out a small handgun from her purse. Her stare was cold as winter as she pointed it. Bianca gasped and raised her hands in the air in a surrendering gesture. She gulped down a breath.

"You just couldn't leave things alone, huh, Bianca?" She gestured with the gun. "Living room. NOW."

Bianca moved quickly, taking care to look back periodically to avoid bumping into her furniture. Hopefully Melanie heard Priscilla raise her voice from in the office. She prayed Casper would keep quiet.

"You had to keep digging, Bianca," Priscilla said, still pointing the gun at her.

"You brought this on yourself."

"What was I supposed to do?" Her eyes pooled with unshed tears. "Martin told me he was still in love with Nicole. Can you believe that? I gave up my Broadway career for that man! He took care of me and Chad. Then… *she* comes along." Priscilla gave a mirthless laugh. "Martin always had a thing for blondes."

"What about you?" Bianca asked. "I saw you with a man at the local gift shop in town. He looked pretty friendly with you."

A *tsk* escaped Priscilla's mouth. "You mean Paul? Of course I had my fun. Paul was my fun when I needed it."

"You had him follow me? Attack me in the park?" Bianca could feel the sweat building on her hairline. This couldn't be the end. Help was coming.

"You should've stopped, but you didn't." Priscilla sneered. "No. That was Luis. Paul's cousin. Thanks to you calling the police, he panicked and abandoned the car. So, I had Paul rent one like Judy's. I had her under my thumb, since I was paying her money to keep their business going. She had no idea what was happening. I even had Paul take Richard's golf club for good measure that last time we played together. I never liked him anyway."

Was everyone blackmailing each other? "Nicole's bracelet?"

"I took it after Jordan left it on the table. She was to bubble-headed to notice. I needed everything I could to shift blame to that *gold digging* Nicole." The tightness around Priscilla's eyes increased.

"Why kill your husband?" Bianca had to buy time.

"It was almost perfect." Priscilla eyed her right-hand glove, as if Bianca's question didn't matter. "I thought I washed all the blood away from my hands that day. I even burned the old ones and put on another pair. Paul dragged Martin's body to the limo and sat him up. The driver was inside during the reception, so he didn't see anything. He'd given me the keys since I told him I had a last-minute *present* for the happy couple."

Bianca gulped down a breath to stay quiet. That must have been when she planted the bracelet under the limo.

Priscilla shook her head as she continued. "I figured Martin would come to his senses about us. Most men go through a midlife crisis. Some act irrationally. They do things on impulse with no regard to whom it affects." Her grimace lingered. "You know how that feels. Don't you, Bianca? You know what it's like to have someone you trust and love leave you for someone else."

A pang stung Bianca's chest. Malcom walking out on her came flooding back to mind. Her high school sweetheart. The love of her life. Yet another woman had turned his heart away. Malcom had left, leaving her to raise their daughter alone. He had found happiness with a younger woman.

How many nights had she spent crying? People had asked her, "What went wrong?" The pain in Alyssa's eyes had torn at her soul. Their family had never been the same.

"See," Priscilla said. "You understand." Her creepy tone made Bianca shiver.

Bianca blinked. A hurt woman stood in front of her. Betrayed. Scorned even, but to take someone else's life? Bianca would never stoop to such a violent act. "No. You're wrong, Priscilla." She squared her shoulders. "That didn't give you the right—"

"He was going to leave me!" she shouted. A tear ran down her cheek. "Don't you understand? Martin *had* to die." Her chest heaved a sigh. "I'm sorry, Bianca. Now that you know, I can't—"

Bark, bark, bark, bark.

Priscilla's head jerk at the noise. Taking her eyes off Bianca for a moment, Bianca shifted out of the line of fire and grabbed at the gun.

"NO!" Priscilla yelled.

Bianca kept her grip on her wrist while her other hand wrestled to take the gun away. A deafening crack of thunder filled the room. Priscilla shot at the table lamp, the coffee table, and the wall. Bianca stayed clear of the bullets. Someone had to have called the police by now in her neighborhood.

She then slammed her foot into Priscilla's. Hard. A yelp escaped the woman's throat, and Bianca snatched the gun from her grasp.

Bark, bark! Bianca pointed the gun at Priscilla, who hunched over, clasping her foot.

"Bianca!" Melanie shouted. Casper continued to bark as he ran into the living room. Melanie had a bat in her hand.

Adrenaline rushed through Bianca's body. When pounding and kicking sounded at the front door, both she and her sister screamed at the sudden noise. Sounded like someone was breaking it down.

"Police! Open up!"

Melanie hurried to open it. Police officers rushed in past her sister and flooded into Bianca's living room.

"Freeze!" Detective Sims pointed his gun at Priscilla, still moaning over her foot.

Bianca put the handgun down on her couch. She raised her hands in the air and gestured at Priscilla. "There's your murderer."

Detective Sims motioned with his hand and the arresting officers with him handcuffed Priscilla.

Chapter 30

Wrapping her arms around herself, Bianca sat on her porch. Melanie held Casper in one hand, while she talked to their mother on the phone. Colorful lights flashed, murmurs from police officers filled her ears, but when she spotted Priscilla sitting in the back of the police, she breathed easier.

Who would have thought? Priscilla had killed her own husband. The woman had pointed a gun in her face. Bianca's thoughts scrambled. What would have happened if Casper hadn't barked or Melanie wasn't in her office to call the police? What if Detective Sims hadn't shown?

Bianca looked over at Casper, who'd settled comfortably in her sister's arms. Bianca sighed.

"I still can't believe it." Melanie shook her head. "Priscilla capable of... murder."

"Me, neither."

Melanie rested her head on her sister's shoulder. "I'm glad that's over."

"Me too."

Casper barked.

Bianca smiled and opened her hands and he came to her. "I guess you came in handy tonight."

"He sure did," Melanie said.

"Ladies." Detective Sims walked in front of them. "We doing okay?"

Melanie bobbed her head.

"I think so," Bianca said.

"Well, we got a full confession." He gestured behind him.

Bianca spotted Priscilla's head bowed, as if she were crying. "The Queen of Tears."

"What?" Melanie and Detective Sims said together.

"There's a newspaper clipping in her hallway at her house from her Broadway days. They called her the "Queen of Tears" and the... Bette Davis of the stage." No wonder Jordan had said it when she'd visited him in the hospital.

Detective Sims made a note on his notepad. "Anything else?"

Bianca tucked a loose curl behind her ear. "She said she gave her Broadway career up for Martin, but when she found out about Nicole, it humiliated her that he wanted to leave."

He bobbed his head.

"A woman scorned," Melanie said.

"Bingo." Then Bianca reached into her jacket pocket and handed Detective Sims a folded picture she'd just printed. "Here."

He took it and unfolded it. "This is a picture from the wedding reception. What about it?"

Bianca leaned in and pointed to Priscilla in the corner. "I took this. With Priscilla's heart condition, her medication can't be mixed with alcohol. I looked it up, so I think she faked her spell at the wedding reception. What tipped me off was her gloves. I saw the stain and took a picture. That's what I had Melanie send you. I wasn't completely sure."

He gave a faint smile. "Thank you for that and the voice recording you sent."

"Recording?" Bianca's eyebrows raised.

"I figured it wouldn't hurt recording the conversation on my phone, although I had to keep this guy quiet." She held Casper close and rubbed his head.

"You're a genius," Bianca said to her sister.

Melanie winked at her. "I'm... going to wait for you inside." Then she took Casper with her and left Bianca alone outside with Detective Sims.

He sat next to her. "Are you okay? Really?"

"I think I'll get over having a gun pointed to my face." She faced him. "I see what you meant though. I didn't mean to—"

He shook his head. "Let's forget that. I will admit, you helped us close a case. Just try not to make it a habit. Okay?"

She didn't answer.

"Don't tell me you're thinking about doing this again?" he asked.

She opened her hands, palms facing upward. "I was in the right place at the right time. I didn't plan on figuring this out."

He raised an eyebrow.

She giggled. "I even thought of consulting with the police department."

He rubbed at his forehead. "Ms. Wallace..."

"I said *thought*, don't worry." She ran her hands down her pant legs. "Do you need anything else from me? I think I've told you everything I know."

"If I have more questions, I'll call you." He stared at her. "I'm glad you're okay."

"Thank you for being here. I don't know what I would have done."

"Good thing we've been monitoring your house." His gray eyes gleamed with a smile. "Well, you don't have to worry anymore. It's over." He stood to his feet. "Goodnight, Ms. Wallace."

She followed, standing to her feet. "Goodnight, detective." Bianca didn't turn around for another look at him as she walked back inside her home, closing the door behind her. She exhaled, leaning against the door.

"We're good?" Melanie asked. Casper was licking up water from his bowl.

"I think so. Priscilla is going to jail. Paul too for being an accomplice, along with attacking Jordan. I already identified Luis from the park and the car chase, so I'm sure it won't take the police long adding the additional charges." Bianca rubbed at her arms. "How bad is the damage?"

Melanie perused the living room and back at her sister. "Nothing we can't replace." She inched in closer and hugged her. "I'm glad you're okay. I was scared."

Bianca patted Melanie's back. "Me too."

"So?" Her sister pulled away from their embrace, eyeing her closely.

Bianca's eyebrows raised. "So... what?"

"What was that with Detective Sims outside?" Melanie grinned.

"I just told him what I knew. Case closed. Right now, I want to soak in a hot bath, and get some much needed sleep. Can I do that?"

Melanie bobbed her head. "If you say so." She turned on her heels, and headed down the hallway.

Bianca waited until she was out of site to peek outside the window. Detective Sims hadn't left yet. He was talking with Detective Atkins. With his arms folded, she couldn't deny the tingle in her fingers. Then when he turned and locked his gray eyes with hers, her body shivered again, but not out of fear. This time... pleasure.

A slow smile built on his face. Bianca blinked, coming back to reality. Closing the curtain she backed away. Sleep. She needed sleep.

Epilogue

Mocha Frappuccino. Just what Bianca needed. Almost three weeks since Priscilla's arrest, and things slowly felt back to normal in Edenville. While Jordan still needed time to recover, she was grateful he'd survived the blow to his head. Chad and Nicole had left for their honeymoon, determined not to let his mother's antics break up their marriage.

Bianca paced herself through the park, with Casper trotting ahead of her. She didn't have to worry about looking over her shoulder anymore since the police had arrested Priscilla's accomplices, Paul and Luis. Both men she'd hired as body guards before retiring from the theater. They'd stolen Judy's car with Luis driving, with Paul ready to pick him up after abandoning it on the road, because of Bianca calling the police right away.

Chasing Bianca's car had been only to scare her, along with Luis following her home in the car he'd rented before attempting to skip town. The original plan had been to keep Judy's car longer prior to returning it. Stealing her car had been a scare tactic on her too, on top of the blackmail. Thank goodness Judy had only been guilty of taking money from Priscilla and nothing more.

How had Jordan known the truth? He didn't at first, but like Bianca, he'd asked too many questions. Turned out Priscilla's hysterics at the memorial service were all an act since she noticed Detective Sims had showed up. Making him suspicious of someone else kept her that much more in the clear, on top of everything else in her plan. Jordan visited Priscilla's home to make an amends after the memorial. Then he noticed she had recently used her fireplace and saw an unusual residue of material inside the firebox.

Pieces of her bloody silk gloves from the wedding. Priscilla caught on to him and had Paul follow Jordan, only to have Paul attack him with the golf club she'd taken from Richard after visiting him weeks prior. That got Jordan out of the way for a while.

Priscilla *had* had the bracelet all along, lying about leaving it on the table for Nicole. She even made up the story of leaving the door open. An actress worth believing. With the same knife set as Richard, it hadn't taken long for her to switch them so she could kill Martin. Since Nicole's prints remained on it from slicing the ham at her bridal shower, it'd been perfect. As far as a witness pointing blame to Nicole, it turned out Nicole stepped away to get some air in the hallway.

Bianca sat on a park bench, relishing in her drink. The worst was over. She stared through the gazebo, taking in the tranquil moment. It was the most peace she'd experienced in a long time. Birds chirped and squirrels leapt from tree to tree.

"I keep forgetting this is a small town."

Bianca turned in her seat to see Detective Sims. She swallowed the last of her coffee and tossed it in the trash bin beside her. "You'll get used to it. Taking the day off?"

"Just getting some air before I head to the station." His eyes scanned the park. "This is one of my favorite places."

She smiled.

Then he stooped and petted Casper.

"Think you'll get a dog?" she asked.

"Not sure. My schedule's unpredictable." Then he straightened and locked eyes with her. "Maybe one day."

"When you do…" Her eyes drifted to her dog. "You'll have a hard time letting them go."

"Is that so?" His eyes beamed.

"It's a fact," she said, followed by a giggle.

"Thank you for the tip." He folded his arms. "Will you ever stop giving me tips?"

"Only when it's called for." She stood. The wind picked up, and she caught a whiff of his manly scent. Not woodsy cologne this time. This scent was fresh. Crisp.

An almost electrical feeling passed through her when she met his gray eyes again. She opened her mouth to speak but stopped herself. "I think I've… I need to get to work."

"How's business?" he asked.

"Booming, so I'm glad. I even found a virtual assistant last weekend. I'm… sure I'll see you again." She backed away a few spaces from him.

He grinned.

"What?" she asked.

"I was thinking of when your heel…" He chuckled.

She pointed to him. "Don't you *dare* hold that against me?"

He held up his hands in a surrendering gesture. "Your secret is safe with me. I don't think anyone else noticed."

"I would have heard around town if they had."

He touched a hand to his chest. "So you know you can trust me."

She tilted her head to the side. "The jury's still out on that." Bianca took another step back with Casper by her side. "Have a good one, detective."

"You too, Bianca." He smiled and then turned his back to walk away.

Bianca. He had called her by her name. An overwhelming tingling went through her core, as she watched Detective Sims leave. Despite the breeze, she fanned herself as she walked to her car with Casper...

To be continued in *Killer Runway* (A Bianca Wallace Mystery, 2)

THANK YOU FOR TAKING the time to read my book! If you enjoyed *Photo Bombed*, please leave a review at any of your favorite retailers.

Best Regards,
Daria

More by Crimson Fox Publishing

Broomsticks *and Board Games* (Spooky Games Club Mysteries, Book 1) by Amy McNulty

Dahlia Poplar is a genuine witch, an unofficial gofer, and Luna Lane's only cursed resident.

With a werewolf best friend, a vampire ex-boyfriend, and a ghost for a hanger-on, Dahlia is far from the most unusual dweller of her sleepy small town, but she's the only one unable to leave. Dahlia has to perform at least one good deed per day—or she's one step closer to turning to stone.

Fortunately, the residents of Luna Lane have plenty of tasks for Dahlia to complete to avert the curse until Cable Woodward, fetching professor and nephew of her elderly neighbor, stops by for the semester on sabbatical. Attempting to help Cable's uncle work through the trauma of losing his wife, Dahlia uncovers the man's collection of board games, which leads to him reminiscing about the long-forgotten Luna Lane Games Club.

Dahlia reestablishes Games Club, only to find evidence of a number of horrible demises connected to the original group. While trying to uncover the truth about the deaths, Dahlia has to fight off her curse, protect her elderly neighbor from becoming the next victim, and most vexing of all, keep Cable from figuring out Luna

Lane's supernatural secrets. Only with eerie board games like these, there may not be a loser—or even a winner—who survives.

Old Flames **(Northwest Magic, Book 2) by Elisa Keyston**

Laney isn't looking for love. She's perfectly happy with the life she's built for herself in the little town of Foreston, Washington. She's a successful businesswoman, the owner of an alterations shop with a clientele across the northwest. She's the chair of the local Victorian house museum's annual fashion show. And she has a reputation for a magic touch: the rumor around town is that anyone who wears one of the period costumes she designs in her spare time will be blessed with good luck.

That's what they say, anyway. Laney knows the truth is a bit more complicated—anything she wills while sewing has a tendency of coming to pass. It's a supernatural gift from the fae who are said to inhabit the woods surrounding the Paine Estate, and it's taught her to keep a guard on her notorious redheaded temper. But keeping her temper becomes difficult when journalist Paul Nelson comes to town to do a feature about the museum. With his stunning good looks and swoon-worthy English accent, Paul is charming, irresistible... and just so happens to be Laney's ex.

Laney wants nothing more than to keep Paul at arm's length, but when she stumbles across a series of break-ins at the museum, she may have no choice but to trust the dashing reporter who once broke her heart to help her catch the culprit. And when a nearby forest fire threatens the safety of the town—and of the woods—will Laney be able to put her old feelings aside in order to protect the magic of Foreston? Or will that same magic lead to an unexpected happy ending?

About the Author

Daria started writing as a teenager. Since she loves sweet romance novels, she figured why not write them too? Now she's including Christian romance and cozy mysteries to her writings! She graduated with a degree in healthcare management, so writing was not in the cards for her. It's rare that you won't catch her reading. Aside from that, she loves Turner Classic Movies, painting, Pilates, the piano, and chocolate.

More Books by Daria

Christmas Therapy

The Wedding Report

Wish for Love

Stay in Touch

My website: www.dariawhite.com[1] and subscribe to my newsletter!

Follow me on Twitter: www.twitter.com/Daria_White15[2]

Follow me on Instagram: www.instagram.com/dariawhite90[3]

---

1. http://www.dariawhite.com

2. http://www.twitter.com/Daria_White15

3. http://www.instagram.com/dariawhite90

Thank you from Daria

Thank you again for reading *Photo Bombed*. Wow! My first cozy mystery. I still can't believe it, but I'm glad I did it! Was it hard? Absolutely, since I'm used to writing sweet romances, but I was up to the challenge. I hope you enjoyed it and are looking forward to the next one. I know I am lol.

If you enjoyed this story, please take a few minutes to leave a rating or a review. If it's only a few words, it's perfectly fine with me. Unbelievably, it helps other readers to decide if they want to read my work or not. I look forward to sharing the next story with you. There's more to come!

God Bless,
Daria

Shout Outs!

WWW.VILADESIGN.NET[1] (Tatiana, you're the best!). Special thanks to my family. You made sure I had the space to finish editing and proofreading. To my writing partners, you rock! Thank you for all your help with my first mystery. To my fans, your support means

---

1. http://www.viladesign.net

so much. I hope this wasn't too out of the box for you to enjoy. Lol. Thank you for reading whatever I choose to write!

Don't miss out!

Visit the website below and you can sign up to receive emails whenever Daria White publishes a new book. There's no charge and no obligation.

https://books2read.com/r/B-A-YNYJ-EXZHB

BOOKS2READ

Connecting independent readers to independent writers.